Also by Jack Beltane

Novels
The Toyland Tales
A Company of Tatters

Poetry
Nightshade & Daylight

Available from Graveworm Press

PENNY HARPER
BY JACK BELTANE

Graveworm Press

Cleveland, Ohio

Penny Harper

Copyright © 2018 by Jack Beltane

The cover art is an untitled work by Faith Klasek (acrylic on canvas), photographed by Tim Arai. Copyright © 2014 by Faith Klasek. Used with kind permission.

The cover title is typeset using Baveuse 3D designed by Ray Larabie of Typodermic Fonts Inc. (typodermicfonts.com). The chapter titles use a custom font designed from Jack Beltane's handwriting.

For more information contact:

Graveworm Press—graveworm.com
Jack Beltane—jackofbells.com

ISBN 978-1-929309-23-8
202303P/fiction

To Phil, the strongest man I know

Penny Harper

Darkness has a weight and presence, a stillness like a massive beast curled and sleeping. When it stirs, it stirs slowly, lumbering toward you. The void is inviting—you run to it, jump into it, and realize too late that its thickness is smothering you; that you can't climb out. That no matter how hard you push back—no matter how long the years stretch between then and now—that vast, unfeeling emptiness will never go away.

In my head, she will always be sixteen. I could see that her profile page said she's thirty-six now, but I didn't understand that. It wasn't possible. Penny Harper would never get old. The teenage girl would always be there, standing in front of her house at the top of the hill, her dark blond hair touched by the sun and stirring in a slight breeze, her smile wide and her eyes bright, her skin tanned to perfection. In my mind, she still looks exactly like she did that first time we ever talked: her left knee cocked just enough to break the line of her legs, the tips of her fingers stuffed nervously into tight pockets. She raises her shoulders the smallest weight that says she's excited to see me but she can't be too obvious.

"I heard that song we always blasted by Mötley Crüe," her message said, "and figured I'd look you up. 'Louder Than Hell'—you remember? I understand if you ignore me."

Sometimes the past is so close it hurts. It hurts because the distance in the air between then and now seems small enough to close, if only we could stretch back far enough.

But that air beyond our out-stretched fingertips is cold and we pull back, leaving the songs we used to play drifting in the emptiness of time like the echoes of a cry for help: A lonely, diminishing sound that fades with each beat of our hearts. It's the long look back and our fear of the darkness ahead that traps us. When the past has that kind of distance, it's hard to turn away.

Slam another shot.

Watch something funny on TV.

Sleep to live another day.

Tobie's smile said that she didn't care that an old girl-friend from high school had looked me up. If anything, she felt bad for the poor girl, if she'd reached that point in her life when looking up exes from twenty years ago filled her time.

"Isn't that what the internet is for?" I checked. "Looking up old friends?"

"Sure, Jack," Tobie agreed.

She grinned inwardly, waiting for me to take the bait, fiddling with her coffee mug at the kitchen table. Her hair was pulled back in a big, bushy ponytail, brown like fox fur. It let me see her face clearly—the light skin, the shining blue eyes, the soft roundness of her jawline.

"So… what?" I wondered.

"Don't be naïve."

"You're practically purring, Tobie," I pointed out. She giggled and shook her head.

"Penny Harper is spying, Bells. She wants to see if you got fat and ugly. She wants to know she made the right choice back in high school by breaking up with you, so that she can feel better about her shitty life now."

"Really?"

Tobie shrugged, her eyes twinkling.

"Well *I* use it to look up old friends that I wish I *hadn't* lost touch with," I said.

"Really?" she quipped.

11

"So… *you* friended all *your* exes to make sure you still like *me*?" I checked with a sarcastic smile.

"I didn't friend any exes."

"Yes, you did."

"*One* friended *me*, I just accepted it. And it was an amicable split."

"So should I accept Penny Harper's request?"

Her face suddenly got serious and I knew what she was going to say: it hadn't been an amicable split. I held up a hand to stop her, but we both knew she had to say it anyway. Penny Harper was different. Not *just* an ex-girlfriend from my teenage career; more like an anchor that threatened to get coiled around my ankle and drag me overboard. But Tobie had been there—a friend back then, my wife now—and she also knew that I couldn't ignore Penny. Or at least, that it might be more dangerous to ignore her than to restore whatever tenuous strain of diplomacy internet sites afforded.

"Just be careful, Jack," Tobie whispered.

"I don't want her back."

"I know. It's not that."

"I know," I agreed. I paused, measuring the intent of Penny Harper's request. "Maybe *you* should friend her, too?"

"Do you think she knows we got married?"

"Maybe."

"I am curious to find out what she wants, but I think I'll stay out of it. Let it unwind naturally."

"You're a strange girl—"

"Don't use Cure lyrics against me."

"Do you come from another world…?"

"Jack!"

She stood up and stormed off in a fake huff, pausing long enough as she left the kitchen to turn back and grin at me over her shoulder. Tobie always had that grin for me, no matter what, and it told me that the world was still spinning and we were still going around with it, so I didn't have to worry.

Somewhere from the direction she'd walked a squeal of childish delight erupted, followed by the guttural giggle only children with no shame can produce: Pure, unsullied joy. Then the patter of tiny feet as "the baby" (now four) joined in on the fun with his big sister and mom.

The memory of Penny Harper was a stain over that morning for me, but you can't scrub a stain away if you're not willing to look at the dirt—that was something Tobie also understood, and feared.

Sometimes stains hide the real damage that lies beneath.

There used to be a bar in Lakewood, Cleveland's closest suburb, that (to hear the owners tell it) was the best place to see live music in northeast Ohio. To be fair, it *was* a great venue—but that didn't change the fact that it had also been the kind of place bands went to die. Or dead bands went to play—bands like Ambrosia, which Gray decided I had to go and see with him before the place closed down. His opinion was based entirely on his love for their song "Biggest Part of Me," which had been sonically pummeled into him at the impressionable age of ten when he heard it repeatedly during a rain delay at a baseball game.

Those kinds of memories are hard to shake: The ones wrapped up with something else that finds an easy hook to sink into you. It wasn't the *song* he loved, after all, it was the *game*—it was that *time*, with his dad and brother, and the magic of a rain delay while soft rock swirled in air that was laced with the scent of hotdogs and nacho cheese. I could see it in his eyes as we sat at the bar, his nose upturned ever so slightly as if straining for an errant whiff of stadium confections.

"You think they have nachos?" I asked him.

"You want nachos?"

He turned and flagged down the bartender before I could respond. She looked completely over being flagged down, but then most of the clientele was the brand of lecherous old man soft-rock acts from the 1970s attracted in the twenty-first century. Not that Gray and I were spring chickens—we'd first met in college just shy of twenty years before—but we carried our ages well and we still weren't quite old enough to be her father.

"Do you have nachos?" he asked her.

Gray's a very charismatic guy, especially after a few drinks. He has an easy way of talking that makes you feel like he knows exactly what you mean and—more importantly—he actually cares to hear what you have to say. Me? I'm not that guy. I'm the asshole who sits quietly; the guy you smile at cautiously to see how he'll react so you know whether or not to run.

"Sure we do," she said, lapping him up. I got the smile; I didn't react.

"We'll take an order—say, were you expecting this kind of turn out?"

She looked around at the crowd and shook her head, leaning against the bar conspiratorially—now we were her only allies in a sea of well-pressed T-shirts, khaki shorts, and dress shoes with white tube socks.

"No, not really," she admitted.

When we'd got there, the line was immense. Like, around-the-block immense. Like, unheard of for some has-been band that, to my knowledge, had a string of hits some-time around when Carter was in office. We didn't have tick-ets in advance, of course—Gray was always up for a whim, a style he'd tempered early in his marriage but had long since given up trying to suppress. I went along with it because his whims often involved live music, and if there's one thing I can rarely say "no" to, it's live music. There's a power and energy at a show—even a bad one—that you can't get any-where else. It feeds me—recharges me—and that was some-thing I really needed after fretting all day about the unex-pected re-emergence of Penny Harper.

Anyway, we got there with no tickets and found our-selves at the wrong end of a sell-out line snaked around the building—not so bad to stand in now that early summer warmed the wind coming off the lake—so we did what any member of the press (Gray) would do: We found the owner and got in free (he reputedly let a lot of people in free, which may have contributed the club's eventual demise). Because of our dubious entrance, we opted to hang out in the back at the bar and buy our weight in bourbon and cheap beer.

"They don't seem like your kind of band," the bartender

admitted, eying me as if trying to figure out my game.

I nodded and smiled in what I hoped was a convincingly nonthreatening way and pulled the sleeves of my waffle shirt down, but she'd already seen the tattoos on my arms and the skull on my shirt (a record store's logo) and maybe had the impression that I was tougher than I was. Gray had never gone the body-art route and looked basically presentable, but still out of place. We both had neat hair—good-upstanding-citizen cuts—but you could see it in our eyes that middle-of-the-road American life would always be a thing we embraced with tenuous arms, like a scary old relative you only saw once a year and had to work yourself up to hug.

"Oh, they are *exactly* our kind of band, right, Bell?" he replied.

"Well... no... I mean..." I mumbled.

"Bell just doesn't want to admit it," Gray confided loudly to her.

"I'll get the nachos," she chuckled and walked off toward the kitchen.

"I think you got a shot with her, man," Gray said.

I shook my head and smirked and turned on my stool to face the stage. Gray was always saying shit like that, even though he didn't mean it. It was some kind of fun for him, like he was in a movie trolling for laughs by making the off-color comment or having the out-of-place reaction.

"She's paid to be nice to the customers," I said.

He patted me heavily on the shoulder and chuckled. The laughs he was trolling for were mine because he could tell I was bummed about something—that ol' charisma he had must have come from some true source, I guess. I mean, he

16

did genuinely care, but he wasn't going to pry.

"You ever had an old girlfriend look you up online?" I asked him.

He was still facing the bar and when I looked over he was staring into the mirror behind the liquor bottles.

"I mean, they're *all* old now," he pointed out, narrowing his eyes. "But like, high-school old? Middle school…?"

"High school. We were sixteen."

"Damn. Out of the blue?"

"Totally."

He turned and smirked at me. "Was she hot?"

I paused long enough to cut him a look, which he de-fused with his own look that said, *No, seriously.*

"Very hot," I said evenly.

"And… still?"

"Don't know."

"You didn't check?"

"Yeah—I mean I saw her profile picture."

"Yeah?"

"She's not sixteen anymore."

He laughed and finished off his beer, twirling on his stool to face the stage with me. We sat in silence, both en-thralled by a man dressed in white. Like, everything was white: White shoes, white socks, white Bermuda shorts, white Polo shirt tucked into said shorts. He had a close-cropped ring of hair around his bald dome and looked like a shorter, fatter Hunter S Thompson (if Hunter S had gone into real estate instead of drugs). He was gesticulating wildly as he talked, as if he needed to draw more attention to himself. The target of his onerous hand jiving was a woman a full head-n-shoulders taller than he was, who looked arrogantly unappreciative of his remonstrations. She was dressed in white, too—white heels, white miniskirt, white tank top—and I couldn't imagine a more nauseating couple, especially since neither of them seemed to be having any fun.

"Speaking of not sixteen…" Gray mumbled.

"Dude," I whispered, leaning in to him. He obliged and leaned over to meet me halfway. "That chick is *not* a chick."

"What?"

He sounded genuinely shocked.

"It's a dude."

Gray allowed his eyes to linger longer on her hips and her chest and her shoulders, and shook his head slowly.

"Yeah," I breathed.

"A she-male?" he enjoined as if catching sight of a real unicorn. He was still trying to goad me into being offended by his off-color remarks. I didn't bite. I scanned the rest of the crowd.

A lot of these folks, you could tell, hadn't set foot in a bar in more than thirty years. They looked like teenagers, wary and unsure they were actually allowed to be there. Some of them may never have set foot in a bar, I considered. Like their fifties were drawing to a close and a band from their heyday coming to town was enough to remind them that there was more to life than being safe and good—that the hidden wonder of living lay not in following rules and order but in tasting the chaos and surviving long enough to tell. I didn't want to be them, I decided: I wanted to do my living now while my body can still recover.

My eyes came back around to the woman and I noticed

that she was watching us—maybe Gray had stared a bit too hard—so I snapped around on my stool and faced the bar. Gray did the same, then stood up, mumbled something about nachos, and vanished. I went cold, my back straightening in anticipation of a firm hand on my shoulder. I turned slowly to glance over my left shoulder and saw the guy who had been messing around in the sound booth walking over. He caught my eye and motioned at the stool, and I indicated that I wasn't going to stop him. He sat down with a huff and waved to the bartender.

"Bourbon," he said. "I have a headache."

"A whiskey headache," I agreed rhetorically.

He looked over and smiled knowingly—he was only a few years older than me, if that. I wasn't sure if he was with the band or the bar. I'm not normally too gregarious, but I was genuinely fearful that the woman had got the wrong impression, so I used the guy for cover.

"You with the band?"

"Yup," he nodded.

"They really pack 'em in."

"They're very good musicians," he said. "This soft-rock shit sure has staying power."

"Yeah?"

He shrugged, playing with the drained shot glass in front of him, twirling it lightly in his fingers and contemplating the worth of sucking out that final golden drop of bourbon.

"Soft rock was the happy end of the sixties, man," he explained thoughtfully. "People were burned out with all the riots and violence."

I could tell it was a pet theory of his that he rarely espoused, probably because no one cared or because someone always ended up offended, and I realized I had him wrong: This wasn't just another roadie gig for him, this was a job he'd *wanted*; a chance for him to be near something he thought was great. It made me reset my expectations for the whole night. I turned and glanced up at the stage, now set and waiting only for the boys to take their places. The crowd had stumbled into their seats—a few aluminum walkers with tennis balls on the legs littered the aisles, I swear to God—and most of the fans were sitting politely, waiting. Back by us, by the bar, is where the action was—near the alcohol and the pretty bartenders.

"I never thought of that."

"Sunshine and rainbows," he said with a smile and stood up. "Who wouldn't want to drift away with that? All the shit the hippies *fought* for, the soft rockers just *did*. Relax, man," he summarized, giving my hand a classic clasp-pull-rock combo. "Enjoy yourself."

Gray returned seconds later and glanced at the guy—assessing the potential danger, to judge by his breathless panting and the wild-eyed look he gave me. He was also holding two drinks: a beer and a very healthy pull of bourbon, straight, in a rocks glass. He handed me the whiskey.

"Thanks," I said, raising the glass to him, but he shook his head and I lowered it again without drinking.

"No," he said stiltedly. "*She* bought them for us."

"Who? The *bartender*?"

I hate to admit that my heart pattered, but as a heterosexual male, the thought of a pretty girl noticing me got a reaction—as it should, I'd say. God forbid I ever become so jaded that I lose that magical rush of nerves—those brief, breathless moments of hope and desire seeming to join forces—despite the fact that I'd never act on them.

"*No*," Gray said, for some reason trying to talk without moving his lips. His eyes widened comically as he added, "*Shim*—the *she*-male."

"*What?*"

He nodded. I glanced around but couldn't see her.

"Well…" I started, raising the glass again.

"We can't!" he cut in, stopping me. "She's a *dude*."

I sighed. "It's a free drink, man. Relax. And I'm sure she's a perfectly nice person."

Raised voices drew our attention as the crowd near the sound booth parted. I saw the sound man shake his head, disappointed at the cause of the disturbance, which was the White Knight in an altercation with a man—clearly a man—dressed in a black sequined halter top and denim mini skirt. It was an outfit no one should have been wearing, least of all a guy in drag. Off to the side and towering over both of them was the woman who'd bought us drinks, looking equal parts aghast and pleased. Clearly, the fracas was over her. And clearly the White Knight was going to lose.

We were stunned. Of all the shows we'd been to, *this* was where we were witnessing a bar brawl? At a soft rock show? Involving a guy in drag? Gray—still shaken from the free drinks—now became convinced that he would soon be summoned to also duel the sequined guy as he stood over the body of the White Knight, blood marring the sparkle of his halter top.

Fortunately, a bouncer showed up and summarily ushered the guy in drag away. And that, somehow, was the most depressing part of it to me, that this man, who was trying to be a lady, or at least look like a lady for the night, was hauled from the room like any other testosterone-fueled brawler, only he was stumbling on heels he could barely walk in, even when he wasn't being strong-armed. It reminded me of a guy I'd known once-upon-a-time who turned up one day, out of the blue, in drag. He'd been going through some shit that didn't involve gender identity. He'd been trying to get attention, plain and simple, but I'd been too young and inexperienced to understand that then. I wondered if this guy was going through some shit, too, and I felt for him.

The White Knight had quietly slipped his arm around the waist of his girl, who was smirking with inner joy. I'd bet the guy in sequins had tried to pick her up, and she was clearly the type of girl who liked to flirt (hence the drinks).

"We need to move. Over there."

Gray pointed into the crowd, in the opposite direction from the couple in white, and I had to agree. Obviously she liked to start fights over herself to make herself seem more desirable or something, and just as obviously the White Knight was willing to play his part in her little game. If that was their thing, so be it, but I didn't see the sense in dragging innocent bystanders into the insanity.

"What about the nachos?"

"Fuck the nachos!"

We ended up over by a small bar—maybe it was a wait station left over from when the place was a restaurant—that was now a merch table, completely out of sight of the pugilistic couple. It was a great spot with a good view of the stage that gave us something to lean against and somewhere to put our drinks.

"So anyway," Gray said, back to his normal self again. (The way his mood cleared was subtle proof that a large part of his reactions were nothing more than that movie playing in his head; a film he made and edited constantly, watched by no one and everyone.) "What's up with this high-school chick? She dumped you, right?"

"Yeah," I sighed. "It was a summer romance and it ended when we got back to school."

"Typical," he spat. I raised my eyebrows, but he shook his head and chuckled. "I mean, no, it didn't happen to me, but it *is* a cliché."

"That's me!" I agreed with mock sincerity as I polished off my shot—that had been more like three shots. "I'm all about the clichés!"

"So what was her reason for dumping a fine man like you?"

"Don't know. She called and told me to go to hell, in almost as many words. Really fucked me up."

"Are you serious?"

I didn't answer and he watched me suck the last few drops out of the bottom of my glass. I may have suspected that her dad had put her up to it because he didn't like me, but that was a theory I tended privately and didn't entirely believe. There was more to it than that—there had to be. I couldn't have wasted so much time and energy on a God damn daddy's-girl who did as she was told over something as serious as young love.

Gray nodded at my silence as if he could help me crack this nut, but it wasn't going to happen. Penny Harper was the one girl who had always haunted me, but not in the nostalgic way young loves are supposed to stay with you. She was a wound that had scabbed and scarred but had never fully healed. It unsettled me how the inexplicable actions of a teenage girl could *still* wake me up at night, twenty years later, running over it all in my head again, trying to see what I'd done wrong; trying to find out why. Because the nagging inner voice that had whispered in my ear back then—and had been whispering in my ear all those years since Penny had last hung up on me—told me that if I didn't figure out what I'd done wrong, I may do it again.

And this time, it would be Tobie who'd leave.

I shook my head to dislodge the thought—it was ridiculous, I knew, but that's what I'd been left with. Gray nodded serenely again.

"Maybe she wants to explain? Maybe she feels bad and she wants closure?"

I didn't react, so he kept fishing for an angle.

"Does Tobie know? Did she know her in school?"

"Yeah, Tobie knows everything."

Tobie had been there, back in high school, to pick up the pieces—Tobie and I had always been great friends first, since we were about twelve years old, a fact that had allowed our relationship to age and flourish in a way that had led to ten solid years of marriage and the promise of a lifetime left to go.

"And?"

"She said I should find out what she wants."

He raised his eyebrows and cocked his head, presenting me with the unspoken solution.

The house lights dimmed and the crowd erupted, but only a few of them managed to stand up. I felt bad for the fans who couldn't stand, and how what might be their last view of their favorite band was being blocked by some healthier fan's ass.

They opened with the song Gray wanted to hear most and it set the house on fire. The sound guy was right: They were tight, and the music seemed real to me in a way it never had when it oozed out of the speakers of my mom's car radio, all full of saccharin bliss. Rainbows and sunshine, indeed—and I soaked it up. I even glimpsed a little of what the sound guy had meant about being burned out with the darkness of the sixties: Ambrosia actually fucking *moved* me that night. Maybe it was the whiskey talking or seeing how much Gray was enjoying himself, or maybe it was that the band really had tapped into some kind of primal joy buzzer with their silky grooves and sweet melodies. Maybe people weren't sick of the darkness so much as the darkness fled from soft rock, like a talisman against the devil—and it worked for me, too.

But then, music often does that for me. There's a restorative power to music that is elevated by the live experience. It gave me hope and solace and commiseration; I felt moved by the communal experience, even if this wasn't my usual crowd—the music *made* them my crowd. Broken hearts surely abounded, and maybe we were all thinking of long-lost loves from the golden-edged summers of youth—the eternal light of teenage desire still glowed deep down in every one of us; there was still fire in the world and love worth fighting for.

We left the club, laughing and talking way too loudly as we walked to Gray's car, and suddenly our laughter seemed too loud, our joy unearned. With a snap, the talisman lost its hold on me and the world came back into focus: the bills, the job, the responsibility of kids… And girls who should be ghosts taking shape before my eyes.

"That's my *youth*!" Gray was saying excitedly. "That's my *song*!"

He shook me and I grunted agreement.

"What was *your* song, then? When you were twelve?"

"Twelve…?" I mumbled. "Probably Led Zeppelin. Or I taped the radio a lot. There was this song, 'Jungle Boy'— that would've been when I was about twelve, maybe a bit older."

"Don't know it."

"John Eddie," I stated. "I only know that because I never knew back then who it was, and I always tried to find out—I only ever had the song on a tape off the radio. I used to fuck-ing *blast* it."

"I suppose you think that's cooler than my rain-delay story?" Gray assumed glibly, then added in a narrator's voice-over, "The loner tapes songs off the radio after midnight, hoping his parents don't catch him still awake…"

"Fuck off, Gray."

"Aw, c'mon, Bell—what happened to your mood?"

I offered him a sneer, but he wasn't having it—he was never having it. Maybe Ambrosia *had* cast a defensive spell over him all those years ago, and it had stuck—he seemed to naturally ward off that ill-defined darkness that followed me. I grinned and shook my head.

"Sixteen, then," he said, opening the car door for me in an exaggerated fashion. He scooted around the front and hopped behind the wheel as I got in and closed my door. "Since you want to mope over girls that don't fucking matter... what was your jam *that* summer? *Her* summer?"

"I was big into the Psychedelic Furs and the Cure, but for some reason I was still spinning a *lot* of Mötley Crüe that year."

Gray narrowed his eyes, trying to reconcile my usual taste in music with glam metal.

"I was a total metalhead first, Gray. Ratt, Ozzy, Dio, Def Leppard, Motörhead, Metallica..."

"I get it! And of course you were."

"And I still love *Theatre of Pain*."

"That's not even their best album."

"You loved Ambrosia, I loved the Crüe. *That's* what's linked to that summer for me."

swirls, tops, full pops, and lollies

On the way to the park from the house where I grew up were two great hills, smooshed together into a trough like waves, so basically you went up one huge hill, then halfway down the height on the other side before you rose back up again on the second hill, then all the way back down the second hill to the level you started at before the first hill—like an M where the center V doesn't go all the way down.

This is important because it was a long haul up one side with a skateboard, but the long-standing quest of me and Niz was to start at the top of the first hump, ride down and back up, and keep enough momentum to coast right over the crest and on down the second hill without having to take your feet off the skateboard to pump. The wheels and bearings of that era made this much more difficult than you'd imagine.

On the day I met Penny Harper, not long into summer break the year I turned sixteen, I was attempting this feat again, on my way to the park to meet up with Niz and my other skate buddy, Sammy. They said that there was a new length of curb around a storm sewer outside the park gates, and for some reason the city had painted it yellow with that thick, almost-plastic paint that makes anything a grindable surface. Add grinding the worn metal of the storm sewer—one of those built into the curb, with a little grate in front and a gaping maw into the basin below—and it promised to be a decent little ride.

Or so they assumed. None of us had tried it yet. It was pristine, and I couldn't wait to get there—but I had to try that hill first. To be the guy who finally notched *that* trick would make me a legend. I was just to the crest of the second hill, moving painfully slowly, when I heard a bright chuckle and turned to see a girl walking some kind of toy poodle or other miniature dog that looked like a fuzzball with stick legs.

"I don't think you're going to make it," she said, then smiled bashfully as if she hadn't meant to say it out loud.

She'd scared the shit out of me, to be honest—lost in my own thoughts as I was, contemplating my woeful lack of speed and wondering if the ride to the park was even worth the effort. It was early summer in the 'burbs of Cincinnati and the southern Ohio heat and humidity had already settled in—summers in Cincy are all a long wash of golden light that burns, endless blue skies, and the incessant whirring of cicadas.

"Where did *you* come from!" I barked much more force-fully than I'd meant to, hopping off my board, my face flush-ing as I realized how stupid I probably looked.

"My house," she said with another smile.

She held my gaze and indicated the house behind her with a tip of her head, her hair catching a hint of a breeze and skittering over her face. It ran shoulder length and was that sunned-in shade of blond that some people call mousy. She slowly reached up and pulled the errant strands back over her rounded nose and pushed them behind a perfectly tan ear—her skin was so smooth and brown that even her ear was the same healthy shade. It was a tan she didn't work on—you could tell. It was the natural state of her complexion—that soft, round color only some girls get, and only during the summer.

The next thing I thought was, *Stevie Nicks*. The girl standing in front of me, smiling a knowing smile that ignited her deep brown eyes, looked like Stevie Nicks on the back cover of *Rumours*: The same rounded cheeks and button nose; the same half smile and shining eyes. Sure, she didn't have the full '70s hair, but it had a similar color: dark blond, almost light brown.

"Jesus," I breathed.

"Pardon?"

"Oh… Nothing."

You could tell by her eyes that she was enjoying herself. I pushed my skateboard over to the curb and moved closer to her. The street on that side of the hill was oddly wide—four cars could've cruised it at the same time, if they didn't mind squeezing—but I still didn't like the idea of standing in the street. If the cops came by, it'd be nothing but questions and scare tactics for the punk-ass skater, and I was trying to talk to a pretty girl.

"You always lived here?" I asked, my heart fluttering in my chest like a caged butterfly. I hoped I sounded cool and unconcerned—the verbal equivalent of James Dean popping his collar.

"Yup."

She nodded and glanced back at her house as if double checking. Her hair was dislodged again and she had to pull it back over her ear, her fingers weaving silent magic as she did so. Her dog walked over to me and barked once then licked my leg.

"Hush, Puffy!" she commanded, giving the dog's leash a slight tug, which alerted me to the fact that I was now only a leash-length away from her. The animal licked its lips, barked once more to prove a point, then snuffled off into the grass behind her.

"Puffy?" I smirked. She caught my eye and giggled.

"I named her Powderpuff when I was, like, six… We always called her Puffy. Do you have a dog? Pets?"

"Dog," I said. "Scamp. She's a beagle. Barks a lot. A *lot*."

"Yeah—beagles do."

We stood looking pleasantly at each other for several seconds. It felt like there should be something obvious I should say or ask or do, but for the life of me, I couldn't pin it down. It hovered just out of reach, a word on the tip of my tongue. With a jolt, I realized it was my turn to talk and we were both waiting.

"Hey—so I'm Jack. My friends call me Bells. So do you…? You go to the high school, right?"

"*Yeah*," she said with a slight gasp of exasperation, but still that smile, her lips slightly parted, not in a big-fake-cheerleader sort of way. "I'm *Penny*. We had *math* together…?"

"Penny and Puffy," I smiled. "Hi, Penny."

"Harper," she added. "Penny Harper."

She held out her hand and I shook it, all very businesslike, except for the weakness in my knees and the strange twist in my tummy as our hands touched. I panicked that I was gripping too tightly, then feared my shake was too loose and pathetic.

"So we had math together?" I asked.

Of course I knew that we had—I knew exactly who she

31

was—but I was trying to play it cool, like I'd never seen her before. Of *course* I remembered her from math class—I remembered that she was the only reason I got to my seat before the bell rang, so I could watch her come in and sit down in the front row, far away from the creeps like me in the back.

She blushed for some reason and shook her head, grinning down at her dog and pretending to be occupied by whatever Puffy was doing, which was nothing except sitting and panting.

"We did," she agreed. "You and your friends are kind of... hard to miss."

I nodded sagely and pursed my lips as if she'd struck upon something terribly serious. This was exactly the kind of entry I needed to show off my amazing wit—or what I assumed to be amazing. It crossed my mind that people were laughing at *me* not my jokes, but I was too far down the path now to turn back.

"It's our careful attention to the rules of our learning institution and how well we display our deep, abiding compliance to society, isn't it?"

"No!" she laughed. "It's the *hair*."

"What?" I gasped sarcastically. "The *hair*?"

"Yes! The *hair*!"

She reached out and sort of touched my shoulder, like she would have given me a punch if we'd been closer friends. My hair wasn't too crazy—close cropped on the sides and long on top, in a sort of neo-*Outsiders* mussed-up look or something—but some of the people we hung out with had more memorable styles.

"Did that one guy—with the red hair? and the liberty spikes?—did he really get suspended for his hair?"

"Allen?" I checked rhetorically. "Nah. Well, I mean, he got sent home, but he wasn't, like, *kicked out* or anything."

"But because of his hair?"

"Well yeah, that's true. They said it was a hazard or something."

"Crazy."

We nodded and smiled at each other, but it was a do-or-die moment for continuing the conversation and it had to be handled correctly or I'd upset the whole apple cart. She couldn't invite me in—we'd only just that second met—and I couldn't say, "Well, see ya," then turn and leave. Tobie had taught me that much: If a girl doesn't find a reason to leave the moment a conversation starts, then she wants to stay. And if she wants to stay, then you better ask her out before you leave. She might say no, but she'd appreciate the gesture, and that beat being rude.

"So... you have big plans for summer?" I asked casually, trying to worm my way in to asking her out. Penny didn't look like the kind of girl who dated skaters and my deepest instinct said I should leave while I was still ahead.

She shrugged. "I play softball, so lots of practices. You?"

"Nah... I'll probably get a job, now I can drive."

"Oooo...you can drive already? I don't turn sixteen until August."

"So you have your temps...?"

"Yeah."

"Can I call you sometime? Maybe we can go for a drive?"

"Sure," she said, her face breaking into a wide smile.

I felt lightheaded. My heart stopped for several beats and my breath caught in my throat.

She pulled a fat ballpoint pen out of her back pocket—bleached denim shorts, by the way—and reached out for my left hand before I could say anything. She wrote her number across my palm in huge, looping, teen-girl lettering then folded my fingers over it and smiled at me, holding my gaze.

That was the moment I expected to wake up. I couldn't believe it was happening. As I looked into her perfect, wide, American eyes I realized that this rock star had given me her number, which couldn't possibly be true.

"See ya," she whispered and backed off a few steps, then turned and jogged back to her house, her hair bouncing in the sunlight, Puffy loping along after her as quickly as its little legs could carry it.

I opened my hand and looked at the number, memorizing the most important digits I had ever seen in my life.

Three minutes later, Sammy licked his palm and gave me five, slathering my outstretched hand with his spit and smudging the phone number.

"Fuck you, Sammy!" I barked, pulling away. "Fucking *gross*, man…"

I looked at my hand, at the smudged numbers, and considered my options: Let Sammy's spit dry or risk wiping the number off on my pants. I rubbed it down my pants once, quickly, and looked again—more smudged but still legible.

"What's the big deal, Bells?" Niz managed to choke out between hoarse laughter—it really wasn't that funny, but Niz looked to be in a mood to laugh for no reason, so he was forcing it. "You wrote it there yourself!"

"*Bull*shit! Her name's Penny Harper!"

Niz had been my best friend since we were seven or eight—who could remember at this point? He lived around the corner from my house and I honestly don't remember a time when we weren't hanging out. He always looked the most presentable of us—sort of like a wholesome surfer, with his loose blond hair and toothy, shit-eating grin—but he liked to cut it up as much as the next guy. I'm not even sure how we met—maybe at recess or something. I seem to remember sitting on the curb with Niz in third grade, picking at the weeds that had taken root along the cracks in the concrete, and there was only one reason to be sitting on the curb at recess: You'd got busted—busted for knocking some Kindergartener on his ass while playing octopus tag, for example.

Sammy, on the other hand, was a relative newcomer. He had long hair that always looked a day late for a shower. He came from the "bad" neighborhood across the state route from me and Niz, though he rose above the reputation with aplomb. We'd met him on the bus in ninth grade, looking all psycho-shy with his skateboard sticking out of his backpack. We'd talked about skaters and skateboards, then started hanging out after school—usually meeting at the park, which took him a good half hour to skate to—and now he was thick with us, like he'd always been there.

"Penny... Harper?" Niz repeated, sobering up instantly. "The chick that lives at the top of the hill?"

"Yeah...?" I agreed suspiciously.

"The really *hot* chick? Blond hair? Nice... eyes? Well... rounded?"

He cupped imaginary breasts over his chest and waggled

his eyebrows.

"Sure. Yes. Her. From my math class."

"Aw, don't pretend you didn't notice her tits, Bells!" Niz chided. "But it's still bullshit. She'd never give you the time of day."

He was voicing the unwritten rule that kids like us didn't date good girls like her. Not that the three of us were *bad*— we got decent grades and hadn't been arrested—but we did get a few detentions here and there, and we did get up to what the movie ratings would call "comic mischief." In other words, not the kind of guys the Penny Harpers of the world usually hung out with. She was very *normal*, with her softball practice and her Puffy dog and her pressed denim shorts. She was a straight-shooter, the first to raise her hand in class and the last to start talking when the teacher left the room.

"Nice try," Niz added, patting me on the shoulder as consolation for what he assumed was a failed joke. "Now let's hit this curb—it's gotta be full pops, I'll bet!"

"Full pops!" Sammy spat. "This shit's not even a top. It's barely a swirl."

Skate spots around our town were reviewed and rated by a senior everyone called Tagger, a guy who lived on Sammy's street and skated with us from time to time. He was older than us—a graduate now—so we didn't cross paths that often. After he checked out a spot, he spray-painted his mark on it, which was a lollipop for some reason. Only he also used the lollipops to rate the spots, and what had started out as his own personal way to remember if a spot was worth hitting again was now a part of our local lexicon. If he'd hit a spot, it got an orange swirl. If he'd hit a spot and liked it, it got a yellow swirl within the orange, making a complete lollipop top. If he loved the spot, he added the stick, making it a full lollipop—full pops. Spots with full pops were then ranked for difficulty or excitement by the number of lollipops he added (the most I ever saw was three). So we had swirls, tops, full pops, and lollies, and any skater in town worth his salt knew the difference.

"I'm totally serious, though," I protested, looking dismally at my smeared palm.

"It's at *least* a top," Niz argued. Sammy shook his head.

"I was trying to get over the hills—y'know?—and she was just suddenly *there*, walking her dog or something, and we started talking."

"What are you going on about?" Sammy cut in.

"*Penny Harper*!"

Sammy narrowed his eyes. He knew this was too far for me to take a lame joke, but he still felt like there *had* to be a joke somewhere in there. He looked equally excited and suspicious and intoned slowly, "And what did you talk about?"

"I don't know—her dog? Allen's hair?"

Sammy's shook his head slowly and squeezed his eyes shut in disbelief, sucking a sharp breath through his nose. "You talked about *hair*? About *Allen's* hair?"

"Well, no, I mean, not *about*, like, *hair care* or sham*poo* or whatever, but—"

"Bullshit," Niz decided. He held his hands wide begging me to argue.

I shook my head slowly. "Look, fuck you, okay?"

"Fuck me, Bells?"

"No no—not here, Niz," Sammy interjected, stepping

37

between us.

To anyone looking on it would have seemed for all the world like Niz and I were about to throw down in a hail of fists and broken noses, but Sammy knew what was really going on. It was Niz's thing, and God knows how or why it started, but if you said "fuck you" to Niz, he'd take it to the next level, every time.

"Fuck me, Bells?" Niz repeated, standing on his toes to glare at me over Sammy's shoulder. His head bobbed into my line of sight and he grinned widely, his eyes sparkling. Sammy sighed and looked genuinely dispirited.

"No, Bells…" (he pulled in a deep breath) "FUCK YOU!"

I really can't explain to you how loudly he yelled it when he dished it back to you in those moments. It was an inhuman caterwaul that seemed to come from another dimension, using Niz as a conduit. It echoed no matter where you were or how open it was. It made dogs bark and babies cry three blocks away. It was the voice of a vengeance demon calling you to war.

"*Jesus*, man!" Sammy whispered harshly, as if his dulcet tone could tame Niz's rebel yell. "This is a *family* park. There are *children*…"

Niz busted out laughing and I couldn't help but join him—poor Sammy looked so damn serious. Worse, I think he *was* serious. He ran his fingers through his hair, dropped his board, and skated off, hitting the curb we'd met up to witness. He didn't land whatever half-assed trick he was trying, but it snapped me and Niz out of it and we rolled off after him. For the moment, Penny Harper was forgotten in a string of tail slides, grinds, and no-complies (and Niz's inex-

38

plicable caveman no-comply) and we tore up that curb pretty well for the better part of an hour. Unfortunately, the paint job looked really slick and beautiful, but it was just as knobbly as unpainted curb and so only marginally better for tricks, but it seemed to absorb our scuffs and damage, which gave it a bump in our estimation—there was one less thing for nosy neighbors to complain about if we didn't leave any visible marks. It was a stupid thing to worry about—show me a curb that's still as pristine as the day it was laid, and I'll show you a skater who prefers a scooter—but worry we did.

When I was sixteen, skating took a certain force of will because it outed you to everyone else as someone they hated on principle, and that principle was almost always the ol' "destruction of property" trope that often wasn't true, or at least was greatly exaggerated. It hasn't changed too much over the years, but back then there was no internet and no celebrity—skaters were seen as nothing more than vandals, time wasters, and unkempt noisemakers, and polite society (everyone but the skaters and other outsiders) had no use for us at all, not even as entertainment.

Now I'm not saying there weren't elements of vandalism and noisemaking in our antics, but the noise was because we usually skated at night when everything else was quiet (it's easier to run and hide in the dark, and not as hot as daytime in the summer) and the vandalism rarely progressed beyond black, waxy scuffs. I do take exception to the time-waster view, however: Anything we can do to pry a little joy out of life should be done, and is never a waste of time.

Sitting long hours in an office and not having time to go out and skate is the *real* waste of time, and I honestly believe that was the linchpin of all the ire levied against us: Parents hated us for not being locked in an office, the other kids hated us for not being locked into activities our parents demanded we do, and the rest of them hated us because we had a wide view of life and living that wasn't too concerned about the things that they felt held society together: fashion, money, and the almighty decree to Act Your Age. It's okay to skate if you're twelve, but God forbid you still enjoy the sport after you could drive or—horror of horrors—hit middle age. At a certain point, Joe Society says it's time to buckle down and act like a man—which I assume means you start working 80-hour weeks and playing golf on the weekends. It means you forget about all the things that make you happy and instead try to buy the things that don't. It means you pop the collar of your polo shirt, tucked neatly into khakis, and laugh the toothy laugh of insincerity, all the while hating your life and anyone who reminds you that there is more to it than what you're doing.

Youth is a state of mind, not an age, I've come to realize, and skateboarding seems to be the thing that keeps that fire alive—skating and live music.

This is why Niz and Sammy came down so hard on me about Penny Harper—she wasn't a skate Betty, so they didn't believe it. We were sixteen and no matter how much we railed against it, we knew deep down that clichés existed even for us. Polite Society simply didn't mix voluntarily with skaters, and she was part of *that* world, not ours. Those people called the cops when they saw us hanging out in groups, or crossed the street and hurried away, or both. They certainly didn't hang out at the top of a hill with their dog and strike up a conversation.

"So you're totally serious about Penny Harper?" Niz asked as we hoofed it up the big hill toward her house, heading back to his house. The "unkempt" complaint fit us well by this point on any given day—after hours of sweating, skating, and picking ourselves up off the asphalt—and I really hoped she wasn't outside again, either by design or accident. We probably smelled as bad as we looked.

"Absolutely."

"That's fucked up, truly."

I shrugged.

"So you're going to call her?" Sammy checked.

He'd stopped and was absently messing around with the wheels on his skateboard, propping it on the ground so he could lean over and spin them.

"This one wheel…" he mumbled.

Niz and I stopped and turned back to him, and I noticed we were right in front of Penny's house. A mild panic set in as I glanced over the windows, checking for anyone spying on us. No one was. It looked empty—or *felt* empty—in that inexplicable way houses do when no one is home.

"Hey look!" Niz blurted and moved into the street, pointing at the opposite curb. "This hill's full pops!"

He dropped his board and pushed off, gliding across the blacktop to a lonely lollipop spray painted into the cupped C of the curb.

"No shit," I said, trying to sound unimpressed so they wouldn't want to stick around too long. "We bomb this hill every day."

"The paint's fresh," Niz reported. "I wish I'd known he

was around so he could've tagged that curb we just hit."

"Pffft!" Sammy derided. "He wouldn't even *ride* that curb!"

"Hey!" Niz shouted over; I cringed and glanced at Penny's house again. "You spent the last hour putzing around there!"

"Let's just go," I suggested. "Sammy, fix your damn wheel at Niz's. Let's try the humps going this way—maybe that's what the pops is for?"

"No way," Sammy decided, flopping his board down. "I'm not bombing the other side of this hill—it's a blind curve to your house. We'll get creamed."

"Unless there's a spotter!" Niz hollered, then pushed back over to us. "The boy's right."

"Fine. Let's bomb the first hill and walk down the other side."

Niz smirked gleefully.

"That's her house, isn't it?" he checked. "Right there." He pointed.

"Cut it *out*," I demanded, slapping his hand.

"Why you?" he asked seriously. "That's what I don't get—no offense. Why's she *your* girlfriend?"

"She's not my girlfriend," I mumbled, then pushed off to the crest of the hill and slid out into the street, crossing to the other side as I angled down the slope.

"Not yet!" he shouted after me. "But you gotta call her!"

Penny and I went bowling on our first date, and I took that as a good sign. She wasn't afraid to break a nail or put on dumb shoes, and by the way she laughed at her gutter-balls, she wasn't afraid to fail, as long as she was having fun doing it.

We'd started off in the park, at the top of the massive sledding hill that was an overlook in the summers, looking down into the city center below us, beyond a long expanse of trees. Everything looked green from up there, and the humidity draped us like a cape. I drove and we sat on a retaining wall and talked: it was far enough from home to seem like a date, but still close enough to back out quickly if it didn't feel right. It also seemed like neutral ground—out in public, at neither of our usual haunts. We sat on the wall, feet dangling, sun burning our skin, and talked the kind of small talk that seems entirely relevant on a first date: *What's your favorite movie? Did you see that video on MTV? Do you have any brothers or sisters?*

She had a younger brother who was into skateboarding, I guess. I asked who he was—maybe I'd seen him around—but she'd shook her head vigorously.

"He's only ten. My parents barely let him go over to his friends' houses."

"Really?"

She shrugged, then cocked her head and squinted at me with genuine interest.

"Well what did *you* get up to when you were ten?"

"I don't know. In the summers it was pretty much, 'See ya, Mom—I'll call you at noon and check in.' I didn't see my house again until dinner, unless I needed to grab something."

"Out causing trouble?"

"Nah…" I considered, gazing off into my memories. "Niz had a rope over a dry creek in his back yard. We went on hikes in the woods—those woods," I added, pointing vaguely off to our right. "Backyard baseball, capture the flag, skateboards—all the kid stuff."

"So what do you do now?"

"Now?"

I looked at her to gauge her expression; to see if I could glean what she was really getting at. She wore a simple smile and her eyes glowed with curiosity, as if she was hearing for the first time what it had been like to be a kid.

"Did anyone ever tell you that you look like Stevie Nicks?" I asked instead of answering, not so sure that what we got up to now was fundamentally different from what I'd just called kids' stuff.

"No," she chuckled and looked away, blushing. "I hope she's pretty."

"You don't know who Stevie Nicks is?" I gasped.

She shook her head, blushing more.

"Fleetwood Mac? *Rumours*? 'The Chain'? 'Dreams'? Come on!"

"Is that a band? I don't listen to much music."

"Oh my *God*!" I exclaimed in exaggerated dismay.

She tutted and sighed back at me. "Oh, stop. What do you know about baseball?"

"Baseball? Nothing. I mean, I know the basic rules, and I can hit okay…"

"The Big Red Machine? Johnny Bench? Joe Morgan?"

"I've heard of Pete Rose…?"

44

We lapsed into silence, gazing at each other and sort of smiling and pretending to be bashful. Finally she sat up straight and fixed me with a determined stare.

"So you never answered my question: What do you do *now* for fun?"

"Skate? Go bowling…? I don't know."

"Let's go bowling!" she decided, and hopped off the wall before I could disagree.

And there we were, her learning to bowl (she claimed she'd never been before), me watching her learn to bowl, and me just watching her. She had a way of smiling that was easy and secretive, as if she was about to let you in on something important and funny. She laughed a lot, too—not in the obnoxious way of someone trying to convince themselves they were having fun, but in the pure way that comes when you're in the moment and oblivious to the world and its expectations. And she always spun a little pirouette after she released the ball—her version of follow through, I guess, as she tried to bolt her lessons from softball onto a new sport.

"So why bowling?" she asked after we'd finished our game.

I watched her unlace her shoes and slip them off, then slide her feet back into her sneakers, blissfully unaware of how that simple action played in slow motion to me, as the lane lights glowed off her skin, her ankles bent demurely like a ballet dancer's. She tied her shoes with precision as well as speed—no doubt from the repetition of lacing cleats for softball practice—and I thought that even her fingers were gorgeous as they twiddled the laces into knots.

"I don't know… I guess it started with 97x and their

45

rock-n-bowl events a couple winters back."

"97x?"

"College radio, outta Oxford, I think."

"I don't know where that is," she admitted plainly, sitting back and smirking at me. She'd pulled her hair into a casual ponytail and her cheekbones caught the odd glow of the alley's lights. She smiled warmly.

"Up by Miami University?"

"Ohhhhh… okay, yeah. I think we went to see a play there once."

"Well, they set up and broadcast from here every so often, so we come out and bowl and listen to live radio. Me and Niz and Tobie and the gang."

"You have a lot of friends…?"

"Yeah, I guess." I shrugged. "I never really thought about it."

I finished tying my Cons, then leaned over and grabbed our bowling shoes and stood up. She grabbed both our balls, and there was a moment when the chivalrous male in me looked nervously from the shoes in my hands to her, but she only smiled and walked off, her ponytail bobbing happily behind her.

I moved over to the counter and returned the shoes, leaning on the scarred wood as the cashier settled up the bill with a massive, old-fashioned cash register that clanged a rusty old bell when the drawer opened. Penny caught up to me and stood right beside me as she leaned on the counter, her arm touching mine, her hip leaning lazily into me. Her eyes dared me to complain, and I damn near kissed her.

"So now what?"

46

"Want a drink?" I suggested, nodding toward the bar that separated the alleys from a small greasy-spoon restaurant.

"Are you *serious*?" Her expression said she was up for whatever—as long as it wouldn't make her look like a fool. Or get arrested.

"Well, I mean, not like a *beer* or anything. A Coke or a milkshake or something."

"Oh. Sure!"

I took my change from the cashier and we walked over to the bar. The guy working was the same guy who was always working, it seemed. His name was Chooka—at least, that's what everyone called him. He looked like a burnout from the last gasp of the hippies in 1975—or maybe a biker gone soft—and he seemed genuinely happy with his lot in life. We loved him because he talked to us like we were adults and he invented cocktails out of Coke that made us feel like we were ordering real drinks.

"Heeeeey!" he said loudly as we sat down on bar stools in front of him. I doubt he knew my name, but he probably recognized the face. We didn't go bowling a *ton*, but I bet we'd averaged a game a week the summer before, and I doubt too many other kids were that regular. He glanced at Penny and gave a her polite nod.

"Where's the rest of your crew?" Chooka rasped—too many cigarettes, I'd wager.

"No idea," I said honestly. "But it's hot out, and Penny's never been bowling before."

"That right?"

She leaned over and nudged me, her shoulder to my shoulder, her face slightly flush with the attention. She grinned at me sideways and shook her head slightly in mock disbelief, as if I was airing some mad, grievous secret. Suddenly, I felt like I'd known her for years—like I knew all her ticks and tells; how she felt; what she was thinking. That kind of closeness isn't something you can fake, it's something that just... happens. Out of nowhere. You realize the person you're with *gets* you.

Behind us, the low rumble of bowling balls and the loud pop of pins being tossed helter skelter echoed through the lanes. It was never busy, and the sound was almost lonely, like a train whistle at night: It felt like a sound you shouldn't be hearing; a sound that should be surrounded by other sounds and people and noise. I reached out bravely and touched Penny's arm so she'd turn to me, so I knew there was life in that bowling alley. She smiled and moved her arm away, then leaned over. My heart beat in my throat as I leaned in ever so slightly to accept her kiss.

"I think I like bowling," she whispered and sat up straight.

"Well, bowling's addictive," Chooka decided, eying me curiously, not sure if he should leave us alone or take our orders. "What'll ya have?"

"What was that one you made with Dr. Pepper?" I wondered. "Fireball?"

"Yeah—that's right!" he agreed, grabbing a couple of beer glasses. He dug into the ice, his face flickering as he tried to remember what the hell he'd put in it. "Cinnamon?"

"I think so..." I said slowly, giving Penny a shrug.

"So you guys hang out here or something?" she wondered.

"Well not really. Sammy's mom started it last summer—

he's the one with the long hair. She'd drop us off and go to work, then we'd skate home. Like once a week."

"That must be *miles*!"

"There's a lot to do between here and my house."

We sat and looked at each other silently, neither of us knowing where to take the conversation. That feeling of comfort with her was just as suddenly eroding and I felt panic rising. Music and skating were my go-tos, but I doubted she wanted to hear about them again, and she probably figured I didn't care about baseball or whatever she liked. Chooka served up our drinks with an expectant grin. I took a long drag from the straw as if really testing the flavor and gave him a thumbs up—it was the cinnamon that did it—and he slapped the bar happily and headed off to the other end to serve some other guys.

"So what do *you* get up to?" I asked.

She took a hesitant sip of her drink but seemed genuinely pleased with it.

"I'm on a softball team. Practice… games…"

"You said that before," I chided pleasantly. "Is that *really* all you get up to? Do all your friends play softball?"

She shrugged. "Most of them."

"And you guys don't ever do anything else? Watch movies? Go on hikes? I don't know…"

"Not really, I guess. We go out for ice cream sometimes, after games and maybe after practice."

"Well that's something!"

She chuckled and looked away, embarrassed.

"What?" I asked.

"Nothing—it sounds lame."

"No it doesn't! Ice cream is *not* lame!"

"You're making it sound *more* lame."

"I'll just have to find out for myself. We'll go for ice cream tonight!"

"Can't," she said guiltily. "I have practice."

"All night?"

"Well, I mean, until, like, eight-thirty or so."

"So…? After?"

She huffed and looked down at her shorts, picking at the frayed edges of her cut-offs. In the glow of the bar lights her skin looked golden. I couldn't help myself—I reached out timidly and touched her arm again, just to feel it, to make sure she was real. She looked up and met my eyes, smiling meekly, but she didn't pull away.

"Well… Can I come and watch you practice?"

Silence stretched for maybe a second—a second that lasted more than a minute in my head.

"Really? You want to watch me *practice*?"

"Why? Is that weird?"

"No," she shrugged. "I'd love for you to come to my practice," she added tightly, me reading too much into her tone and the way her back seemed too rigid.

She sucked up the rest of her drink.

"Okay… Where?"

"Up at Harbin Park."

"Cool—I mean, if you don't want me to stay, maybe I can walk you there? And back?"

"My parents usually walk with me."

"Oh… Well maybe we can hang out after?"

"I don't think so. My parents…"

I probably should have seen then that it would be hard to date her—that her parents were always there, or always wanted to be. Not that I have anything against parents being around, but sometimes kids need to be kids—they need to fuck up every once in a while and not get caught.

"I better get home," she said suddenly, standing to go.

I waved down to Chooka: "Two bucks cover it?"

"Sure, that'll do!" he called back. I put two dollars and all my silver on the bar and got up.

"Will they mind if I walk you to practice, though? I mean, if it's the only way I can see you tonight…?"

"Stop it," she whispered.

"I'm sorry… Did I…?"

"You didn't, Jack," she said sweetly as we walked toward the door. "I have to get ready for practice, that's all."

I felt like I'd taken something too far, but I didn't know what. She chuckled politely and slipped her hand into mine, catching my eyes and daring me to say something—maybe even willing me to tell her to defy her parents—but I couldn't. The way she held my hand—it's hard to explain—made it seem more important than it was, so I stayed quiet and squeezed her hand back and smiled, holding on for dear life. Maybe she felt it, too: The slow tug of my hand against her parents. I wish this had all been clear to me then, but it wasn't. All I knew was that I'd almost scared Penny off and only by gripping her hand tightly would she stick around.

Outside the light was dazzling and the heat draped over us like a blanket—I always love that feeling, when you leave air conditioning in the summer and go back into the real world. I associate that feeling with escape—getting out and doing something, *any*thing, so I don't have to go to sleep without something new to think about. My reflexes told me to drop my board and push off, but I grinned and caught Penny's eye instead.

"What?" she asked, dropping my hand as I opened her car door.

"Nothing... Just having fun."

"Me, too," she agreed, and I believed her.

You know those jerks in the bowling alley having too much fun, bellowing over every strike and split? That was us—me and Gray and Gray's neighbor, a guy I've only ever known as Shaggy. I assume he got the nickname because of his goatee, but he also had longish hair and walked with a lanky gait. He didn't solve mysteries, though. He worked at a local microbrewery as some kind of quality-control overseer or something. All I know is, when we went to his house to play cards, he had an endless supply of rejected beers—bottles with missing labels or labels stuck on upside down or something. He'd hand you an unlabeled bottle with a big grin and say, "God knows what it is—take it slow." Some of the beers would knock you on your ass—twice the alcohol of a shitty beer—so you only failed to take him seriously once.

"Suck *that*, Beltane!" he hollered at me as if I had trouble hearing. "Two strikes in a *row*!"

To be fair, the bowling alley was part of Mahall's, a bar that was also one of Cleveland's most unique concert venues, so obnoxious drunkards were not uncommon. We were taking in a game before the show we'd come to see, and we'd already had some mystery beers before we stumbled up the block on foot from Shaggy's house.

Gray and Shaggy lived in Lakewood, a suburb that hugged the western border of Cleveland and seemed to benefit from equal parts city living and white picket fences. They hired a relatively staggering number of cops, which kept the riff-raff in control, and the city had a healthy rotation of young families to keep it alive. Tobie and I had lived there for a while, before we'd had kids and fled to the far-flung suburbs. But Gray and Deet had held their ground and sometimes I envied them for the night life a few blocks away.

I have fond memories of Lakewood—I'd lived there even before Tobie moved in with me—and in some ways it felt as much like home as the house I grew up in. It was where I first truly struck out on my own, cut free from the tethers of parents and school friends, and those first-time adventures always gain a higher level of romance when you look back on them. They were fraught with joy and misery, too—good times always are—but the misery hadn't seemed as raw to me then; maybe I'd already formed the callused husk of adulthood, even in my early twenties. Whatever the reason, the city hadn't had any expectations of me and I'd had none of it; we'd just gelled and had a great time, and I missed it.

"Two strikes, Shaggy?" I goaded. "Is that impressive?"

"Just fucking roll," he stated grimly, hiding a smirk behind the rim of his beer bottle as he drank.

"It's Gray's turn."

Shaggy nodded and flopped down in the seat next to me. For as much beer as he drank you'd expect him to weigh three hundred pounds, but he didn't: He was doughy but slim. We all were, but only Gray seemed to actively work at fitness.

"So this chick—she friended you online and then… *poof!* Nothing?"

"Yeah, basically."

Gray had brought up Penny Harper earlier. We didn't see each other as much as we used to and he'd been curious to learn what had happened since we'd last talked, back at the Ambrosia show. Tonight it was my pick—Bass Drum of Death. Something loud I could use to drown out the nagging realization that I may be turning into my parents.

"I never got into that online-friends thing," Shaggy decided, offering himself a slight, private nod of agreement.

"Why's that?"

He shrugged. "I can't think of anybody that I want to keep up with that I don't already keep up with."

"Nobody?"

He sipped his beer and squinted down the lane, then yelped when Gray tumbled all but one pin.

"Nobody." He looked at me again and smiled. "Your roll."

We notched our last frame, drained our beers, traded for our shoes back, then shuffled over to the concert venue, which was the old automotive bay of whatever the building was originally, still with massive glass garage doors. Heavy curtains were now drawn over the doors—for privacy, but also to deflect anything that might smash glass.

Gray and Shaggy found a spot back by the sound booth on an L-shaped wooden bench that had probably been filched from an abandoned bus station somewhere along the line. I drifted over to the merch table and poked around to see if there was any tour vinyl. There was a 7-inch I grabbed and also a pocket liquor flask embossed with the slogan "Bass Drum of Death hates you." The flask seemed more likely to be rare than the vinyl. Not that I bought it to resell. I bought it for its uniqueness, because it's easier to hang a memory on something you don't see every day. I bought it because when I'm ninety, no matter what kind of mush my brain may become, I feel like that flask will always remind me in some way of that show at that club at that time. Maybe not in an obvious way, like the details I'm filling in now, but the *essence* will remain, latched onto that flask the way smells and sounds bring you back to specific moments—seconds made memorable because they weren't like the others; because they stood apart from the mass of hours that made up a weekend or a vacation or a summer.

"Don't we look pretty damn hip?" Gray observed as I plopped down beside him. "Three old dudes hanging out in the back of a club. We have to be the oldest people here."

I glanced around, not really concerned, and saw that he was right. I figured as long as we didn't seem assed-up, like most parents our age, we'd be fine. Besides, a good chunk of the kids were too hip and self-involved to care. They wanted to see and be seen with each other—as long as we looked envious, they wouldn't give a shit. It was kind of sad really, and I wondered how many times at shows over my life some middle-aged guys had said the same things about us—about me and Gray, and good ol' Joe from the coffeeshop.

"Those were the days, huh?"

"Wazzat?" Gray asked studiously.

"When we were young and making a paycheck at shows like this."

Gray spat a laugh and nursed his beer, but I could tell he enjoyed the thought. Once upon a time we'd both worked for the same alternative newsweekly, him taking the photos and me writing the reviews.

"Speaking of kids… That reminds me," Shaggy said, pointing his chin at me. "You got a fancy phone?"

"Fancy how?"

"You know—takes pictures, pulls messages from the air?"

"Messages from—*what*?"

"The air, man! I wanna send my daughter a picture, show her I'm cool."

He pulled an old clamshell flip-phone out of his pocket and waggled it at me.

"Oh, Jesus," I said. "Gray? Why do you hang *out* with this guy?"

"He gets me to church on time."

"Sure," I said, more to Shaggy than Gray, and dug my phone out of my pocket.

Shaggy hoisted his beer and Gray leaned in for a kiss and I took the picture, the flash obnoxious in the dark club, but if anyone noticed they didn't care. I guess the kids were used to people taking pictures these days. In my day, it would as likely get you punched.

"So who'm I sending this to…?"

"My daughter."

"How old is she?" I asked suspiciously.

Shaggy shrugged. "Fourteen, almost fifteen—why?"

"So you want me—a stranger—to text a picture to your daughter? Haven't you taught her to ignore that kind of shit?"

"Fuck!" Shaggy mouthed. "Fine—I'll call her first and let her know it's coming."

"On that thing?" I asked as he opened the clamshell. "Good luck. Sure you don't want to make change and find a pay phone?"

"This phone has served me very well, Jack. Very well."

"Just stop waving it around," I pleaded. "Talk about looking old…"

"Gah!" he deflected, swiping my comment out of the air with a lazy hand.

He dialed the phone and stuck it to his ear, plugging his other ear with a finger against the background music. Honestly, it wasn't that loud—we could still talk and I could hear the overdone laughter of the hipsters near us. The rest of the crowd looked more my speed: College educated drop-outs who'd learned that a higher education had only prepared them for a life of low-rent corporate slavery, which they were avoiding. This was their last stand against that future, and I wanted to tell them to live it up, because eventually life would catch you, and it had deep claws that drew blood with a scratch.

Then again, we were at the same damn club to watch the same damn show, so maybe they'd be okay.

"Send it," Shaggy said. "She's expecting it."

I sent her the picture ("Your dad says he's still cool") and we laughed some more about Shaggy's phone. Gray went and bought another round, then Shaggy disappeared to find the restroom. Gray and I sat and talked about old shows and the Clubs of Cleveland Past. I commented that no club in their right mind should be serving beer in bottles at Bass Drum of Death (but they were doing exactly that) and Gray tried to convince me that crowds were friendlier now, which got me off on a tangent about how crowds were never *un-friendly*, it's just that all crowds at shows are excitable.

"It's always about time and place," I considered.

"So crowds at shows are allowed to be violent?"

"Rowdy," I corrected. "And at this kind of show? I expect it."

"Well that's why I'm sitting back here."

"Where's your sense of adventure?"

"Shit, Bell, I never got into the mix like you did."

This was true. In college, Gray hung out in the back with Deet—now his wife—while I dove in. Not that he was holding back or unwilling to cut loose, it just wasn't his thing. He once told me he didn't like getting sweaty at shows, and that about sums it up: Gray kept it clean.

The opener started up and I left him with Shaggy and drifted toward the front. I wasn't much for the pit myself these days, but I like to be closer to the action, just in case. Midway through their set, sure as shit, a beer bottle came flying across the room and pegged the girl standing next to me right in the forehead. She looked about to faint and I steadied her, asking if she was okay. She waved me off—mostly out of embarrassment—and walked over to her friends, who all looked mortified. She didn't look like she'd come to this show for herself, in her nicely pressed shorts and white summery tank top, and I glanced around for a boyfriend, but if he was there he wasn't anywhere close by. The girls she was with didn't get up to find anyone either, so I figured this was a girls' night out or something. She saw me still watching her and smiled bashfully and waved a thank-you, and I fled to the back of the room to Shaggy and

Gray before she got the wrong idea.

After the opener Shaggy leaned in and asked me seriously, "Who's the chick?"

"What chick?"

"Oh, come on! The hot little number standing next to you the whole time? I saw you whispering to her."

"Dude, she got *beaned* with a *beer bottle*—like I *said* would happen," I added for Gray. He grinned.

"Yeah—that's a good excuse, anyway," Shaggy replied. "You should go check on her."

"Oh, he's not trying to get laid, Shaggy, don't worry," Gray jumped in. "Jack has more sexless girlfriends than anyone I've ever known."

"Shut up, Gray."

"Seriously! In college, his two best friends were girls, and he never even kissed either of them."

"Maybe I find female conversation more stimulating."

"Hey—there's nothing wrong with it!" Gray defended, holding up his hands. "Just setting Shaggy here straight. Don't want him to get the wrong idea about you."

"So you didn't even notice that she was hot?" Shaggy asked with utter disbelief.

"Well shit—what *am* I?" I squawked. "*Yeah*, I could tell she was hot, but what difference does *that* make?"

"Forget it," Gray said. "You've had too much whiskey. Don't start yelling at Shaggy about sex and love and all that bullshit."

Now I was pissed. I either sounded like a prude or a lech, and somehow Shaggy sounded like the normal one for insinuating that I should be trying to make it with a girl maybe five years older than his daughter. That makes Shaggy sound like a bad guy, which he wasn't. I really think he was hoping to live vicariously through me or something, because the man didn't have a cheating bone in his body, but the whole thing still riled me. He didn't know shit about how I treated girls, and the assumption that I came to shows to score didn't sit well with me. Is that what everyone here thought? Did I look like a wolf on the prowl? Can't a guy just enjoy a God damn show for the show's sake? And show a little concern when someone gets hit in the head with a bottle, without it having an ulterior motive?

"I woulda done the same thing if it had been a guy," I said pointedly to Shaggy.

"Now that's true," Gray spoke up. "Girls used to think he was flirting all the time, then they'd see him acting the same way with some dudes. Half of them thought he was bi."

"Oh don't start *that* shit again!" I begged, getting agitated all over. "No one thought I was gay."

"Lots of people thought you were gay—or at least open to it."

"Bullshit."

"Who was that girl junior year? Didn't she tell you she thought she was just another one of your friends?"

"How does that prove anything? We *date*d!"

"But she was always jealous."

"And that's why it didn't work out."

"I was always scared when he dated a girl," Gray confided loudly to Shaggy. "If he dated a girl, I knew he *really* liked her, and I knew it wouldn't work out for whatever reason, because it never does at that age, and I knew he'd end up depressed—"

"Fuck off, Gray!"

I stood up and started to walk off to find the bathroom or something, but Gray caught my wrist.

"Shit, Jack—forget it! I'm just kidding around!"

"Yeah—sorry I brought it up," Shaggy added, his voice full of genuine apology, his eyes wide circles of guilt.

It had all been good-natured ribbing and I'd taken it all the wrong way. Now I felt like an asshole. But Gray didn't know how truly he spoke, and I hadn't known how obvious it had always been. I've never made friends easily, but once I do, the bond runs deep—be it girls or boys or girlfriends—so when they leave, it hurts. I don't make friends because I don't trust most people—I figure they'll leave me; that they aren't as into it as I am.

Maybe I expect too much in return.

"Fuck it," I said. "It's my round and I gotta piss. Don't worry about it, Shaggy."

"It's that girl, isn't it?" Shaggy asked with mellow insight, his face oddly lit by the glow from the stage. "It's that girl you friended online? Was she an ex?"

"Yeah," I admitted. "Yeah—I'm sorry. Forget it."

Gray narrowed his eyes but remained silent, maybe trying to gauge his responsibility for my mood since he'd been the one who brought her up. Shaggy nodded that he understood, but his expression said that while he didn't *truly* understand, he thought he understood enough to stop prying.

"So what'll you assholes have?" I asked.

As I waited for our drinks at the bar I got the sense that someone was looking at me and glanced around in my typical paranoid fashion—ask an introvert what they most fear and it's that someone has noticed them. I didn't see anyone looking at me, though—just a collection of hipsters covered in beards, flannel, and beanies. As I turned back to the bar I noticed her, the girl who'd got pegged by the bottle—she was the one looking at me, standing right beside me. She smiled.

"Thanks," she said.

"Oh, it's okay. Are you okay?"

"Yeah, yeah—I just didn't want you to think I was a jerk, y'know?"

"Sure..."

"I mean, my friends said I should buy you a drink."

I smirked and nodded at the bartender, who was tending a sloppy pour of Guinness for Gray. "Too late."

Shaggy's voice echoed in my head (*The hot little number standing next to you*) and I saw that she *was* quite pretty. Not in any ostentatious way, but in the subtle way of a girl who's more concerned about her brains but not oblivious to her looks. She blushed, and I knew that if I was another man or in another time and place, I would have bought *her* a drink instead, and we would have talked about music and movies and all those get-to-know-ya things that can make or break a date in minutes. But I wasn't a different man, and this wasn't another time or place, and I could only see a girl who was grateful, who didn't want me trying to get in her pants, who only wanted to thank me. Gray once told me my biggest problem was that I couldn't recognize flirting... Looking back, he's probably right, but I'm not sure it would have made any difference. I'm not built for one-night stands so I assume girls want to talk not fuck.

"Well, thanks anyway," she said. "My friends didn't even want to come to this show. They said we should act our age. We're not in college anymore."

She rolled her eyes. She was feeding me info, paying out her line to see if I'd bite—a subtle play to tell me she was older than she looked, because no one would put her a day over nineteen. Out of college, long enough to think of it as the past... Twenty-four? Twenty-five? So maybe ten years younger than me, not just a few years older than Shaggy's daughter.

"Well, my wife gave up on telling me to act my age long ago," I explained with a smile. It was a shutdown; a spike over the net for the kill shot. I was married and I was happy. She nodded, her lips pursed into a wry smirk—message received. Her shoulders relaxed and she straightened up.

"Not many guys look out for girls at these shows," she admitted. "It's like, they figure we should man-up if we're going to stand on the floor."

"Most guys are assholes," I confided, slipping the bartender a twenty in exchange for our drinks.

"Yeah?"

I shrugged and organized the drinks for transport—Gray's glass in one hand, Shaggy's bottle in the other, and my rocks glass between my thumbs.

"I mean, my wife could kick any one of their asses, if that's what 'man-up' means."

It was true. It was a factual statement—Tobie was beautiful, but she didn't take any shit from anyone, least of all me—but I hadn't intended it to be a re-enforcement of my marital status. I'd figured we were just talking now—but she got the message if she had intended to flirt. She collected her drinks and flashed another smile. I felt my heart jump. How could I not? Anyone who says they don't want another breathless chance at a first kiss is full of shit.

"Thanks again."

"Be careful out there."

Jesus, I sounded like a fucking dad.

I can't fully remember these things later, no matter how hard I try. Not the details, not the points and lines that sketched a complete image. They're nothing more than pictures in a photo album, these memories—stills from some time so far gone that the colors start to fade and the faces lose shape, fuzzing out along the edges like an ink drop in water.

The light was golden—sparks firing off green leaves in sunlight—that I remember. She was dressed in white shorts and a pink-striped tank top, the even tan of her legs against light white tennis shoes, her hair pulled back in a lazy ponytail. We were at a park, but not Harbin Park near our houses—this was a date, our second date, and we'd driven somewhere else, probably Winton Woods, to make it seem more special. I remember the light skimming off the water, and her face, her eyes smiling above rounded cheeks, her lips so perfectly colored they should have been used as the shade for a subtle lipstick.

"I don't have time for makeup," she'd commented with a grin when I told her how perfect her lips looked. It was the best response I could have hoped for from such a stupid compliment.

"I want to kiss you," I admitted in response, and she slowly closed her eyes and moved toward me, and I closed my eyes and found those lips. They felt every bit as perfect as they looked, and we kissed delicately at first and I was afraid I wouldn't match up to her expectations and I pulled away, and we grinned at each other. Then we kissed again, and her lips parted and her arms were around my neck and my hands were on her hips and she pushed her body against mine, and all I could hear was the soft sound of tiny lake waves lapping against the rocky shore.

"Jack," she said simply as she pulled away, but it wasn't a question or a comment, it was a declaration, an admission that I was with her and she wanted me to be there.

I took her hand in mine and we continued sauntering down the trail along the lakeside. All the nerves and questions had evaporated with that kiss—holding hands felt natural; walking side-by-side with her seemed like the way the world had always been.

"We should go out for dinner," I suggested.

"Oh, my parents are big on dinner time," she said, tugging my hand. "I don't want to rush them."

"*Rush* them?"

"Never mind…" She shook her head but held my gaze, begging me to make her explain.

"What is it?" I asked playfully.

"I mean, I guess you should know, I wasn't allowed to date until I was fifteen."

"Oh…? I don't…"

"So they aren't used to it, Jack."

She liked to say my name, and I loved to hear it. I stopped and turned to her and gave her another kiss—a deep, lingering kiss. She certainly didn't kiss like she'd never dated before, if that's what she'd been trying to say. She pulled away and looked at her watch—a big Swatch watch, white like her shorts and in perfect contrast to her tan.

"We'd better head back. But I really liked this."

"Me, too. How about after dinner…?"

"I have practice."

"Right…"

Setting schedules, making plans—the fact that I'd told Niz I'd head over to his house to watch some new skate video he'd bought never even crossed my mind. Not with Penny's eyes locked on mine, her lips parting as she breathed gently and smiled.

"So… tomorrow, then?"

"Absolutely."

"I'll call you when I get up."

"Let's finish today first," she decided, and she kissed me again, and her hand on the back of my neck felt like sunlight through the trees, and her hand on my waist felt more real than anything I'd ever known, and her cheek still smelled like soap.

Somewhere in there, that memory is complete, spooled around other frozen moments from that summer: Penny in her softball uniform, Penny running away so I'd chase her, Penny stepping out of my car, Penny jumping off her front porch to meet me. Penny's lips, Penny's skin, Penny's gentle soapy scent, Penny's face flushed after softball practice.

Somewhere, it's all still complete, but it fades like a soft dream of yesterday; like a bright white dandelion head drifting toward the sun and blurring into the summer sky.

At least I can remember her lips—God granted me that tiny mercy.

The soft, even glow of American summer nights is like a pool full of warm water: You simply float in it. You reach into darkness and bathe in humidity, the earth a warm-blooded lap you're curled up in. Everything seems like liquid in those moments, and not because of the sweat that breaks out immediately across your neck and brow. There's a molten quality to the world in summer nights, but in a soft way, unlike the harsh glare of the sun in daylight hours. It's like being wrapped in a warm blanket on a winter night. It has romance in it, even if you're out alone, stargazing—but I was rarely alone that summer. Penny and I would sit in the park, long after her softball practice had ended, and we'd talk and we'd kiss.

It was easier to see Penny by hanging out after her softball practices because sidestepping into a date was simpler than making an actual date: After softball she could tell her parents that I would get her home, and they couldn't exactly say "no" without sounding like complete bastards. But pre-planning a date gave her parents time for an excuse: I wasn't there already, so why bother?

Penny didn't really like me watching her practices, though. Her parents still walked her up to the fields, and it immediately became clear that wasn't going to change. She was trying to figure out where her parents fit in to us dating, and that was one line she wasn't willing to cross, for some reason. Maybe it had echoes for her of being dropped safely at school by her folks—who knows? Only a few parents stayed to watch the practices, like Penny's did, and you could tell they were the kinds of parents who also walked their kids right up to the gym doors at dances instead of throwing open the car door so they could hop out. Once, I watched a full practice instead of only showing up in time to take her home, and I could tell it made Penny self-conscious, and it made me self-conscious, too. And it made her *parents* nervous, like it was only okay that I existed as a shadowy boyfriend instead of a real person—which is some kind of fucked up thing only her parents could be okay with. Seeing me made me real; not seeing me left open the potential that I was only a figment of the imagination of their lovestruck daughter.

But *after* practice was perfect: her parents didn't expect her home until ten and everyone else on the team wanted to get home and shower and watch TV and go to bed. That left a good hour or so for us to hang out in the park (as long as I left my car on the street outside the gates, so the cops didn't know we were in there). I'd drive up around eight and sit in my car, and when they got done she'd practically skip over to me, pulling off her ball cap, her hair fanning out around her face as she leaned in the driver's side window and gave me a quick kiss before I got out. She'd toss her glove and hat on the passenger seat, then take my hand so we could walk up to the overlook.

It all felt very cinematic, like we were star-crossed lovers stealing defiant minutes together. Like I was her secret lover on horseback waiting to take her away from it all—to a life of romance and European sunsets. Later, that image didn't seem so great, but for those first few weeks it seemed like the dream was real.

We'd walk up to the overlook at the top of the park, me stealing glances at her legs and her pretending not to notice, and we'd plop down in the grass at the top of the sledding hill and talk as the summer light faded to purple around us.

And we'd kiss—of course we'd kiss—and the scent of the humid air on her skin was soft and lovely; her skin glistened in the fading light like magic or ruin.

"Let's go out tonight," she said once, her hand running through my hair, our noses an inch apart, my hand gently resting on her waist. We were sitting in the grass facing each other like bookends pushed together, night slowly bleeding the color out of the sky.

"Yeah? Are you allowed?"

Usually she wasn't, not on practice nights—or whatever excuse there was that day—but softball was almost over, so she'd either taken a stand or her parents had started to soften. Sometimes I'd take her home to change and shower and we'd go down to Big Boy—a sort of high-end diner—and get milkshakes and fries. She'd sit and tell me whatever excitement there was to be had from the Reds and the baseball season; I'd tell her about something I'd read in *Thrasher* or some new song I'd heard on the radio. With anyone else it may have felt like our conversations had crossed purposes, but not with her. With Penny it felt right somehow, like we were two explorers out on our own adventures who couldn't wait to see each other and share everything that had happened. Big Boy was our travelers' tavern, our wide eyes brimming with tales over milkshakes as big as our heads.

"I can stay out until *eleven* now," she explained, and her tone had said she meant more than another trip to Big Boy.

"*Eleven*?" I checked. "Wow—what happened?"

"Nothing," she chuckled lightly, straightening her back and ducking her head away as if really embarrassed—and maybe she was. "But I have to go home first and check in." She looked at me and smiled. "And shower. I feel gross after practice."

"Well you're not," I stated, running a finger along her thigh. "Not even close."

"You wouldn't say that if I didn't dump water over my head before we met up…"

"Try me."

"Gross!"

I could see she wouldn't be convinced.

"But eleven is like a whole new world!" I exclaimed, changing the subject back. "We could catch a movie! Hang out with Niz and the gang! What would happen if you were late?"

"Gosh, I don't know."

She looked mortified, like I'd asked what would happen if her parents caught her smoking pot.

"No, I mean, we *won't* be late, but what if the movie was longer than we thought? And we didn't get home until, like, eleven-thirty or midnight? Would you be grounded? Banned from ever seeing me again?"

I was smiling and she laughed distractedly, picking at the grass by her knee. It had been a flippant question, mostly. It wasn't that important—I'd get her home on time even if we had to miss the end of the movie. I'd never met a girl like Penny before—athletic and tan and vibrant and so God damn *American*, like in all the movies—and I didn't want my idea of wiggle-room ending what we had. I liked being with her and seeing her smile and seeing her eyes sparkle and feeling her lips on mine. Most nights, after I'd seen her, I'd lie awake trying to think of some detail—some moment—that would pin down the night forever and prove later that it had happened, because most nights it felt like a dream—I needed that single moment to use as an anchor to reality.

"They're not that bad, Jack," she said softly. "This is all new for them."

"I just don't want to blow it for you—for us—if I piss off your dad."

"He's not *that* bad," she said quietly. She stopped picking the grass and looked at me suspiciously. "How old were you when you went on your first date?"

"Shit, I don't know…" I said vaguely, which was really true. "I mean, what do you consider a *date*? I've been to school dances. I've hung out with girls…"

"No—like for real."

"For *real*?" I shrugged. "I guess last winter."

"See? So you were fifteen, anyway—I didn't miss anything cuz of my parents."

"Yeah, but…"

I stopped because the truth is, Tobie and I had gone out on dates—what we sometimes called dates, and sometimes we hung out and didn't call it a date—since we were kids in middle school, and I'd technically dated other girls here and there, but it hadn't felt *real* until the winter, when I'd taken Tobie to the King of Hearts dance, our first high school dance together. So while on the one hand it felt like I'd been dating girls for a while, on the other hand I'd really only

73

dated one girl.

"Okay… So how many girls have you kissed?" she wondered casually.

I glanced at her and she was grinning devilishly; it was a game of truth-or-dare to her, only it was all truth. Maybe it was a test. I could feel panic rising in me.

"Three?"

"Including me?"

"Four…? How many boys have you kissed?" I snapped, trying to divert attention from my answer.

"Two."

"Including me?"

"*Two*," she giggled, ducking her head. She was being playfully embarrassed and I liked the glee that rimmed her eyes.

"How old were you?" she checked.

"What?"

"When you first kissed a girl? How old?"

"Eleven," I said without hesitation, a weird resonance fighting for my attention as I realized that the first girl I'd kissed—and meant it—had also been Tobie.

"Eleven," I repeated. "We were sledding and we went off in the trees across from my house and we kissed. I mean, it wasn't *planned* or anything…"

I trailed off and she was looking at me in a satisfied way, a half smile across her lips, like she was pleasantly surprised to discover the specimen she'd chosen to study was entirely human, after all.

"What about you?" I asked slowly. "Who was the other boy?"

"A kid at church. We were thirteen. We were at a lock-in.

74

I think it seemed like we should be doing something, you know, *dangerous* with all those kids—boys *and* girls—on a sleepover. We snuck off to the back of the chapel and kissed in the dark, in the back pew. It was *such* a big secret…"

She giggled at herself and gazed off wistfully down the hill, looking out over the lights of the town center below us, a breeze puffing her hair ever so slightly. She closed her eyes against it and smiled.

"That's really kind of beautiful," I admitted.

"It's silly," she decided, suddenly standing up and holding out her hand for me.

I took it and stood up and pulled her to me, kissing her slowly, seriously, proving to her that this was real, more real than anything before. I don't know if she understood that, but she met my kisses and dropped my hand so she could hold my head. I put my arms around her and squeezed her against me, her body humming like a live wire. She gasped and broke away and I let her go. She looked at me with heavy eyelids, her face a blur of satisfaction and relief.

"I take it back," I said softly.

"Take what back?" she asked, confusion flickering across her eyes.

"I've only ever kissed *one* girl."

"Including me?"

"One," I replied.

She smirked proudly and stepped away, taking my hand again and pulling me toward the street and my car.

"I want to go get changed so we can go out," she explained. "We're probably too late for a movie, though."

"Nah—we can still make it," I said.

"Okay—it's a date."

"So *now* it's official?" I joked. "We weren't dating before?"

"I guess we were just hanging out," she agreed with a lingering gaze.

Later, after the movie and after we were safely back at her house, standing on her front porch, she pulled me lightly toward her and I met her eyes, her lips parted with the slightest grin. She may or may not have twitched closer, so I leaned in and kissed her, quickly, nothing more than a peck on her lips. She pulled away.

"What's wrong?" I checked. Had I misunderstood?

"Nothing," she said quickly. "I mean… my *parents*."

I glanced at her front door and shrugged. Did she really think her parents were under the delusion that we'd never kissed? Worse… did she really think her parents were *spying* on us?

"I didn't mean to call you lame before," I said instead of talking about her parents again. "It's just lame that you can't ever stay out late."

"It's not late?" she asked with perfect innocence. I glanced at my watch. It was 11:05—not late, by my estimation. I was heading over to Niz's after this. The night was young.

"Can't you ask them if you can come and hang out with us? Tobie and Jess are there, too."

She sighed nervously but pointedly and waggled her

head.

"I don't want to push it."

She moved closer and placed her lips on mine. Her hands drifted into my back pockets. I kissed her harder. Her mouth opened slightly, her tongue found mine, and she yanked herself back and stepped away.

"My *parents*," she hissed, looking at her feet as she pulled her hair back over her ear. "I mean, they *know* we're going *steady* and all, but..."

My breath caught in my throat. Had she said we were *going steady*? She'd never said that before, not even in private, and never when we ran into her softball friends at the park or the movies or something. She never introduced me as her boyfriend; never even said we were *going out*.

"I like kissing you," I blurted.

She snickered.

"I like kissing you, too, Jack."

She touched my hand, glanced up at the porch light— either waiting for it to come on, or willing it to.

"Let's go to Niz's, huh? He's just right down the street. Just for a half hour, so you can see what you're missing?"

She shook her head no—bashful, apologetic—and then she was gone, her front door closing over my smile.

I drove to Niz's and sat in my car for a minute before going in. They all wanted to meet Penny and I knew she would come around eventually so there wasn't any reason to upset the apple cart. They'd give me a hard time, though, I knew that. Niz would say he didn't think Penny was a real girl, Jess would agree, and Tobie would laugh but not actively join in. I wasn't sure I could handle it again. It was starting to seem like a chore, like I should just go home and go to bed; like I should go home and call Penny and apologize for giving her a hard time.

I sighed heavily and opened the car door, my left foot dangling out toward the street, still undecided. I finally touched the pavement and inertia had me: I got out, I slammed the door, I plodded down Niz's dark driveway toward the maw of his garage, the garage door always open, the door to his house always unlocked. I knocked anyway, *knock nuh-nuh-knock*—our "secret" knock so he knew who it was—and he called out "Yo!" so I knew who I was walking in on.

"No Penny?" he surmised before I was even through the door.

"Dude, she's not real." (Jess.) (Laughter.)

Someone threw a can of Coke at me. It missed and skittered into the utility room by the garage, into the darkness; I left it and walked into the family room. Niz was holding court in a wingback chair, Jess and Tobie were slumped on the couch. A pizza box had two pieces left in it. It was just like every night. I wished I was still with Penny; her stories seemed new, her ideas fresh and wise.

"Couldn't get away from her parents," I half lied. "What's on?"

"*Evil Dead*," Niz said.

"Again?"

"Everything okay with Penny, Jack?" Tobie asked softly.

"Yeah… She just—"

"Has strict parents," Jess finished. "We know, Jack-o. Sit down, for God's sake."

"Where's Sammy?"

"His dad said he had to stay home."

"His *dad*?"

"Yeah—he thinks Sammy's on drugs."

"Wow."

I couldn't get into the conversation and I didn't know why. I wasn't sad or upset—I was actually tired. Normally news that Sammy's dad thought he was on drugs—and cared enough to notice—would have set us off into twenty minutes of nervous ribbing in his absence, but I wasn't feeling it. I motioned to the pizza and took a slice as Niz waved for me to take what I wanted.

"There's a Coke in the utility room," he added.

I ended up going home around midnight anyway, as if Penny had been there all along.

After nine in the summer, the darkness falls in full. Dusk is a slow build and a sudden drop-off into night. The air didn't thin any—not in summer, not in southern Ohio—but the sun was gone, at least, and that's when we slipped out of our houses, after dinner and chores, when our parents were watching sitcoms.

Before I got my drivers license it was harder to get out after dark, but now that I could drive back home by myself, there was no need for my parents to go out and get me, so I didn't need to convince them of anything. My world became larger simply because I could drive myself. I had a shit-brown 1980 Malibu sedan that had probably never seen better days, and it felt like a standing ticket to everywhere: The mall, the record store, the movie theater, even to Tobie's house, way out in the township beyond the stretch of suburban lights.

That's how we ended up at the police station in town, helping Tagger with his latest project. And by helping, Niz and I sat and watched Tagger and Sammy. Tagger's plan was simple: He'd made a bunch of bumper stickers with his lollipops on them and he was going to stick them onto the bumpers of any police cruisers parked in the lot. It was his way to get back at them for harassing us, I guess. My job was the getaway vehicle—he'd reasoned that the cops already knew his car so I'd be able to make a cleaner getaway.

"It's cool," he had reasoned. "If they catch us, I'm

eighteen. I'll take the fall. But if they *don't* catch us, they won't find me later cuzza my car."

"Wouldn't it be better for a minor to take the fall?" Sammy offered. "You could go to jail, right?"

We ended up with something of a compromise: Sammy would help. One minor, one adult. Niz and I would keep the getaway car warm.

"I don't think I could evade the police," I admitted to Niz, understanding both the limits of my car and my ability to drive it.

I figured I should come clean with him in case a high--speed chase presented itself. We were sitting in the dimness between two streetlights looking every bit as suspicious as we feared. Across the street we could see Sammy and Tagger dodging between cruisers, running hunched over, slapping stickers onto bumpers as quickly as possible.

"This is massively stupid," Niz decided. "No way they don't get caught. *We* don't get caught."

"I don't know—it actually looks pretty dead for a police station."

And dark. I guess they figured no one was dumb enough to try something at the actual station, and this was long before cameras recorded every move anyone made.

Tagger and Sammy suddenly emerged from the other side of the building and sprinted straight to the car, grinning ear-to-ear. They hopped into the back seat without a word and I carefully pulled out and drove away. Totally undramatic. No yelling, no sirens, no chase.

"I swear if I see a cruiser driving around with that sticker on it...!" Tagger chuckled gleefully.

He was a wiry kid with long, dark hair and his clothes never seemed to fit right—always a bit big. He was the kind of kid my mom would call a hoodlum, which always made us snicker. For one thing, skaters weren't hoods, though we ran along similar paths and crossed lines from time to time. For another thing, no one called hoods "hoodlums" anymore; this wasn't 1957.

"You know, they check their cars before they drive off—taillights and all that?" Niz said.

I shrugged.

"Still…"

"Yeah—at least we *did* it!" Sammy enjoined, patting Niz heavily on the shoulder. "Maybe one of 'em will let it go for a day! Officer Oler or someone!"

"How many did you get rid of?" I wondered.

Tagger held up his empty hands. "Well we started with ten and now we have none! Good driving, Jack," he added, and I got the sense he'd assumed we'd bail as soon as they got to the cruiser pen.

I glanced at Niz. His expression said this might have been the dumbest thing we'd ever done, and we'd done some pretty dumb things.

"No sweat," I said to Niz, but Tagger assumed I meant him and snickered again.

I could tell Niz was worried in a fatherly way and I was trying to let him know that this wasn't the start of a slippery slope into adolescent vandalism that would descend into drugs and chaos. It was was just a dumb idea that ballooned up and burst before anyone really thought about, and now it was all over.

I hoped.

"Don't they have closed-circuit cameras at the station, though?"

"Nah," Tagger said glibly.

I could fully imagine a camera pointed at my car, its lens whirring and turning slowly as it zoomed in on my license plate.

"It *was* a pretty dumb stunt," I said.

I felt like I needed to have Niz's back, but I didn't glance at him to make it too obvious.

"It's cool, man. Look, if they had cameras, they would've come out while we were back there creeping around. Right? And nothing happened. They didn't even turn a light on."

We drove in silence for a few minutes, each thinking of our own possible version of a worst-case scenario.

"Look, man," Tagger finally spoke up. "If they come and ask you questions, you have my full permission to rat me out. Say it was all my idea. Corrupting the youth and all that bullshit—they'd eat it up. They'd *expect* it from me."

He wasn't wrong. It was exactly the kind of story parents and the press would fall for, and Tagger—being from one of the neighborhoods on the other side of the state route— would be an easy scapegoat. Somehow, the solidity of this escape plan didn't make me feel any better—I couldn't put it all on Tagger, not with all the shit he already had to put up with because of his address, and I didn't think Niz or Sammy would either.

"Don't worry about it," I decided. "I mean, you're right, no one even followed us, let alone chased us."

"Look, man," Tagger said, his tone contemplative and honest. "I'll take you to my favorite spot—full pops, seven lollies. My highest rating. I don't take *any*one out there, man."

We were all silent again. Niz looked excited but for some reason I was waiting for Tagger to burst out laughing and admit to joking about a veritable skate Valhalla.

"*Seven* lollies?" I checked.

"You're *serious*?" Sammy choked—he'd assumed it was a joke, too.

"One lollie for each obstacle—there's a wicked curb, a steel bench with no back, an easy fucking rail, and even a sweet little bank around a sewer grate. Plus lollies for being dark, distant, and quiet. *No one* knows about it—and you better keep it a secret."

I was more amazed at learning how his system roughly worked—lollies for obstacles, plus more for location—than with the idea of being taken to some top-secret skate spot. Niz was all ears, maybe trying to make up for coming across like a wet end before.

"Why would you take us there?" he wondered.

"Y'all earned it! I've been trying to get that asshole Timmy Toderman to take me to the police pen for *months*."

I shot Niz a look because I knew what he was thinking: If Timmy Toderman—*aka* The Toad—hadn't gone along with the plan, it really *must* have been stupid. The Toad was going to be a senior and all of the skaters kind of looked to him as their moral compass, probably because he had a job and better things to do than skate—like, he worked hard and got good grades but he still found time to skate with us.

My eyes darted to the rear-view mirror but it was dark behind us, the streetlights fading to yellow blobs along an empty road.

"Turn right after the library, then hit the first street on the left."

His directions were easy to follow, but I'll be damned if we could find that spot again without him—our li'l 'burb was actually pretty big. I guess we were only half paying attention, driving around with the windows down and the music loud, making sudden turns when Tagger commanded. The only time I could have taken a moment to get my bearings was when I'd stopped after taking a corner too fast—there'd been a squeal of tires and a *pop* like a huge cork erupting from a bottle, and I slammed on the brakes. We were completely alone—no cars, no houses. Well, no finished houses—we were out in one of the new developments that was still being put together, so there were a few framed-out houses and a couple of dark, empty show homes, but other than that it was us and the crickets.

"What the hell was that?' I breathed, cutting the music. We could hear a strange whirring, metallic sound nearby, like a spinning top losing steam.

"Dude!" Sammy exclaimed. "You lost a hubcap!"

He was right, too—the turn had put enough pressure on one of the tires that it had popped the damn hubcap off and sent it rolling down the street ahead of us, where it now swirled into its resting place.

"Can you grab that, Sammy?"

He did, and as soon as he was back in the car, I gunned it and got out of there, irrationally afraid that someone had

85

seen us. From there, it was a blur of paranoia as Tagger directed me, and when we finally got to Seven Lollies it was indeed dark, distant, and quiet—a forgotten park on the edge of town waiting patiently for houses to be built up around it. The streets were unnamed and unlit; the bench and rail perhaps evidence of a project that ran out of money, or need, or both. The banked curb was the best part, I thought: Built into the crook of a sharp left in the street, like a mini pool around a flat storm-drain cover with a grate. The in and out was smooth and if you were lucky—or good—you could nab a tail slide at the top. And if you fell, which I did, it was only a couple of feet to the pavement. Traffic was nonexistent and people seemed like a dim rumor of another world.

Seven Lollies ended up being like a mythical summer paradise; a weird time and place I can't forget but can't ever have again—one of the shining highlights of my first summer of independence. We tried to find it again on-and-off through high school, after Tagger was gone, and we never could. Tagger only took us there a couple of nights—he guarded Seven Lollies with an almost jealous intensity. And the streets, they take on a tunnel-like, featureless quality in the dark that can't be fathomed in daylight—it all looks different in the sunshine and it all looks the same later, if you go back after sundown without directions. There were a lot subdivisions being built up in those days, too, constantly changing the landmarks and visual cues.

"Why don't you tell everyone about this place?" Sammy wondered as we stopped to catch our breath. We must have been hitting it for a couple of hours straight by that time, taking breathers only long enough to cheer each other on.

86

"Are you *kidding*?" Tagger asked almost angrily. "Look man, if I tell everyone, then everyone comes out here all the fucking time because it's *seven* fucking lollies. And then the cops find out, and then it's all over. No way, man—this is *mine*. And you better keep your trap shut!"

"We won't tell," I assured him.

He looked around suspiciously as if we'd already told everyone, then nodded slowly to himself as if he'd arrived at the only logical conclusion he could think of.

"I'm thirsty anyway," he said, turning back to us. "Let's go get something."

Niz and I exchanged glances—"something" could mean anything—and Sammy, either sensing our unease or innocently making an honest suggestion, blared, "Slushies!"

And so I followed Tagger's directions out and eventually swung my massive Malibu sedan onto the main drag into town—it heaved itself around the last curve like a mastodon cornering at a slow gallop.

The nice thing about driving a beater is that it didn't matter too much what happened to it—the whole thing was held together by used parts and duct tape—and I drove it kind of hard. Not in a pedal-to-the-metal way—God knows it topped out around sixty-five—but just in hard turns and sudden brakes and trying to come off the line at a sprint, like any red-blooded American with a new license does. The beast whirred and coughed as it got up to speed, but even a shitty V8 is still a V8, and when it was humming along at a cruising altitude somewhere between twenty-five and sixty, it was all good and all power. That damn car held out until my last year of college, when a trip up a massively steep hill finally killed it in a whiff of fried spark plugs and burned engine oil.

After hitting the main drag, it was a straight shot all the way down a long-ass hill into the city center, with an all-night convenience store on the corner in the middle of town, by a bank and a grocery store. My hometown had already started to sprawl, blossoming as it had in the late '70s, but the city center hadn't yet gone over to corporate-owned strip malls. I mean, there *were* two strip malls in town, but they were owned by local landlords and city bigwigs, one of whom lived in the house right behind mine—and God bless him for not wanting a McMansion in one of the rich neighborhoods, I suppose.

We rolled up to the convenience store laughing way more than was required at absolutely nothing—the place looked deserted so I wasn't too worried about pissing anybody off. Inside, the guy behind the counter eyed us warily, not saying a word as he watched the four of us trail back to the pop coolers for a chilled case of Coke. There was another customer back there, it turned out, a hunched guy in a light longcoat that may have been a bathrobe. His hair was longer and stragglier than Tagger's and he hadn't shaved in days—a classic bum with a look on his face that was either panic, surprise, or concentration.

Convenience stores are perhaps the greatest American invention. Once, in college, Gray and I hatched a plan to see the country by working our way from convenience store to convenience store—we figured we'd live and work in one town long enough to make enough money to move to the next town. Working in a town, we decided, was the better way to truly experience America and all it had to offer. The linchpin of the plan was that every city, town, and burg in America has an oasis open twenty-four hours a day, all year long, and the secondary assumption was that no one really wants to work the graveyard shift at an all-night convenience store, which meant (we figured) they'd always be hiring.

This plan, I know, had its hoary origins in the summer I was sixteen, with my newly minted drivers license and my crew along for the ride.

"Don't let him bother you," the bum advised us, nodding and winking. "Don't let him."

"Okay," Niz agreed amiably, reaching past the guy for our Coke.

"You know, they put them here to watch us, right?"

"Who?" Niz wondered, looking around. Sammy and I chuckled, but tried to keep it to ourselves. Tagger was over in the chip aisle looking for some snacks.

"The man behind the counter—there's *always* a man behind the counter. You ever notice that?"

"Well sure," I offered. "I mean, they work here, I guess."

"That's what they want you to *think*," the man agreed with widening eyes. "But you need to *think* to see what *they* see!"

That stumped us. We all stared at the guy, and he stared back, waiting for what he'd said to sink in and make sense; waiting for our epiphany. It never came.

There is another thing about convenience stores and American nights, other than hotdogs and Coke: Entertainment. Those long, slow hours between midnight and sunrise get a bad rap as prime hours for stickups and vampires,

89

but we only ever ran into your usual crop of nut-jobs and drunks—people who didn't want to brave the world in the daylight, either out of fear or some innate form of self-p-reservation. And the thing is, those midnight denizens are really good for conversation, if you enjoy pretending to believe every word they say.

Sammy finally mumbled something and Niz backed away with the Coke. As I turned to follow them to the counter, the guy caught my eye and nodded sagely, then whispered, "That girl will *get* you."

"What?"

He nodded once more, then turned back to the pop cooler, his finger pointing and his lips moving, as if he was counting the cans. I caught up to the others, who were chuckling to each other about the bum, but they stopped when they saw my face.

"What'd he say?" Niz wondered.

"He said, 'That girl will *get* you'!"

"What girl?"

"How should *I* know?"

"He meant Penny—obviously," Sammy cut in.

"*Obviously*?" I barked. "What the hell does *that* mean?"

"Calm down, fellas," the man behind the counter said—the bum was right, they were always watching.

"Grab some Cheez-Its, Bells," Niz said. "Sammy's just messin' around."

I slumped off and found the Cheez-Its and I almost went back over to the bum to see what he'd meant, but when I glanced back up at the counter I could see they were all waiting for me—especially the counter man, who was watching us. I snatched up the Cheez-Its and strode back to the counter, thrusting them at Niz, who took them and relayed them to the counter-man, where he took them and rang them up with a light rattle of the register keys and a sullen *beep* that the price had been entered.

Outside, it was still humid—the air seemed thick enough to mold and the stars looked puffy through the moisture.

"Let's sit here and have a Coke," I suggested.

"Sure," Sammy said. "Look, I didn't mean nothing about Penny—that dude's crazy."

"I know, man—don't worry about it."

Niz popped open the passenger door and dropped the case of Coke on the seat, then tore into it and passed me, Sammy, and Tagger a can. Tagger eyed me curiously, but we all four sat on the parking block in the next spot over, popped our Cokes, clinked cans, and drank to the summer and the night.

Around us you could hear the sounds of the city center echoing off the buildings: Car tires squealing, sirens in the distance, a truck down-shifting as it left the state route and hit the speed zone. There's always life in the world, if you sit and listen for it. Good life. The sounds of activity, of humanity. And somewhere back there, in my neighborhood, I assumed Penny was snoring softly...

"So why would that guy bother you, anyway?" Sammy asked.

"Leave it alone, Samuel," Niz growled.

He was afraid Sammy was treading into water he'd inadvertently tested and found sour: Niz had made some comment about Penny and I being "all wrong" and I'd kind of lost it; told him to fuck off in a tone that didn't engender his usual retort. Maybe I was afraid of the same thing, and maybe I didn't want to be reminded of it, and maybe Niz understood all of that in the silent way true friends do, because he apologized and even gave me an awkward hug, and then we forgot all about it.

I glanced at Niz; he looked angry for me. Funny thing is, I wouldn't go off on Sammy the same way I'd gone off on Niz—Sammy and I weren't that close yet. Besides, with Tagger there I wasn't about to go off on anyone.

Niz chugged his Coke and ripped out a massive belch, so we sidelined the conversation long enough to congratulate him on its length and resonance.

"Anyway," Sammy said. "For some reason she is *totally* into you. For now, anyway."

Niz sucked his Coke loudly.

"What does *that* mean?"

"What?" Sammy asked innocently.

"'For now'. What's *that*?"

He looked to Niz and Tagger for support, got none, and shrugged.

"Dude, I don't know—these kinds of things always burn hot at first. It's like a match."

"A match…?"

I actually respected Sammy's opinion now that he was stating it. Sammy always had—how do I put it nicely?—a lot of girlfriends. Not all at once, just a constant parade, like he never had to worry about getting a date. So maybe he knew a thing or two about fleeting relationships and how they looked at first.

"Matches go out real quick," Sammy concluded. "And

sometimes they burn you before they do."

"Yeah—you're dating Penny Harper, right?" Tagger said suddenly. There was something in his tone that seemed like he'd been waiting for the right time to ask, but he felt that moment slipping away and finally blurted it out.

"Yeah," I replied suspiciously.

"You're not?"

"No—I mean yes. I mean… how do *you* know?"

"My sister's on her team," he said dismissively, waving me off. "She figured I knew you—said Penny was dating some skater named Jack."

He grinned kindly and sipped his Coke. "And I *do* know you."

"Oh…"

I didn't know what to say.

"She is fucking *hot*," Sammy illumined loudly. "Like… *hot*."

"My sister says she's kind of a bitch," Tagger added, getting right to his point. He nodded apologetically but didn't look like he was about to take it back. "I mean, just so you know. Kind of stuck up. Never hangs out with the other girls; doesn't like to cut loose."

"Oh, I think she's just shy. Besides, her parents don't let her go out much. She has to be *home* by eleven!"

"Hm," Tagger considered, nodding thoughtfully.

"What?"

"I mean, that seems *way* early for a fucking *junior.* Sounds more like an excuse to me."

"Excuse for *what*?" I snapped.

Niz sucked in a sharp breath; Sammy stopped grinning. I

93

think they were both waiting for Tagger to deck me.

"Don't know," he shrugged, standing up.

"Well why did your sister bring it up?" I wondered.

He shrugged more vigorously. "I don't know, man. I just wanted you to know—girls like that…"

He didn't finish the thought.

I sighed heavily.

"I don't get why y'all are bagging on her. Maybe she fucking *likes* me?"

Niz straightened up and said nothing. Sammy nodded slowly. Tagger shrugged—it was no thing to him, one way or the other.

I diverted the conversation by looking sidelong over at Niz and grinning.

"What?" Niz demanded.

"You know… *Jess*?"

"What about her?"

"Is there something brewing or not?"

Niz forced a sharp laugh through his nose and sucked down the rest of his Coke, shaking his head. "I don't know."

"She will *punch* you if you try anything," Sammy said very seriously.

"Where does this come from?" I wondered loudly. "We've known Jess for years and she's never punched any-one!"

"Never?"

"No! Never!" I stopped and thought and Niz caught my eye, smirking with the shared memory. "Well, okay, maybe once—but it was *totally* justified."

"See!" Sammy squeaked. "See!" And he looked from me

94

to Niz to Tagger, fishing for support.

"Counter man says you gotta go," the bum suddenly said from behind us. He was standing on the sidewalk and pointing at the sky. "Gonna call the cops, he says."

"Seriously?" Niz sighed.

"Counter man says you're trouble and you gotta go."

And he wandered off around the corner of the building and was swallowed up by the shadowed maw of the empty grocery store parking lot. I no longer felt any desire to chase him down and ask him to spout additional pearls of wisdom.

I stood up and glanced through the massive windows at the clerk, and sure enough he was glaring at us, watching us.

"Look, I gotta bail anyway," Tagger decided. "Would ya mind giving me a ride home?"

He'd been quiet since his comments about Penny and I felt bad for cutting him out of the conversation—that hadn't been my intent and I wasn't really upset with him for sharing his opinion. I felt bad that maybe *he* felt bad.

"Look, I'm sorry, man…" I started, but he shook his head and waved me off.

"It's cool—I don't know her… I shouldn't have said anything."

It was an awkward ride home and by the time we got back to Sammy's no one had said a word for several minutes. Tagger slunk off back to his house down the street without more than an errant wave at the night and I almost chased after him to apologize again—but I didn't know what I was apologizing for.

"I hope that's not the last we see of him," I said quietly

as he rolled off on his board.

"Nah," Sammy dismissed. "He's cool. We're all just tired, man. It was a long night."

I glanced at my watch and saw that it was five to midnight.

"Shit! Sammy, I gotta call my folks."

He eyed his house curiously for a second and sighed.

"Okay, but be super quiet. If you wake my dad..."

"I won't—*promise*. But if I don't call my folks and let them know where I am, I won't see you guys for the rest of the summer."

We all knew better than to hang out at Sammy's—his mom was great, but his dad made you feel unwelcome—so I made my call and headed home with Niz.

On the way back, I asked Niz about what Tagger had said. He didn't think it was that amazing that Tagger knew about Penny and he also didn't think Tagger had any particular insight.

"We don't know Tagger's sister," Niz summed up. "Maybe *she's* the bitch and that's why Penny avoids her."

I couldn't say much in response, so I let it go.

Maybe I always overthink things.

"Nope."

Niz was adamant, but he was caving.

"Oh, come on! It's only a softball game—it'll be over before dark. We can skate there and skate after!"

He weighed his options; sucked in a deep breath and blew it out slowly—deflating, almost.

"Fine. Fine! We'll go *this* time, but only so I can see for myself that this whole girlfriend thing isn't just bullshit."

I hadn't been to any of Penny's games yet, mainly because I hadn't been able to convince Niz to go with me. Not that I'd tried that hard, but now that I'd been seeing Penny for a while and softball season was almost over, it felt like I really had to get my ass up to the park and see her play. That wasn't entirely my fault—I guess her league was like the all-stars or something and they traveled to a lot of away games on the weekends, and sometimes during the week.

"Look, just be cool, okay?" I begged Niz as we coasted along the straightaway to the field—off a side road right before the gates to the park.

"Be *cool*?"

"Yeah. None of yer damn swearing."

He grinned at the irony but understood my sentiment and nodded once.

At the field, we had no idea which set of bleachers was home or visitors. I saw Penny's parents and figured it would be better to sit far away from them—I assumed on the visitors set of the bleachers. We sat quietly for the first inning or so and got into the groove, listening for the ping of the aluminum bat against the ball then watching the slow arc as the ball got lost in the blue sky, then found again in someone's glove. The people around seemed to cheer at everything, no matter which team did it, and I began to wonder if I understood the fundamentals of softball as well as I thought. Somewhere in the third inning I huffed and glared at Niz.

"Is it just me or is everyone cheering for everything that happens?"

"Dude, Penny looks *hot* in that uniform." He looked at me, then scanned the crowd, then watched the game again. "Yeah, it's weird. But seriously—you have *got* to hook me up with one of Penny's teammates."

She'd given me a small, secret wave (that was obvious to everyone) when we'd first sat down, so Niz was at least convinced that Penny knew me. I'd waved back, trying to look all cool and uninterested, but my heart had pounded so hard that for the first inning, I assumed I was having a heart attack. She'd smiled at me again since, and I'd waved, and now I had managed to come to some plateau, very much aware that everyone on the bench was talking about me and Penny and me-n-Penny, and loving every minute of it. Niz was right: She looked great and I couldn't believe I was dating her.

"I don't know, man—we don't hang out with the team at all. We go for a walk sometimes, then I drive her home."

I wanted to help him get a date, but the truth is, I didn't *know* anyone on her team—not properly, not like we'd ever been introduced or anything.

"Sounds boring. Her. Right there." He pointed with such determination I actually had to pull his hand down.

"*C'mon*!" I cautioned him. "Act cool."

"I like a girl who looks like she could kick my ass, Bells."

"Oh boy," I breathed.

Niz was starting to sound like one of our other friends, Jolly, who often opined way too loudly about which girl he wanted to bang (his word) and exactly why. It made us uncomfortable—no doubt that's why he did it, because he wasn't a bad guy at all, but he did get a huge kick out of making people squirm—and now I was afraid Niz was taking up the mantel. Or maybe he was confessing something; I gave him a sidelong gaze and narrowed my eyes.

"Seriously—you didn't tell me there'd be *so... many... hot...*"

"Stop. Please."

He grinned maniacally at me and twiddled his eyebrows like Groucho Marx.

"Okay—so Penny. I don't get it, Bells. I don't get it."

"What's not to get?"

"Where are her parents again?" he wondered, gazing down the bleachers.

The way he was flitting from one subject to the next, I was starting to get worried. Maybe it was heat stroke. I shielded my eyes against the sun and picked our her dad, standing behind her mom with his arms crossed, her in a cheap folding chair with a magazine shading her eyes. I wondered if she brought it because she found the game boring.

"Down there—it doesn't matter."

I motioned vaguely.

"No—I just figured there's some daddy issues or something going on and I wanted to see him."

"*Jesus*, Niz!" I hissed. "What the *hell*? And I'm not at *all* like her dad, anyway."

I looked around—we were tucked off to one corner of the first row of the bleachers and there was no one particularly close to us, and no one giving us the stink-eye like they'd overheard our conversation.

"So it's a rebel thing," Niz decided.

I shook my head and narrowed my eyes, so he nodded again.

"She's dating the *opposite* of her dad to get *back* at him."

"Or maybe she saw me in math class and liked me?"

"Why would anyone like *you*, Bells?" Niz asked with a serious undertone that he hadn't intended. He must've heard it, too, and quickly added, "Anyone like *her*, I mean. Everyone *loves* you, of course. *I* love you."

"Why are you being so weird? Can we just watch the damn game?"

He shrugged, and we did. In fact, to preempt any further odd conversations, I started cheering for Penny's team—whether or not I was cheering at the right times be damned. She grinned over at me once after Niz had joined in, and her friends clustered around her in the dugout, glancing over at us and grinning. Niz puffed out a breath and rolled his eyes—yeah, sure, they were acting like a bunch of basic girls in a dumb teen movie, but I suddenly didn't mind, since it looked like I had a lead role.

After the game I sidled over to Penny. Her teammates kind of peeled away from her and drifted off in clumps, like they weren't ready to meet me yet. Niz smiled at them but no one seemed to care. Penny came in for a hug and a breathless "We won!" and it felt good to have her arms around me; to smell the soft brush of sun on her skin and the harsh nylon of her uniform, and still the faint perfume of her shampoo.

"Good game, Penny," her dad said. She let me go and turned to him.

"We won," she agreed.

"Good job, Penny—really," her mom added, smiling at both of us.

"Is it okay if I go with them for ice cream?" Penny wondered. "Heather can drive—"

"I don't think so," her dad decided, his eyes flickering from me to Niz then back to me then to our skateboards then to Penny, obviously nervous as to which "them" was going for ice cream. "It was a long game."

Penny sighed and glanced at me, jigging on her toes like a child unsure if she should disobey. She dropped to her heels, flatfoot, and sighed again.

"Okay, I guess."

"We have to collect your brother on the way home."

Collect? Like he was a package or a forgotten umbrella?

They turned and walked off toward the parking lot.

"Thanks for coming, Jack," Penny said with a wide smile and glowing eyes. She leaned in and gave me a peck on the cheek. "Call me tomorrow."

"Damn," Niz breathed once he assumed they were out of

earshot. "That *ass*..."

I punched his arm. Hard. He cried out and reeled back from me, stunned at the force and intent of the blow—he knew I wasn't kidding.

"Don't be a *dick*," I stated, even though we'd both said the same exact thing countless times as girls passed us in the halls at school or at the mall or in the park or walking down the sidewalk.

"Sorry, Bells! Jeez!"

"Look, I'm trying to make a *good* impression—her dad hates me."

"I get ya," he agreed, still rubbing his arm. "Play nice with daddy so you can play nice with Penny later..." He waggled his eyebrows comically again and grinned. I shook my head and sighed.

The exquisite hormonal pain of being a teenage male may not be fully understood, even by the boys it debases, and it may not be right or proper, but the thing that makes us men is how we overcome it; how we begin to enjoy a girl's beauty for more than a nice ass. Penny had turned from an object of lust into a woman of big ideas, simple pleasures, and an unbridled future. I wanted everything for her in that moment: I wanted her to go out for ice cream with her friends, I wanted her to hang out with me at the mall, and I wanted her to never know how hormonal teenage boys who didn't know her wished they knew her, because it cheapened her in a way that wasn't fair.

Maybe Niz was right, maybe she did want to date some-one like her dad—someone who loved and respected her. Only that didn't feel quite right—I didn't think he respected her. I think he *wanted* her to be an object of lust, but only for the right kind of boy, the kind that would make her a rich housewife, and that wasn't me. I think she liked me because I *wasn't* like her dad: He was trying to trap her into a way of life that mirrored his own, and I was trying to get her out.

I looked at Niz and his grin dropped slowly.

"It's not like that," I tried to explain to him. "She's not just a piece of ass."

I watched her hair swaying as she jogged to catch up to her parents. I wanted my friends to know her like I'd come to know her. I wanted everyone to know how great she was; how bright and alive and carefree. And I especially wanted her parents to see that, and to see how they were stifling her.

"Ah shit, Bells, I think you're in love!" he joked, slinging his arm around my shoulders and guiding me back toward the street. "And I think you're too young to fall in love."

I shrugged his arm off. Everything he was saying seemed as right as it was wrong and it was pissing me off.

"Look, just forget it, okay? I *told* you to act cool."

"He wouldn't have let her leave with us—you know that, right? No way he'd let her leave with two boys like us. But this was fun. We should do this again."

"Forget it, okay?" I said again. "Let's go skate."

"My mom says I have to get a job."

Tobie looked at me, waiting for me to finish, and when I didn't she asked, "Yeah?"

"Yeah."

"And?"

I shrugged noncommittally.

"And I guess I have to get gas money from somewhere."

When I inherited the piece-of-shit sedan, my parents had given me the same deal as they gave my brother: they'd pay for the insurance, but I had to pay for the gas. I made the mistake of asking how I was supposed to do that, and my mom for once had been decidedly calm and succinct. She'd said simply, "You get a job," then hoisted the laundry basket to her hip and disappeared into the basement.

It was the first time I'd ever felt guilty about my parents caring for me. That wasn't her intent—she was only stating facts—but that was the effect. I stood in the kitchen and looked out at the summer—at the thick, golden light and the deep blue sky—and heard my mom fussing around in the basement, doing the laundry. They'd let me coast for the first month or so, but now the party was over. Now it felt like the summer was no longer mine, or not mine alone.

"That's rough," Tobie agreed, her voice edged not with sarcasm exactly, but with a faintly derisive tone that said she was only being polite because she really didn't see what the big deal was.

104

Tobie's uncle owned a farm out in the township and she'd grown up working the weekends for him. Nothing heavy, just light farm work for a few hours here and there, but work nonetheless. She didn't even have to drive there—her parents had a plot of land and a house on the other side of a huge hay field from her uncle. We were sitting on her back porch in the sun like a couple of old coots, watching the grass in the field bend and sway in the breeze.

"But it's nice that you can drive out here now," Tobie added, trying to make me feel better. "You can go *any-where*," she stressed.

"As long as I have the gas," I pointed out. "Say, is your uncle hiring?"

She puffed out a "be serious" laugh then looked at me. "Oh come *on*—don't give me that look. *Farm* work, Jack? You?"

"Well *you* do it!" I protested.

"Yeah—and he's got *me* to do my work. If he needed any help, it'd be *hard* labor."

"Never mind," I pouted.

"So tell me about this girl, anyway. She's a jock...?"

I narrowed my eyes and searched her face for signs of a trap. She grinned expectantly, her eyebrows slightly raised.

Tobie and I had dated pretty seriously the past winter—well, seriously for us, anyway. We'd sort of half-dated for years, in the way friends of the opposite sex do when they grow up together: A stolen kiss here, a hug there, holding hands in the mall that one time. I don't think our parents knew what to make of it, all the times they drove us to the mall to hang out, and I was flushed with sudden joy to think

105

that now I could drive myself and not have to worry about our moms sharing a knowing (or so they thought) look.

But no, back in February we'd decided to try a sustained relationship—it all sounds very calculated, I know, but it really wasn't. We kissed at a school dance for Valentine's Day, a bit longer and a lot deeper than we'd ever kissed before, and that spark kindled into a fleeting, heavy crush. A few weeks later, we had a very serious talk, and very seriously decided that maybe dating wasn't the best thing for our friendship.

I think the fact that neither of us could remember who decided to break up was the one thing that made it work; the one thing that made the fabled "let's just be friends" stick. What she didn't know is that I'd been really down about the break up, mutual as it was, and I think I returned her calls and hung out with her at school in the hopes it was all a misunderstanding and we'd get back together. Then it had suddenly been longer since we'd broken up than we'd actually dated, and the spark died back down to a single, glowing ember of friendship—a slight warmth that sustained us through high school and eventually drove us back together after college, when we were finally old enough to realize that love cuts so much more deeply than mere convenience and attraction.

But back then, age sixteen, a few months since we'd broken up...? I expected her to be mad, that's why I hadn't talked much about Penny before.

"What have you heard?"

"*Noth*ing," she chided, lazily brushing my arm with her fingertips. "Niz talked to Jess and Jess talked to me—you know how this works. It's been the same rumor mill since sixth grade."

It was true. Niz and I—best friends since forever—had met Jess and Tobie—also best friends since forever—at a middle school dance, the first real school dance of our careers. We'd hit it off, and since Jess had lived a few houses down from me back then, and Niz was right around the corner, we'd all started to hang out, even in the summers.

"Well, her name's Penny Harper."

"Hmmmm," Tobie mused, narrowing her eyes and focusing on the far side of the field. "I know *that*."

"She's in my math class," I said dismissively. "Or she was… last year."

"Oh that's right—you dropped honors algebra."

"What's *that* supposed to mean?" I barked, even though there hadn't been any kind of tone in her voice. It was sort of a sore spot with me, though—I'd almost failed algebra freshman year. I had, in fact, made a deal with the teacher that he would pass me only if I promised to drop honors math—a strange lunchtime meeting that had been facilitated by Niz, who'd been trying to tutor me and obviously felt some blame for my failing. Of course, I knew I'd failed because I hadn't tried at all. I was too busy having fun with the stoners and metalheads from shop to actually study.

"Nothing," she said blankly. "I'm trying to place her."

She turned and offered me a kindly smile.

"Is that why you called me?" I asked. "To find out about Penny?"

"Niz said it seems serious. I have to make sure she's good enough for you, not some heartbreaker."

107

"Says the girl who broke my heart."

She cut me a sour look, wrinkled her nose at me, and pretended to sit back in a huff. For the first time in months I realized I didn't want her, not in the way I'd been simmering about since the breakup. It was weird, because it was also the first time in months I realized I *had* wanted her like that before Penny. I still felt a special bond with Tobie, don't get me wrong, but having someone else to focus my attention on gave me an odd sense of clarity, like I wasn't there for *me*, I was there for *her*.

I settled back in my chair—one of those low-slung Adirondack chairs—and closed my eyes, the sun warm on my face, the breeze only a whisper through the hay field.

"Penny's nice," I said softly—it seemed wrong to speak too loud all of a sudden.

"Niz seems to think so, to hear Jess tell it. I think he's jealous."

"Niz? Naaahhh…" I disagreed. "He's happy for me."

"Okay, Bells… sure."

I didn't feel like arguing. We both sat there for several minutes, soaking in the sun.

"So what does this Penny do?" Tobie finally asked. I heard movement and looked over. She'd sat forward and was getting ready to stand. "Lemonade?"

"Sure."

Her mom made the best homemade lemonade; turning it down was not an option. The kitchen let out on the back porch where we were. I watched Tobie as she got up and went inside, sliding the patio bug-screen aside with casual finesse then closing it behind her, leaving the opening a black hole of shadows to the inside. Sounds came out of the blackness, but I couldn't see shapes.

"Niz said she plays softball?" Tobie called from inside as she puttered around and poured the lemonade. She was back before I could answer, working the door with her toe. I got up and closed it behind her and took a glass from her.

"Yeah, she does. I dragged him to her last game."

"I'm sure he loved *that*," she quipped as we sat down, slouching back in our chairs.

"We didn't go for *him*, we went for her parents."

"Her parents?"

I shrugged, lost for the moment in the sweet, tart taste of the lemonade, then gasped for air after I drained the glass, offering Tobie a smile. I always chugged it, unable to drink it fast enough for the pleasure to keep up with my taste buds

"Good?" she guessed.

"Always." I sat forward and put the glass down by my chair and sucked the last remaining drops of flavor off my lips. "I don't know. I don't think her parents like me, like her dad doesn't."

"How do you know that? Have you met him?"

"Not really. I mean, she introduced me cuz he came to the door once or twice when I picked her up. I don't know. It's not like we stay out late or anything. She's kind of a goody-goody."

"Hm," Tobie considered. "Well I think you need to meet them. *My* parents like you and we *do* stay out late, especially now you learned to drive…"

"Well that's why I went to the game. I went over to them so I could say hi, y'know? On common ground or something. Like, we're both rooting for Penny so we'd have... I don't know..."

I slumped back and sighed heavily. Who knew where gut feelings came from? But I had one about her dad—maybe something in the way he looked at me, or the way he had straightened up rigidly when I had walked over to them. Her mom had looked kind, but sort of too polite, like she was waiting to be yelled at and hoping you'd take pity on her.

"I said, 'Hi, Mr. Harper. Missus Harper,' and he almost didn't even look at me. She was in a lawn chair and didn't stand up. He stood there with his arms crossed and didn't un-cross them. I thought maybe he's one of those dads that is *way* too into their kids' sports, but he wasn't cheering or any-thing, he was just standing there, brooding."

"Weird," Tobie decided.

I glanced over at her. She was shielding her eyes with her left hand so she could watch me, her lemonade glass raised in her right hand, her elbow propped on the arm of the chair.

"Yeah, so I thought he didn't recognize me, and I'm like, 'I'm Jack. I've been hanging out with Penny,' and he cuts in like, 'Hi, Jack,' but he only glances at me and doesn't shake my hand, and her mom turned away like she's embarrassed, and I'm like, what did *I* do?"

"Well just how goody-goody is goody-goody?" Tobie asked very seriously, which struck me as immensely funny, seeing her sitting there with her hand to her eyes, saying that.

"What? I'm *serious*!"

"I know," I chuckled and took in a deep breath. "I don't know. She said she'd never had a boyfriend before."

"You believe that?"

"Why would she lie?"

"I guess…"

Tobie had stopped shielding her eyes and squinted at me for a few seconds, then smiled wistfully as if she'd decided to let me learn something the hard way.

"I'm sure that's it. You're a threat to him just by hanging out with her."

"So what about you, Tobe? Anyone on the radar?"

"Shit, Jack—after Richie Dolovar? See… my dad *should* have hated him."

"He didn't?"

"I guess my dad hates all my boyfriends on some level—that's his job."

I laughed lightly. Tobie's parents had always made me feel so welcome, but then like I said, we'd been hanging out for years. Maybe I'd worn them down.

"So she's *never* had a boyfriend?" Tobie checked in a rhetorical tone. "But she was standing outside waiting for you that day?"

"I don't think she was *waiting* for me. She was walking her dog or something. It was fate."

"Fate," Tobie stated.

"You don't believe in fate?"

She gave me a coy look and sipped her lemonade.

"Do you *know* something?" I asked, paranoia seeping into my tone.

"I know that girls don't hang around in their front yards with their dogs unless they're trying to make it look accidental."

"It was luck," I decided.

"Jack…"

It was a slow, deliberate tone. Her eyes sparkled in the sunlight—she was enjoying herself. She was enjoying my naïveté. I didn't answer, I only glowered.

"Look, spill it, if you've got some dirt. I'm not in the mood for games."

She recoiled sarcastically and grinned.

"I don't have any dirt. I'm just saying, as a girl, and as your friend, Penny obviously wanted to hang out with you. Maybe she wanted to see how the other half lives."

"Other *half*?" I questioned. "Is this a stupid movie or something? What 'other half'? We live in the same damn neighborhood!"

"You have to admit, you're not exactly her type. She's the type who thinks she's better than you because she has nice clothes."

"She's *not* like that…"

Tobie looked at me curiously.

"Look, Tobe… I can't explain it. When we're together we *gel*, y'know?"

She nodded, not with understanding but to denote that she had heard what I said. I grunted with frustration and sat forward.

"I don't get why everyone thinks we're such an odd couple."

"Because you are," Tobie said quietly

"How? Why?"

"Never mind…"

I let it drop for the moment while I collected my thoughts.

No one really knew her, I decided—and sure, that was because we never hung out with anyone, but that didn't make her stuck up, did it? She was shy. She was emerging from the shadow of her parents and squinting at the future, skittish and ready to run back if it got too weird. And maybe that was it: Maybe she liked me because I was so different from everything she'd come to know, but I was also safe; I was a good guy. Girls can sense that kind of thing... Girls, I knew, could sense *lots* of things. I eyed Tobie suspiciously.

"She doesn't think she's better than anyone," I mumbled. "I mean, look at *you*—am I *your* type?"

I motioned vaguely at her nicely pressed khaki shorts and crisp T-shirt, but I knew Tobie meant something more than clothes, and I knew Tobie was more like me than her clothes let on.

"We're not dating," she stated dryly, thoroughly enjoying whatever it was she was doing. I was confused, suddenly finding the conversation less than helpful.

"Jesus, Tobie... Maybe it was fate and maybe she *likes* me—who fucking cares?"

"I *said* she likes you, Bells—don't get upset."

"I don't get why you're *bagging* on her!"

"I'm not bagging on her!"

"Or on me! On *us*! Maybe it works because it's not *supposed* to work!"

"Maybe... I didn't mean—"

She reached out and touched my arm, tentatively, like she was afraid my skin would burn her.

"When did you start wearing a watch?" she asked softly—if there was going to be a full apology, it wasn't happening yet. Tobie knew she didn't have anything to apologize for, so she changed the subject and I think that fact, more than anything, affected me. Tobie simply knew she was right, in whatever way it was that Tobie always seemed to know what was right.

I glanced at my watch.

"Look—I gotta go."

"Jack!" she gasped, grabbing my arm before I could stand up. "Don't be mad."

"I'm not mad," I said.

"I'm glad you're happy."

"Thanks. She's pretty great—you guys have to meet her."

"I'd love to meet her, Jack."

"You'd probably get along—she likes nice clothes."

Tobie cocked her head and gave me a sour smirk.

"Har har, Beltane."

"Seriously, though… She does. I mean, *you* do."

"I do."

Her hand was still resting on my arm, willing me to stay. Maybe she felt me pulling away, like she knew Penny and I worked for whatever reason, and it scared her that I was happy with someone she didn't quite understand. I twitched my head to clear the thought—it wasn't true, and I knew it.

"What?"

I turned to her and she let go of my arm.

"People don't understand why *you* hang out with me, you know that?"

"People know *exactly* why we hang out."

"Right. Because we get along."

"Is that all? I get along with Barb and Kammy, but we don't hang out a lot."

"So what is it, then?"

She narrowed her eyes and sighed through her nose, knowing I was getting my own back for her previous comments.

"It's just easy to hang out with you guys. I don't feel like I'm being judged."

"Exactly."

She grinned and stood up as I stood up. "Okay, Bells—you win. I'm judging her, I get it."

"Niz told you to call me, didn't he?"

We stood looking at each other for a few seconds—she wasn't going to lie, she was figuring out how to admit it gracefully.

"Kind of. He said you were acting weird. He thinks you're in love."

"Would that be so bad?"

"No, not as long as it's true."

The concept of "love" is a monumental thing to a teenager—a huge, life-changing thing that no one seems to be able to recognize, which means no one ever truly knows when they have it. What scared Niz—and me—is that because it was so unknowable, we had no idea how it would affect us, and we had no idea what it took to keep it or to lose it.

"I think you guys should meet her, then you can tell *me* what it is."

Tobie smiled broadly and gave me a hug. I held it until she broke it, dimly aware that Niz and Tobie may well be jealous of Penny, but that wasn't a thought I was willing to let fully form—it seemed too vain and, frankly, ridiculous.

"I really do gotta go," I said when she stepped back from me. "I have a job interview for *work*."

"Go get 'em, Bells," Tobie replied sarcastically, touching my chin with her fist and clicking her tongue. I winked at her and we laughed at our own stupidity.

a thousand tiny moments
like stars in the night

Her hand slips into mine, her skin smooth. Our fingers interlock—the French kiss of holding hands. We walk across the lot, away from her parents, her dad driving home with a scowl, having reluctantly agreed to let me drive his daughter home.

"He's her *boy*friend," her mom had hissed in a stage whisper that said it was only the latest volley in a long-running discussion about such things.

But it had done the trick, and after that, when I showed up—when we'd planned it—I got to take her home. But first, the walk—the slow amble from the ball fields to the over-look at the top of the sledding hill, the sun drifting slowly toward the horizon, its heat blocked by the trees and trapped in their shadows.

We'd talk about things—the things that seemed important to a couple of teens who suddenly didn't need parents to drive them around. We made weird predictions of the future, where we tried to include each other but also knew, deep-down, that the odds weren't likely we'd still be together to call each other on it. We talked about movies and movie stars as if they were our friends. We talked about the things that mattered then but completely slip my mind now—the strange, whirling eddies of teenage conversation.

It felt so real. It felt so grown up. It felt like everything I'd ever wanted—everything I'd heard the singers sing about and read the writers write about. It was finally mine, right there beside me, her hand holding mine, our arms swinging unconsciously to the beat of our hearts.

She always tossed her hat and mitt in my car, and some-times she pulled out the band and loosed her ponytail, as if the tightness of her hair was painful against the wind. She worried at first about being sweaty from practice, but it never bothered me, not after summers out running around with Niz all day, and she got used to it, too. The scent of her shampoo is all I remember, like a tiny whirlwind of heaven, and I'd walk closer so I could smell her, and she'd lean in with a grin and a sparkle in her eyes, as if she knew exactly how crazy she drove me.

"What do you want to be when you grow up?" she asked once.

"Jesus, I don't know, Penny…"

It was the truth, but sitting in the grass at the overlook watching the sun set and the sky fade to purple, I wanted to be able to answer that question for her. But I didn't know, and I couldn't lie.

"What about you?" I wondered. "Do you know?"

"I think I might be a doctor—like a team doctor, for a baseball team or something."

I kissed her. It was the only response that I knew she'd accept. I kissed her and we rolled over into the grass and she pushed her body against mine.

Once we had to run from the cop who came through near dusk to make sure everyone was gone. My car was still in the lower lot, so he knew we were there, but we scooted across the street behind his car and dashed across the field to the lower lot, laughing and breathless at the same time, and we crouched down and waited to see if he was going to come back and park and get out and look for us, but he inched on by and left us behind, maybe giving us time since it wasn't truly dark yet.

Sometimes on the way home we'd take a detour and go down to Big Boy for shakes and fries. If we ran into anyone she knew, she'd say "hi" and introduce me as Jack, as if they already knew who I was. But we never sat with them, and we never seemed to run into my friends.

"We don't usually go out for food until nine or ten," I explained once, an idea that perplexed her until her curfew was relaxed to the point that it made sense.

It suited us fine. We could slurp our shakes and make each other laugh, and there was no one to take the attention away from us. We always shared the same big plate of fries, sometimes dipped in barbeque sauce and other times in nacho cheese. Those were the times it seemed like we gelled the most, when we had to talk instead of kiss. It made the kisses sweeter, anyway, when she'd lean in before we got out of the car at her house, and I could still taste the ice cream on her lips.

Those nights blur into the sky like sunset, fading around the edges of a cool breeze; a thousand tiny moments like stars in the night. If I dreamed a million days I could never touch the essence of them again: the long, drawn-out silences between kisses; the fire in her eyes; the simple sense of wholeness and being that makes the world seem new, the sunrise fresh, and the storms like magical tinderboxes describing how your heart flies to her.

And beneath it all, the slow steady drumbeat of the days

119

since then; the soft throb of yearning for something that once was there, yet will never be again.

She felt the most free when we went to the mall—you could tell by the spring in her step and the way her hair furled around her head, barely able to keep up with her stride—and I loved to see her feeling so free.

I had my hot spots—the skate shop and the record store and the dollar store and the food court and the arcade—but for Penny, everything at the mall had merit. She flitted like a hummingbird from storefront to storefront—she liked to dangle those re-enforced paper sacks from her arms, and I liked the way it made her smile. I loved how excited she got when she found *that top* on sale and it happened to perfectly match *those shorts* that were also, unbelievably, *on sale*.

We held hands. We laughed. We hurried to sale racks she'd spotted from across the way, her dragging me and me feigning exhaustion. We ate frozen Cokes from the hotdog stand and—God bless the mall in my hometown—we rode a God damn carousel. That mall even had a Ferris wheel. And mini golf—all in the food court. Penny liked to play mini golf—it was the competitor in her. She always beat me, so she started trying to out-do her own previous score instead, like I tried to beat my own high score on Galaga.

"I'm serious, Bells," she said once as she lined up a shot on one of the easier holes. "We're going to be juniors next year—haven't you thought about college?"

"*College*? Christ, I'm not sure I'll make it through high school!"

"Jack!"

Her head was tilted with anger, but her face was a bright,

smiling aperture of loving bliss.

"I'm serious, Penny! I don't know what I want to do—I want to avoid doing anything." I shrugged. "I like poetry."

"That's cool," she agreed, nailing a hole-in-one off a bank shot. "But you can't get a job as a poet."

"Is that all there is after high school?"

"What?"

"Finding a job?"

"I think so," she laughed, and it made it seem like such a trivial thing; she misread the horror of my expression as sarcasm. "*Seriously*, Jack! What are you going to *do*? My dad says you need to have it figured out before senior year so you know what you're working for."

"Working for...? I mean, I'm working for graduation, isn't that enough?"

"Maybe..."

"What do you think I should be, Penny?"

"You'd be a good teacher."

"A *teacher*?" I implored. "Are you *nuts*? Why would I become a *teacher*? Why not just a damn *cop* or some high--powered *sales* douche?"

She leaned in and gave me a peck on the lips, to let me know she wasn't offended before she explained, "My dad is a high-powered sales douche."

"So you admit he's a douche...?"

"*Jack!*"

And on and on. I worked most evenings at my new job—the four-to-nine shift at a big-box hardware store—and I think I spent almost everything I earned on gas and lunch and games at the mall with Penny. I'd pick her up around ten in the morning—her parents felt that any earlier was too early—and I'd drop her off after lunch, then go home and crash on the couch for an hour, then to work, then to Niz's after work for movies or skating or both. It was the perfect setup. On the nights I didn't work, I'd still drop her off in the afternoon, then trundle up to the park and catch up with her after her practice or her game. It was the rhythm that kept my joints moving; it was the strange beating tattoo that proved I had it all: The girl, the car, the job.

"I think this is it," I told her once, sitting in the food court, eating a basket of fries with our frozen Cokes.

"What?"

"This is what I want—I want to hang out with you. You become a brain surgeon and I'll hang out with you."

"Be *serious*."

"I'm totally serious. I'll write, you can work."

That tilted-head look of loving contempt again. That grin spreading across her lips as if she got a joke I hadn't made.

"You think I can be a brain surgeon?"

"Sure. Why not?"

"I told you I wanted to go into sports medicine."

I shrugged. "Why stop there? Why not brain surgery?"

"I think I like you a lot, Jack," she said very seriously and planted a firm, lingering kiss on my lips. My heart began to beat so rapidly I could barely swallow or I felt like throwing up or both.

"I like you a lot, too, Penny."

"Is this what it feels like?" she wondered cryptically, her nose an inch from mine.

"What?" I whispered.

122

"The future?"

"I hope so, Penny."

That summer, that mall, those eyes, that smile.

Sometimes when I'm gazing into the embers of a dying fire, I remember her. I consider a dying fire and I remember Penny Harper.

I remember her as she was then, laughing at my jokes and goading me into the future. I think about the embers of the fire and how even by morning, there'll still be something glowing under the piles of ash; something hot and ready to reignite a flame.

Then I wonder how much ash has piled up since I was sixteen and I wonder if there's anything left of those embers for me. Not for her, not for Penny, but for me—anything left of my fire and energy that was so willing to fling itself blindly into a future I couldn't even comprehend, let alone plan for.

But first, the fire. First, the youth.

First there were endless nights of promise and surprise, and a hundred ways to think of her when you knew you'd see her soon again.

The show was at the Beachland, in the tavern—Cleveland's best place. Not just best concert venue, but best *place*. If there were a zombie apocalypse, I'd want to go to the Beachland for one last drink, just to say goodbye. I sometimes go to shows there only because the show is at the Beachland.

Maybe it's the wood floors—it's like standing *inside* the speaker. Split into two venues—a ballroom for the bigger shows and a tavern for the club shows—the sound in both is always perfect, which I can't say for most venues and definitely would never say of the corporate chain of concert clubs that sprang up across America like acne in the 1990s.

Or maybe the Beachland felt like an odd sort of home because the people there were like me: music lovers. It was about the only place I didn't feel too shy to speak to random people. Or maybe that was the whiskey talking. Or maybe it was because people spoke to me first.

Gray and I ended up getting there before the doors opened, so we sat on the front step and watched a finite niche of Cleveland go past. The neighborhood had definitely seen better days—or maybe it hadn't. Maybe it was one of those neighborhoods that started out rundown. Across the street was a pizza place—a real mom-n-pop joint—but we couldn't be bothered to drag our asses over there.

"So who are we seeing tonight?" Gray asked.

"The Soft Moon."

"Punk?"

"Not exactly. I'm not sure what you'd call them. Throw-back new-wave shoegaze?"

I honestly hadn't expected him to come to this show with me. He didn't know the band and he always seemed to have something better to do, but I was glad to be there with him. We'd spent a lot of time on a lot of stoops in college, watching the world go by. It felt like a thin sliver of time I'd won back, and I smiled at the thought.

"So how's the family?" he asked. It never sounded like small talk coming from that guy, I swear.

"Oh, fine. They're great."

"And Tobie?"

"Also fine."

Me? I completely suck at small talk, even when it isn't small talk. Thankfully, they opened the doors and let us in, so we settled at the bar. It turned out we hadn't pulled the handle hard enough—the place had been open all along, and the usual crop of barflies was already buzzing around. It looked like some local band was the first opener, and their moms and dads had come out to watch. It made me feel good that their parents supported them, but also a little bad for them that no one else seemed to care. I knew how that felt. My mom and dad loved everything I wrote, which made it hard to tell if it was good or just them. I was broaching the topic with Gray (he said I was being "surly") when a woman behind me said my name. I thought. Gray half turned—we were sitting at the bar and to actually turn around and look would take some effort.

"Jack? Jack Beltane?"

Now I couldn't ignore her. I expected someone from work.

"Penny?"

I choked on the word. Gray turned around on his stool so fast I wasn't sure he'd ever been facing the bar.

"Yes!" she smiled widely and nervously shuffled her feet, giving Gray a bashful glance. It all seemed a bit too rehearsed. "I thought I saw online that you'd be here tonight."

"You come here often?"

It was the most sarcastically delivered cliché line you can imagine. I seriously doubted she'd ever been there in her life, but I was supposed to believe this was a chance meeting? Just an oh-my-gawd moment of stunned disbelief at the massive coincidence the universe had rolled up and spat out?

"Well... no. Not really."

She smiled again. The years had been very good to her, and I could tell Gray had noticed, too. She hadn't used a ten-year-old photo for her online profile, she really did look like she was still in her twenties. She hadn't got fat or even out of shape. She stood there in form-fitting jeans and a cute blouse—untucked—with hair that ran down to her shoulders in a sleek curtain. In the dim lighting, she almost looked exactly like the last time I'd seen her—only the look in her eyes revealed age and regret; the innocence of youth was gone from them, despite the tight skin and elegant face that said otherwise.

"Oh... uhhh... Gray? This is Penny Harper. An old... friend from high school."

"Hey, Penny," Gray said very politely, with just the right amount of I-don't-like-you in his voice. Gray could sense something—it's probably what made him such a good conversationalist—and he obviously remembered her name from our previous chats. My heart was pounding in my throat—the last thing I'd expected to see at the Beachland was a ghost of this caliber.

"Are you here alone?" I asked.

"No," she cooed, flicking her head toward the wall opposite the bar, where a couple of two-top tables were huddled. There was a woman at one of them who may have smiled at us; she looked nervous and unsure, like she'd been dragged here by a crazy-ass friend.

"I gotta piss," Gray stated gently and slid off his stool. Penny took the hint and slid onto it in his place, still trying to look bashful. Hell, maybe she was.

I was dimly aware that to an outsider, this all looked completely normal: Dude at a bar talking to a girl who looked a decade younger than him, leaving the world wondering what the hell he had, to be able to attract someone like her. I also couldn't help but register that I'd once touched her in exactly the ways that outsider would imagine. I'd put my hand on her flat stomach and watched the wind disturb her hair. I'd kissed her slowly and watched her jog over to her front door, casting a batted-eyelashes glance over her shoulder at me. It felt like waking up from a weird dream with a long sense of dread that evaporates when you realize everything is still exactly as it should be.

Only it wasn't, and like a moment punctuated with the low swell of horror-infused keyboards, I understood that she had no idea what she'd done to me when we were only sixteen. She had no idea how long those years between then and now had been, and how long it had taken for the memory of her to echo into the distance, like a fading light on the far shore; how hard it had been to try and reconcile wanting to forget a summer that I never wanted to let go.

"What are you doing here?" I hissed at her, more pleasantly than I'd intended to. She misunderstood me.

"Will your wife be mad?"

"Tobie? Why would she be mad?"

"Nothing."

The flip of her hair said I was supposed to buy her a drink and this would be our little secret, but I didn't bite.

"I saw your post about this band," she said carefully. "I looked them up and I liked them, so I thought I'd come out."

"From Cincy?"

"Oh no—I live in Akron now."

"Oh."

She watched me watch her and smiled a somewhat apologetic smile. It was my turn to talk, apparently.

"So are you a team doctor at the university or something?"

"No," she giggled, reminded of the dreams of her teenage self and slightly embarrassed by them. "I *am* a doctor, though."

"No shit?" I didn't mean to sound so glib, so I quickly added, "You have your own practice?"

"Oh no, not yet," she corrected hastily. "I work at an urgent care facility."

"Fancy."

I literally didn't know what else to say; judging by her expression, I may have said the wrong thing. If she was offended, though, she got over it pretty quickly.

"What about you? Did you ever publish a horror novel? I've checked from time to time, just in case."

That stopped me. She'd checked? She'd looked me up over the years to see if I had a novel published? It was a strange realization, to know that she had cared enough to... well... care. She smiled pleasantly at my silence, her eyes holding mine, and I almost apologized for trying to brush her off.

"Not yet," I finally replied. "I'm a technical writer now. For a software company."

"Fancy," she said without missing a beat, grinning deviously.

"Look, I just wasn't—"

"My dad died," she blurted, and her whole expression and attitude shifted down a notch. "I guess it got me thinking about better days."

"Jesus, Penny—I'm sorry to hear that."

She hadn't meant to blurt it so forcefully, she'd just wanted to cut off the inevitable small talk about parents and whatnot.

"My mom seemed relieved," she admitted.

"Oh—was it a long...? Did he have cancer, or...?"

"Yes..."

Her eyes got misty and she sucked in a deep breath, looking off into the bar where the opening band was rigging the stage.

"He was strict," she said, as if agreeing with something I hadn't said.

I didn't know which way to take the conversation. An

awkward silence built up, and I still thought maybe I was being played—that maybe she'd come here to see about an old flame because it felt like the safest way to cheat—but as she gazed off toward the stage she took on an almost defeated cast. She looked more like someone trying to figure shit out than a middle-aged woman trying to hook up with an old beau. After all, she wasn't particularly *trying* to be hot—no way-too-tight T-shirt or tiny spaghetti-strap sundress with no bra—and I figured my interpretation of her actions had more to do with my hormones than her desires.

"I'm sorry, Penny," I offered, trying to start over again. "Really. And not just about your dad. I didn't expect... I mean, I never thought I'd see you again, y'know?"

"I know," she admitted, turning back to me. "I didn't mean to make you uncomfortable. I just wanted... I needed a reminder of... something. My son turns sixteen this summer. I told him that was the best summer of my life."

She gave me a watery smile. I couldn't stand hearing her say that, not after how that summer had ended for me. She didn't have the right to romanticize that summer, even if her dad had died and her kid was suddenly...

"Sixteen?" I asked no one, probably not even meaning to say it out loud.

"Yeah," she giggled and cut me a dare-ya look. "I was twenty, if you can't do the math. Total cliché—tried to save myself for marriage, caved, got pregnant on my first go."

"Your parents must have loved that."

"They actually surprised me. I couldn't have raised him and finished college and med school *and* residency without them. You did alright, though. I think I remember your wife...?"

"Yeah, I know you guys met that summer."

I met her eyes long enough to look away again.

To her, this was us catching up, and it hurt that she had no idea. That summer probably had been the best of my life, too, but when she'd broken up with me it had left a stain that the years couldn't fade or wash out. In my head, that summer is a bright yellow fire with endless blue skies and a sense of the *rightness* of the world. But the golden glow tarnished suddenly into a blackness that had shadowed me for the last twenty years. She had no idea that seeing her there, acting as if we'd only been having our fun back then, cut like lightning and stung like cold rain.

I saw Gray at the other end of the bar, carefully studying the billboard of upcoming shows. The bartender, sensing the need for a sale, hovered nearby.

"C'ni get a shot of Jack?" I asked him, sliding a twenty over.

When I looked back at Penny she was looking in the mirror behind the bar. I'd always loved her profile, the way her hair fell and her nose tucked up at the end just a bit, and the way her lips always seemed to hold the perfect amount of color and the perfect definition of shape, like the crisp edges of a cartoon. I wanted to kiss her badly, but what was weird is, it wasn't *her* I wanted to kiss so much as it was those *lips*. I'd forgotten how ridiculously inviting they were. She felt me watching her and her lips parted a shade, then our eyes met in the mirror.

"And whatever you want, Penny."

"Oh…" she said, startled. "Uhh… Rolling Rock's fine."

He got Penny's bottle and poured my shot.

"Thanks," she said, raising the bottle. "To being sixteen, even just for a summer. It was a good summer, wasn't it, Jack?"

"Sure," I agreed.

She chuckled with amusement. "It wasn't? That July Fourth at the park, with all your friends…? Best July Fourth ever."

She had me there and I clinked her bottle with my shot glass, then downed it. That had been the one-and-only time we'd hung out with my friends on my terms, despite my efforts to get us all to hang out more, and *now* she thought it was the best time ever…? But I couldn't disagree either and it worked to soften me up.

"We were together the *whole day*," she recalled happily.

"Only because you wanted to get to the mall and play Double Dragon Two before the line formed."

"That's *right*!"

"Do you still play video games?"

"With Jason? Yeah. I can kick his ass."

She smirked with a mother's love, and I wondered what I'd be doing with my kids when they turned sixteen. It was a nice thought.

"You played all morning," I recalled.

"But they kept kicking me off, remember?"

"Sure—but never for long. That's the benefit of being a cute girl in an arcade."

She might have blushed but took a swig of beer instead.

"Then we got lunch—"

"Hotdog on a stick!"

"And frozen Cokes."

"And you wanted to ride the carousel but I was afraid I'd throw up—"

"From too many hotdogs!"

We laughed contentedly, our gazes lingering on each other, lost somewhere between then and now.

"Then what did we do?" I wondered; it was a rhetorical question. Now that we'd started, I could remember every second of that day, and I couldn't help but smile. Gray, sensing a change in the air, moseyed back over and stood by us.

"We went up to Winton Lake, but it was too hot to walk around."

"Right! But we didn't have bathing suits either—"

"And you tried to get me to skinny dip!"

"Not *skinny* dip!" I protested with a glance at Gray. "I simply pointed out that underwear was basically a bikini and I was wearing boxer shorts…"

"So you were *always* a thinker, Jack?" Gray chimed in. He motioned at his empty bottle as the bartender walked by, then put a five on the bar between us.

"Sure he was." She smirked and nudged my foot with hers. "It had nothing to do with trying to see me naked."

"Pipe down, Gray," I deflected, dodging that particular avenue of memory.

It was probably true, and I had probably assumed I was being subtle. She took the hint with a smirk as I changed the subject.

"So… Jason?"

"Yes! He's a great kid. I'm sure you've seen him on my page."

"Yeah—he looks like a good kid. Studious."

133

"He gets good grades," she allowed. "Like his mom did. He's not out causing trouble—like *you* did."

"What?" I stammered with mock offense. "I *never* caused trouble!"

Gray snorted and nursed his beer but didn't interject—he seemed to be enjoying this glimpse into my life before we'd met.

"You were always running around with Sammy and that other guy…?" Penny mused. "With the weird name?"

"Niz."

"Yes!" She laughed and her eyes sparkled with the memory. "All you talked about was finding good spots to skate!"

I laughed lightly and nodded, looking away.

"Oh my God!" she declared with another laugh, reaching over and grabbing my arm dramatically. "Do you *still* skate?"

I shrugged. She glanced at Gray, who said nothing.

"When I can… I mean, Niz and Sammy aren't around…"

I couldn't tell if she was amazed in a good way or a bad way—whether she thought it admirable that I'd not given up my childish hobby, or pathetic. Most people thought it was pathetic, I knew. Kids are supposed to grow up into acceptable adult sports like skiing and golf, not keep riding a skateboard like a punk who is probably on drugs. If they only knew. If they only knew how much trouble skating had probably kept us *out* of back then, and how relatively fit it kept me now.

We chatted about nothing for a while longer—how we still felt young, mostly—and Gray filled in the awkward si-

134

lences like a professional talk show host or something. I saw Penny look at her friend a couple of times, just to check on her, to make sure she wasn't being harassed by some douchebag or something. The way her hair moved when she turned to look back like that, it struck a long-dead note in me.

"I'm glad to see you stuck with your real color," I said awkwardly, motioning at her hair—almost shoulder length, maybe a bit longer than when we were kids, and definitely straighter; more businesslike. Anyway, I could tell the conversation had run out of steam and I wanted to leave her with a kind word.

"Yeah…"

I'd sort of given her a hard time that summer, after she dyed it back to her natural dark brown color, so the fading browns and Sun-In blonds could grow out without anyone noticing.

"It looks good—always did," I added, saying now what I should have said then.

"Thanks—I always thought you hated it."

"I never hated it."

It suddenly felt like her hair had been a symbol of something too precious for us to grasp exactly. There were other things I wanted to say, of course—other half-apologies I wanted to make—but I let the color of her hair shoulder that burden for now. I wasn't trying to make up with her, after all, I was only humoring her because she'd said her dad had died and because she looked lonely.

"It *was* a good summer," I agreed.

"I didn't like the way it ended either," she admitted quietly, reading my eyes and my expression. She tried to giggle but I didn't share her laugh.

"Oh, don't tell me I was the first girl to break your heart, Jack."

She looked at Gray as if he could offer evidence in her favor, but he hadn't known me then and he could only shrug.

"So you admit it?"

"Admit what?"

"That you broke my heart."

"And that I wasn't the first?"

"Does it make it any better if you weren't?"

"Was it really that bad, Jack?" she cooed sympathetically, finally sensing something in my tone.

I had sucked the energy out of the conversation, anyway, and I think she understood that the summer had ended differently for each of us—maybe it was the first time that it had occurred to her that young love affects people differently, or just that that's how it is with breakups: one side gets what they want and the other side gets a broken heart.

Of course, now that we'd broached the topic I wanted to hide it. I would never tell her how it had ended for me. No matter how sorry she was, I would never let her know how much it had hurt. But she must have seen it in my eyes. She sprung at me and wrapped me in a hug, her arms around my neck, my face forced into her hair. I hugged her back awkwardly, but it felt good. It felt like a thick coat of sludge from years of regret suddenly sloughed off, except the exposed skin it left behind hardened instantly and I felt anger swell almost as quickly. I pushed her away.

"I'm sorry," she admitted. "I'm sorry I did that to you,

Jack."

Gray tried to melt into the background, but without actually turning and running away, he was stuck, unsure what to do and knowing there was nothing he could say. Penny may have actually formed a few tears, or she had that typical girlish habit of always running her fingers under her eyes to fix her makeup. She tried to laugh then took a swig of her beer.

"I remember what I said," she agreed. "I remember. I practiced it a hundred times before I called you. I don't know, Jack. I'm sorry. I had to make it final. I was… I don't know."

She looked at me and offered me a weak grin.

"*That's* why it broke my heart," I whispered.

She sucked in a sharp breath and stood up with a crisp nod.

"Thanks for the drink, and the memories. I should get back to Jill…"

She grabbed her beer as she started to walk back to her friend. Gray stepped out of the way as I reached out and touched her arm, her fingers brushing mine as she moved away. She stopped and turned back, smiling and raising her beer to me.

"I just wanted you to know how much I missed that summer, Jack. And I wanted to tell you in person. I owed you that."

I think she was honestly crying.

The Soft Moon played in complete darkness, which is one of the most memorable concerts I've witnessed—like Bowie said, with only the beer lights to guide us. They bulldozed through a solid set of pounding rhythms and hypnotic guitars in complete anonymity.

I lost myself to them, like I do in all good shows, letting the music transport me to somewhere without bills and worries and ex-girlfriends. Somewhere where I could feel ten years younger again, or I could feel sixteen. I could forget who or what I was, and who or where I came from, and I could just *be* for that short span of time—be like a kid on the hill by my house, cloud-busting with Niz on a summer afternoon, age ten, before anything bad had happened to us.

But even in that ageless dark, I felt myself tethered to a past that had always pulled taught when I tried to run away from it. A hard knot pulled tight by my struggles, with all its ropes running back to that summer, back to Penny, back to that July Fourth at the heart of my sixteenth year. And now that past had a face again, and now there was a new shadow in the darkness painted the color of Penny's regret—a strange blotch of different darkness in my darkness showing me that my memories were incomplete. It was incredibly brave of her to show up like that, and to swallow her pride long enough to say she was sorry. It was amazing to think she'd even cared enough to bother.

Penny had become a *thing* to me over the years, an icon of a summer I'd never live to see again, a symbol of both the brightest day and the darkest night. Seeing her again made her real in a way she hadn't been since that time twenty years ago—seeing her again turned her back into a person, and I wanted to speak to her as a person once more, not as a thing, not as an amorphous shape in the darkness.

But when the lights came back on Penny was already gone.

nights like that, they get set in amber in our minds

Our days hang like spider webs over the dark expanse of years, a matrix of threads crisscrossing into a net of memories and regrets, circling taught knots that punctuate the darkness like the first rippled drops of rain on a still pond. Those knots are the lights in the darkness: Shining silver embers of hope that highlight the greatest moments, the incidents and celebrations upon which the whole webbed history of a life is built. We all have them, but sometimes they can be difficult to see in the gloom. We must strive to look harder in those slow slogs through the bottoms of our souls. We must strive to find those lights in the darkness and touch them again, no matter how painful the sense of loss, so we can understand that knots just like them are constantly being tied. A favorite teacher, a loving parent, a best friend, a night out with friends, a girlfriend who was once the center of that vast web—they all played their part in forming the future, and there will be others who play their parts in the future to come. Grasp those stars for what they *were* not for what they *became* because all of those tangled threads, forming tiny hearts in the past, have a dark twin that shows what happens when you move on: Loss, regret, pain, static.

The summer I turned sixteen is one of those knots for me: A great, shining beacon of the past with its twin dark gravity-well of a collapsed star. The ripples of that knot seem to emanate from a single day in the middle of the summer: the fourth of July.

July Fourth isn't so much a celebration of independence as it's a celebration of summer, at least that's how it seems to me. I guess that's what happens when the war for independence was so long ago, plus the country you broke away from is now your best friend. But hell, any excuse to party— better yet: fireworks. Every town in America has them, no matter how small.

I remember one year, the power went out on July Fourth, and we could hear all the fireworks in all the cities around us banging and thudding and crackling, and the sky flickered like lightning. It was kind of eerie, to be honest, and it gave us a glimmer of what the actual war for independence may have been like for the bystanders.

But that wasn't the summer I was sixteen. No, that summer Penny and I spent the whole day together, from dawn to dusk to her curfew—the only full day like that, not broken up by softball or work or family obligations.

It started at the mall, like most of our days did that summer, and we ate lunch with some of her friends from softball—one of them Tagger's sister—and then we spent time alone at the lake, doing our best to uphold the traditions of young love. We ate dinner at her house—her dad grilled hotdogs and hamburgers, but he barely looked at me, never spoke to me, never smiled. Her mom tried to be nice, but she looked nervous, like she was afraid for me. Then we left my car at Penny's house and walked up to the park to watch the fireworks.

The hill we always sat on after her practices—the sledding hill in winter—was a perfect overlook of the field by the city center where they set off the fireworks, so they

140

decked it out with striped bunting and food trucks and a weird little obstacle course built for the occasion that I never fully understood—maybe to keep the kids occupied? We ended up at the same spot where we hung out after her practices and packed ourselves in with tons of other people. Her parents stayed at home—they said her little brother was afraid of fireworks, but I saw the look on his face.

"You sure?" I checked. "He can come with us, right, Penny?"

"Yeah—sure!" she said happily.

"No," her dad said. "You know it will get him worked up, Penny, and then he won't sleep."

I thought the old man was full of shit, and I felt bad for the poor kid—a chance to go out with his big sister and her boyfriend and stay up late to see fireworks…? *Yeah*, I thought. *He'll get worked up and you don't want him to understand that life is more fun when your parents aren't around.*

Penny tugged me lightly and mumbled "I guess you're right" as she led me toward the door. I shrugged at the poor kid as I stepped out of the house, and he smiled the long-suffering smile of a child with overbearing parents.

"Why is it that parents go too far?" I asked Penny as we walked up to the park, her hand in mine and no rush in our step.

"What do you mean?"

"Aw, nothing."

"What?"

"They either don't care at all, or they care too much."

"Is that bad? Caring too much?"

"Well, why couldn't your brother come with us?"

"He's only ten, Jack. They're right. I think you forget what it was like to be ten."

"No, I remember being ten very well, hanging out with Niz all day in the summer—we never even saw our parents until dinner. I think your parents need to lighten up. They're going to drive the poor kid *nuts*!"

"Why do you even care?"

"Kids should be out having fun, that's all."

"So your parents don't care at all?"

"Nah… My parents care, but they don't over do it. They have rules, but it's like, 'Call and check in' instead of, 'Don't go out at all'."

"And what if you don't check in?"

"I don't know. Why wouldn't I check in? It's not like they've ever told me to come home when I called."

She sighed heavily and smiled.

"Forget it, okay? He'd've probably been a pain in the butt. I think that's more what they were worried about."

"Well… maybe…" I agreed.

But it was a weird thing to me, stopping your kids from being, well, *kids*. I knew there was a balance. For as much as my parents—and Niz's and Tobie's and Jess's and Sammy's—let us go out and do whatever we wanted, they also seemed to be around a lot. Not spying on us or judging us or yelling at us—just *there*. Other kids would tell horror stories about their parents at lunch, and I didn't get it—I didn't understand why they had to be like that. Like the one kid we hung out with sometimes, he got straight As but he was never allowed out past nine on a school night, he couldn't

142

listen to music out loud in his room, and he couldn't use the phone after eight. Once he called me at like ten, and he was whispering and talking about nothing that couldn't wait until the next day at school—I think he wanted to feel like he was getting away with something.

My parents? As I said, they were around but not bothersome. My dad came down to my room the night my friend called at ten and asked who it was, not to be nosy but because he was concerned—he figured if I got a call that late, one of my friends might need help. It made me feel good—and responsible—to know that my parents were there and ready to help... but only if I asked. Most parents, I think, confuse invasion of privacy with "parental concern." They think that harsh rules teach kids to be good, but overbearing rules only teach kids how to cheat.

When we got to the park I kept a look out for Niz and Tobie and the gang because they'd all said they were going, and I was nervous as hell because none of them had hung out with Penny yet. Niz had barely met her when he went to her softball game with me, but he was the only one—and that wasn't even long enough for a "heya" or a "see ya later." Tobie probably felt like she knew her because we'd talked about her, but that wasn't the same. So I wanted to see them first and get a bead on the situation so I didn't overwhelm Penny. I mean, *every*one was going to be there and I was actually considering avoiding them if I could, if too many of our larger circle of friends had coalesced to watch the fireworks. A couple of my friends I figured she could handle, but sometimes our crowd bloomed to ten or fifteen kids, and that might freak her the hell out.

"There you are!" a man's voice growled and I felt a hand clamp the back of my neck. Swear to God, I thought Penny's dad had followed us and had seen us sneaking kisses as we walked, or saw me put my arm around her, my hand low on her hip and an inch from her ass.

I whipped around and saw Tobie's dad backing off, laughing. Tobie and her mom were a few steps behind shaking their heads.

"I got you! I got you, Jack!" he was yelling, and my immediate assumption was that he was drunk. Not that he needed to be drunk to have fun—or ever got drunk around us, for that matter—but because he was actually yelling.

"Yeah," I breathed. "You got me."

"I'm sorry," he said, sobering up instantly—so, not drunk, after all. "I had to. It's the *Fourth*!"

"Go...! America...!" I agree lamely.

"He got a good raise at work yesterday," Tobie explained as she caught up. "He's still giddy."

I let go of Penny's hand and motioned to Tobie.

"That's Tobie. We've been friends since, like, sixth grade, I guess. And her parents, Mister and Missus Malloy. This is Penny Harper."

"Hi, Penny," Tobie's mom said.

Penny smiled shyly but didn't speak; I put my arm around her and squeezed her in close and looked at Tobie and said a bit too loudly, "This is the girl I was telling you about!"

Tobie looked momentarily perplexed and her mom mumbled something about finding fresh-squeezed lemonade then hooked her husband's arm and dragged him off. He

144

waved and laughed again about scaring me, then it was just the three of us.

"Your parents seem nice," Penny said. I gave her another squeeze.

"They're okay," Tobie admitted. "My dad really did get a big raise or something. He's been like this all day."

"Loud and kind of obnoxious?"

"Exactly—and you *know* he's not usually so outgoing."

"No, he's not," I agreed somberly.

"So you two hang out a lot?" Penny guessed.

I relaxed my oddly protective grip and she slid away from my side, but kept her arm around my waist. I hooked my thumb into her back pocket and she kinked her hip toward me—all very subtle, but it was the kind of posture all young couples have when they finally feel comfortable at each other's touch. It wasn't lost on Tobie, but she fumbled the ball.

"Yeah, we do," she said, then added quickly, "We *did*. I mean we're still *friends* so we hang out a lot—not a *lot*, but... you know—"

"Straight up, Penny?" I checked; she looked at me and raised her eyebrows with curiosity. "Tobie and I dated for a little bit. Not long. I mean, we realized we were *way* better off as friends."

"Oh... okay..." Penny answered, and that's when it struck me: She had no idea why that should seem weird because she genuinely had no frame of reference. Like she *truly* had never dated before. She didn't understand that being introduced to an ex-girlfriend your boyfriend still hung out with should be a big deal. She had no mutual friends, no

145

gossipy acquaintances, no crazy ex-boyfriends, no one to measure up to in her mind. For her, jealousy hadn't started to filter in yet… or maybe she was a better person than most of us.

I looked at her and grinned sheepishly, as if apologizing for something I hadn't done. There are subtle ticks and cues that tell the world you are dating, no matter how secretive you're trying to be, and I suddenly saw them in the way Tobie and I acted, but we weren't dating and I didn't want Penny to assume anything was going on.

I mean, that's what jealousy really is: The realization that something special you thought you had with someone—the way her parents treated you or the unspoken looks that served as communication—wasn't special after all. You felt duped somehow, and I was trying to let Penny know it was okay, that she hadn't been duped, that Tobie and I weren't hiding anything. But I needn't have bothered. To Penny, right then, the weirdness was in meeting my friends, about whom she'd only heard stories. The only reason it was any other kind of weird is because Tobie and I were making it weird by trying to *not* make it weird, in a weird way.

"Tobie also helped me pick up the pieces when I got dumped at JP," I added, as if it helped prove something.

"Jay-pee?" Penny asked softly, embarrassed that she didn't know.

"Junior Prom? Did you go to Prom…?"

"Oh no," she said simply. "I wasn't allowed."

"Right… I mean…" I turned to Tobie. "So, have you seen Niz? Sammy? *Any* of the guys?"

"Jess said she was getting here early to claim our usual spot. I saw Niz and his parents and brother heading toward

146

her. Sammy's coming with Jolly, and I think Barb."

"Well that's everyone!" I declared.

We started to wander over to the top of the hill—we always grabbed a spot off to the left, not technically in the visual center of the display, but it gave us more elbow room. As we walked it struck me that baseball and fireworks and America go hand-in-hand-in-hand, and I felt bad for not even asking if Penny's softball friends were here, I was so focused on fretting about her meeting *my* friends.

"What about you, Penny?" I asked. "Are you friends here?"

"Probably," she replied lightly, not in the least bit concerned, it seemed.

"Do you want to try and find them? We could all get together into a huge band of teenagers and scare the hell out of our parents!"

"No," she chuckled. "I'm fine. Besides, you met my friends, but I've never met yours."

"Well, sure... I mean, I don't know... We've never *hung out* with your friends."

"It's fine, Jack," she said with more conviction. "Just as long as *we* get to hang out."

I caught Tobie's eye and she was smiling privately, then blushed and looked away as Penny gave me a quick kiss on the lips. It was a territorial move—as subtle as it was instinctual—but she looked kind and innocent and you couldn't hold it against her. Or maybe it was nerves; maybe she didn't know what else to do and it seemed to fit a theory of expectations she didn't understand because she'd never experi-

147

enced the situation before.

Or maybe I was over-thinking it because that's what I do.

We found the gang with no trouble. Tobie's and Niz's parents were having a loud, jovial conversation a respectable distance away from the kids, and Sammy was there already with Jolly and Barb. This kind of event always brought out the wider gang, beyond the core of me, Sammy, Tobie, Niz, and Jess. Jolly and Barb, and her best friend Kammy, often hung out with us, but not as often as the five of us did. I don't remember how we met Jolly—he skated some, so I guess that was probably it—but Kammy and Barb had found me and Niz in drama club. Niz had a penchant for the spot-light, while I toiled away behind the scenes. Kammy and Barb usually had parts in the plays, and both helped with makeup and costumes, too. Tobie and Jess weren't into drama as much, but they'd help work the ticket desk at per-formances or pound a few nails during set construction, if needs be.

Jolly was a character, though. He played soccer on the high school team—the closest thing to a jock in our group—and had a lust for life I was never able to fully parse. He had a somewhat turbulent home life, thanks to his dad, but it never seemed to dampen his spirits. Sure, he sometimes tracked us down because he had to get out of his house for a while, but it never seemed to bring his mood down.

He was also genuinely kind and generous, as if making up for the deficiencies at home, and he never drank or took part in any of our hijinks, but he also encouraged us and loved to hear our tales. Sometimes I feel like I wasn't as nice to him as I should have been, like he was a better friend to me than I was to him. Not that I ever did anything mean or hurt him in any way, but in those few bright moments where it became really obvious that he'd got my back, all I could think was that I'd never fully reciprocated. Sure, you could say that was because I'd never had the chance to, but that didn't necessarily let me off the hook.

We called him "Jolly" because he was so damn happy all the time and we knew he didn't have to be, and it also worked well because his real name was Roger: "Jolly Roger" Brimley. I hadn't seen or talked to him since Penny and I had started to date, and his eyes got wide when he saw her—not in a creepy way: he'd seen us holding hands and he recognized her.

"Penny?" he said, walking over and leaving Barb right in the middle of a story, to judge by the expression she gave him. "Penny Harper, right?"

"Oh, you know each other?" I assumed. Penny looked shyly away and shook her head slightly.

"Not really," Jolly admitted. "They have spring softball scrimmages on the diamond by the soccer field. You were an underclassman, right?"

She nodded.

"Yeah, so us underclassmen spend most of the time on the benches, bored."

He looked at me suspiciously, trying to figure out my game, then added, "You know how guys are, we all know the names of all the pretty girls on the other bench."

She blushed deeply and put her arm around my waist, trying to hide behind her hair or her hand or my shoulder or whatever she could find.

149

"Oh hey! Sorry! Don't be embarrassed!" Jolly stammered. "Jack, I didn't mean—I'm sorry."

"It's okay," she said quietly, recovering. "I shouldn't be embarrassed."

"I keep telling her she's the perfect girl," I said, squeezing her to me. "Don't you think she looks like Stevie Nicks?"

"She *does!*" Jolly exclaimed, maybe a bit too loudly, but glad to have the conversation deflected. "Holy shit! Like '70s Stevie Nicks!"

Barb had wandered over to see what was going on, and the others had clumped around us, too, so Jolly took them all in, begging them to agree. "She looks just like Stevie Nicks!"

"I didn't even know who that was before Jack," she admitted with a grin. I had finally played "Dreams" for her and had shown her the back cover of *Rumours*, and while she still denied that she was as pretty as Stevie Nicks, she had grudgingly accepted that there was some resemblance.

"Yeah, Jack has a pretty wide rock streak running alongside his punk streak," Jolly agreed. "It's cuz he hangs out with the stoners and hoods in the art wing."

"Oh, you're just jealous," I snapped jokingly and Jolly laughed with his signature high-pitched cackle. Coming out of anyone else, it would have annoyed the shit out of me, but with Jolly, it was just his thing and we loved him for it.

Penny flickered a smile over at me. Something in the look made me drop my arm, and her arm slipped away from around my waist. There was nothing mean in the look, but it made us realize how close we were standing, and we were afraid of looking too clingy and so had to prove we weren't.

"You guys really sit over there talking about us girls?" she asked Jolly.

"Well… I mean…"

"No, no—I'm not mad. We always wondered. Kallie always joked that you were sitting over there talking about us, and I think it's kinda funny that she was right."

Barb huffed a disgusted breath and whirled around, storming back over to the blankets Jess had spread out. I raised my eyebrows and looked at Tobie, but she shrugged and mumbled something, then followed Barb.

"What was *that*?" I asked.

"She's got a crush on Jolly," Sammy whispered, leaning in to us.

"Oh my God! Me and my big mouth!" Penny gasped, a touch overly dramatic.

"Baloney!" Jolly spat. "She does *not* Sammy, I *assure* you."

I looked over at the girls—Barb sitting looking huffy and Tobie trying to calm her down—and I remember distinctly realizing that Barb's behavior was exactly why she didn't hang out with us more often. Tobie was being nice—and trying to save the night from a bad turn—but Jess was standing there with us, rolling her eyes. We weren't used to dramatics in our core group, which is probably why we all gelled. Some people seem to thrive on drama, and Barb was definitely one of those people, making a big deal out of things that weren't even a deal to begin with. Sammy thought it was funny when she huffed off, as did Jolly (even though he'd go and try to smooth it over soon enough).

"It's probably someone else on the bench with me that she's worried about," Jolly decided. He sighed and added, "I'll go talk to her" in a defeated tone, then slumped over to the blankets.

"So Bells," Jess finally spoke up. "I hope this is the girl you've been going on about? Because if it's not, she should know that."

Sammy groaned loudly at the presumed burn of her question. Jess was a somewhat classic tomboy, right down to the short-cropped hair—a pixie cut that gave her jawline strength. As a kid, she'd been all tomboy, but now that we were in high school she was embracing her girlishness more, but she still held her own with the guys, throwing punches and hurling burns at us.

"Yeah, this is Penny," I said slowly, then added to Penny, "And I'm sorry for my friends."

She smiled at me but didn't say anything.

"They're loud and obnoxious," I joked. She laughed lightly; politely.

"Let's go talk with the girls," Jess decided, grabbing her hand and pulling her toward the blankets, leaving us boys behind.

"Damn, Jack," Jolly whispered. "Penny fucking *Harper*? So it's *true*?"

"What? Why?"

"Dude, everyone on the damn *team* wants to bang her!"

"Jolly—*Jesus*!" Niz begged.

"Are you saying you *don't* want to bang her?" Jolly quizzed Niz. Then turned back to me before he could answer. "Did *you* bang her, Bells?"

"Okay, okay," I cautioned, holding up my hands. "Niz is

152

right—you're coming on a touch heavy, man. And if you say 'bang' one more time, I'll punch you."

Sammy huffed out a heavy breath. He was gazing up at the darkening sky, his long, unkempt hair hanging down to his shoulders in stringy clumps.

"Jolly, can we *not* talk about banging chicks for *one* night?" he wondered.

"Exactly," Niz echoed.

"Oh, come *on*!" Jolly protested. "*All* you talk about is ba—uhhh—*screw*ing chicks!"

"Not true, man," Sammy stated simply, looking right at him. "And that's Jack's girlfriend—have a little respect."

I felt like there was something else going on all of a sudden, like something had happened in the car between Jolly, Sammy, and Barb. Niz looked as perplexed as me.

"So Niz—what's up with you?" I asked him. "You seem nervous."

He looked at me and glanced at the others. Had it been just the two of us, he wouldn't have hesitated at all, but now he had to weigh letting Sammy and Jolly in on it.

"I've just..." he started, then shrugged and shook his head. Now he had us all hooked and he knew it—there was no backing out of telling us. "I've just, I don't know, been sort of trying to ask Jess out. Like, for real."

"*Jess*?" Jolly whispered excitedly.

"Why does every mention of a girl shock you, Jolly?" Sammy mumbled. He wasn't wrong, but we ignored him.

"Yeah... I mean, she's... you know..."

"She'll eat you alive," Jolly decided. His tone said he was one hundred percent serious. "*Alive*."

153

"Forget it," Niz snapped. "Never mind. Where's my brother?"

He turned and wandered off without another word, so the three of us moseyed over to the blankets and the girls.

Whatever had been bugging Barb had obviously been cleared up—maybe there was a hint of sourness when she looked at Jolly, but it could have been my imagination. Tobie and Penny seemed to have hit it off, and Jess looked frankly out of place, girl-talking with the girls, but Jess was also a peacekeeper and she wasn't going to let her own opinions of the conversation potentially scare away Penny, and I totally respected her for that. She might tell me later, privately, that Penny was an airhead, but she'd be civil and make her feel welcome all the same. I guess that's why some people said she was manipulative, but they just didn't get her. She was *diplomatic*—she kept the peace, but she didn't manipulate people into getting what she wanted.

In a funny way, she was kind of Tobie without the girly overlay, which is probably why they got along. Tobie was a girl's girl—shopping at the mall and worrying about her hair and all that kind of stuff—but she didn't take shit either, like Jess didn't. She might go along with it for longer than Jess, but eventually Tobie would strike back. So I guess to *look* at her you might think Tobie was a girl's girl, but to *know* her you would never think it. Hell, most guys found a reason to escape if they saw Tobie and Jess coming down the hall because together they were unstoppable.

Now Barb was basically at the other end of the scale, a *total* girl's girl, complete with all the cliché marks of teenage girlhood: the drama, the tears, the eye-rolls and oh-my-

154

gawds. Sometimes I think she took shit—or even invented shit—so she had something to be dramatic about. So if you're looking for the dynamic that held the three of them together, it was Tobie kinda getting where Barb was coming from and being a shoulder for her to cry on, while Jess was there to hoist her up and give her some tough love, and Tobie was ready to back Jess up, and Barb was ready to be over it, her strength coming from their strength.

And then there was Penny. It hadn't struck me until that moment, seeing Penny with the other girls, that she wasn't like my other friends. Barb and Kammy, and even Tobie, were *our* girl's girls, but not like you might expect. It's like how people who didn't know me and Niz and Sammy, and probably Jolly when he was with us, thought we were nothing more than a bunch of skate rats, up to no good. But to us, within our group, we knew who was the clown and the genius and the slacker and the drama queen. Every large enough group of friends ends up with their characters, and sometimes those characters blur the lines between cliques— like Jolly being on the football team or Kammy being a wrestlette—but your crew acquires the same *shade* of those differences, and that keeps you together; keeps you distinct from the other cliques. Like when you put light through a prism and it shows the colors that make it real: everyone else sees white, but you see that rainbow in your crew.

But Penny, you could tell, was a stripe of color from someone else's prism, and the realization scared me. She sat there with Jess and Tobie and had no idea how *different* she was from them, with her tight curfews and her odd social awkwardness around people her own age. I had a sudden

155

overwhelming empathy for Penny, who had no idea these girls sometimes snuck a can of their old man's beer onto the back porch, and lay on the hoods of Chevys with boys to watch the starry night unfold toward midnight. And she had no idea I was the same way—and it made me feel immature, and it made me feel like a shitty liar for not telling her who I really was. But I couldn't tell her now because I wasn't sure it was who I wanted to be be any longer. Penny seemed like the better half of me, and I wanted to be more like the kind of person she expected, not the person I was.

It was selfish, I suppose, but in that moment I wanted to hold onto her—to what seemed to me like her innocence and how I should be—for as long as I could, and seeing her there with my other friends put the fear in me that if she got too close, she'd end up like one of them: we'd daub her with our unique shade, and she'd be marked for life as an outcast, a loser, a ne'er-do-well.

My expression dropped. Penny saw me staring at her and smiled brightly. She patted the blanket next to her, and I dropped to my knees, shifting into a mostly sitting position practically in her lap.

"What's wrong?" she whispered barely loud enough for me to hear.

"Are you having fun?"

"Yeah," she said sincerely. "Your friends seem nice."

I glanced at her with a smirk to gauge her expression and she was looking at me with an open face, her brown eyes glimmering and her lips creased into a tiny, private smile.

"People don't usually call us nice," I half lied.

Niz and I had done some pretty stupid things in our

156

years together, but causing *real* trouble had never crossed our minds. I mean, yes, we'd known some of the things we got up to would get us into trouble—maybe even big trouble—if our parents found out or the cops caught us, but we didn't do it *because* it was trouble, if that makes sense. We did it because it was fun. People who didn't know us certainly judged us—Sammy with his long, messy hair; Jess looking like some punk-ass rock chick; me in my thrift-store fineries and untidy hair.

Penny looked over at Tobie and Barb and Jess, and watched them for a few seconds, considering. Niz had wandered over and was self-consciously hovering near Jess, while Niz's mom was trying to do something to Sammy's hair to show him how good it would look cut.

"Do you want to try and find your friends?" I offered again, compelled in a way to throw Penny back into familiar waters.

"No…" she mused distantly.

"So what do you and your friends do, anyway?"

"Nothing," she said, looking back at me. "I told you, I was never allowed to go out before last summer."

"Just with boys, though, right?"

"With anyone."

"No sleepovers even?"

"Well, sure, when I was little. But I'm a bit old for sleepovers now, aren't I?"

I didn't answer. I mean, we called it "crashing" now, not "sleeping over," but the effect was the same.

"So this summer, before you met me, what did you do?" I pried, aching to find some wedge of light that would prove we really were the same, deep down where it counted.

"*Nothing*," she chuckled. "People got used to *not* inviting me places, and I got used to staying home."

"I can't believe that."

"You can't *imagine* that," she corrected.

It was true. I couldn't imagine not hanging out with my friends. It helped that Niz lived right around the corner, and Sammy didn't mind riding his skateboard a couple of miles to reach us, but I couldn't remember a time—ever—when I wasn't running off to do something with some friend or other, and usually without parental supervision. I looked over at Niz again and grinned—he was completely unaware of me, fixated as he was on talking to Jess. Thing is, the way she was acting, I wasn't sure she minded his new-found attention.

"You really *can't*," Penny repeated, bringing my attention back to her. She looked like a proud parent who knew she should be mad. "You've always been surrounded by friends."

"I guess I have, yeah. Is that weird?"

"No," she dismissed. "But a lot of the girls on the team can't hang out all the time either—and certainly not with boys mixed in like this. Do you know what I had to do to get my dad to let me come here tonight?"

"No…?"

"It's not important. But it took a lot of convincing—and that's how most of the girls are. Well, not *all* of them…"

"But the ones you hang out with?"

She nodded slowly.

"I did call a couple of them. I thought it would be nice to

hang out here with you and them and their boyfriends. Sharon—she's my best friend, I guess—wasn't even coming. And Cassie said she was going to be with her boyfriend's parents, so… you know…"

"Yeah…"

"So whose parents are those again?" Penny wondering, motioning with her head.

"Oh—Niz's and Tobie's. Niz and I go way back—like, second grade. We met Jess and Tobie in sixth grade—Jess used to live right down the street from me back then. So we all hung out a lot. Tobie lives out in the township—our parents actually all get together every so often and hang out. Now *that's* weird."

"I don't even think my parents have friends," Penny said. I could tell she was exaggerating… Maybe. "I guess they go to work parties and out to dinner now and again."

"Well never mind," I decided. "I'll teach you all about the fine art of hanging out, and when we're old, we'll still all hang out and embarrass our kids."

She blushed and I was about to splutter something about not meaning *our* kids but she looked away, and then Tobie caught her eye and said something and they both giggled, and Penny scooted a bit closer to her so they could huddle, and Barb scooted in, too, sensing a girls-night moment, so I stood up and found Sammy and tackled him for no good reason at all, and he sort of fought back but was too surprised to do much more than laugh, and then Niz leaped over and pulled us apart, pretending to be a grumpy old man.

For some reason, that moment more than anything else is how I remember that summer, balanced as I was between childhood and being an adult. I had a wallet that I temporarily lost in the scuffle with Sammy and we had to find it because it had my drivers license in it. I actually had money in it, too—money I'd earned—and I needed that for gas so I could drive my girlfriend to the movies—the girl sitting on a blanket, bathed in the last rays of the dying summer sun, her skin a golden brown like sunset on a beach.

I felt young and alive and grown up and responsible and ridiculous and childish all at once. I had everything a teenage boy required to make life right, and though I may not have thought it directly, I certainly felt it, and later, as I lay in bed drifting off to sleep, I'm sure I was grinning ear-to-ear, because everything was finally beginning—*life* had finally started to happen.

The fireworks, ironically, were the least memorable part of the night. Oh, they were beautiful, even from our vantage point on a hill overlooking them, and I loved that I watched them with my arm around Penny, but they seemed tainted somehow, like the moment at a sleepover when you're told you had to turn in after the movie was over: No matter how awesome those last minutes were, you knew it was the last round and you started to calm down, to prepare for the next hour when all the fun you'd been having was gone. Those fireworks were the final minutes of our movie that night, the spectacular close to a long day together, a day of moments vast enough to be preserved forever.

After the fireworks we politely declined rides from Niz's folks and Tobie's folks so we could stretch that last hour to a breaking point, and we walked home hand in hand, the summer night humid and thick around us. We didn't want to let go of each other—or I didn't, anyway, and I'm pretty sure Penny felt the same way. There was a lightness in the way she walked. There was unbridled joy in the way she was talking fast and telling me all about everything I'd just been with her for, with me breaking in and going along with it, like we hadn't thought of that night in fifteen years and we wanted to remind each other of how much fun it had been.

Nights like that, they get set in amber in our minds; cast in the hot-breath breeze of a summer night, with the crickets and cicadas droning on and on in the background; cast in the slow, deliberate steps of youth, marching the condemned walk of burgeoning adulthood; cast in that look in her eyes and that smirk on her lips that said you were everything, and this night would shine forever in the starry darkness of memory. And it *was* a great night—the final tether that tied that day into a knot at the center of the biggest ripple my life had yet produced.

We stood on her front porch, still holding hands, and looked into each other's eyes, the moths pinging into the yellow light above us and the night bugs whirring and chirping in the bushes and trees, an unseen chorus to our closing scene. And even though we'd kissed before, *that* kiss seemed more special than all the rest. It was slow and resplendent and the only thing that mattered to me right then—not who may be looking out of the windows at us or who may walk out on us or what she was thinking and if she happy with me.

All that mattered was her lips on mine, the warmth of her breath on my cheek when I kissed her neck, the precious touch of her skin against mine.

I sat on the patio with Tobie, sipping coffee and watching our kids playing in the yard, our little boy taking down his big sister with whole-armed tackles around her legs. They'd both giggle, then she'd crawl free and run away, stopping after a few steps and goading him to chase her, which he did with gusto.

Those quiet summer mornings, sitting outside with Tobie, sipping coffee and reading comic books, will be among the moments I'll recall when I'm lying in whatever deathbed enjoys my final repose: The way the sun rose gold-on-green through the summer trees and dripped from the warm air like amber; the way the insects whirred and clicked; the way the birds and squirrels played chase with their arcane chatters and chirps, lost in their own concerns like our children were lost in theirs. The world was nothing more than everything we could see, and it all looked sun-kissed and fine.

"Five more years and Ophelia will be the age we were when we met," I mused out loud.

"Hmmm," Tobie agreed, paging through her magazine.

There's a strange tunneling of time when you pass a certain age, or maybe it happens when you have kids, no matter how old you are. There's a moment when you start to look backward instead of forward, counting the years that have passed instead of looking toward the years ahead. Life ends at forty, the old cliché says, and sitting there watching my kids, it seemed to ring true. "End" didn't feel exactly right,

162

but the wonder certainly got sucked out of it somewhere around thirty-five. There were no milestones left: Forty was the last mark, the sign that said only, "This is the last sign." No more looking forward to being a double-digit age, or being a teenager, or driving, or becoming a legal adult, or voting in your first election, or buying alcohol legally, or leaving college, or turning thirty (the magical age that marked you as an *actual* adult, not just a legal one)… No, after that, it was a lot of looking back to all those things that had got you to the present point—all the living, all the joys and regrets.

"Did Penny mention the show online…?" Tobie asked with half interest, as if sensing where my thoughts were going. She flipped another page.

"Not yet."

"What did Gray think?"

"He agreed with you."

"Yeah?" She looked at me sidelong and smiled, flipping another page dramatically. "And what did *I* think?"

"That it seemed a bit stalkery."

Tobie nodded and looked down at her magazine, smiling privately. She knew that it would eat at me if Penny acted like it never happened. That's how I'm wired: I can't let something like that go. It was like the frayed end of a label on a beer bottle waiting to be picked at and peeled back.

"It *is* weird to think…" Tobie started.

She looked up and watched Ophelia for a few seconds, her smile widening with that soft love only mothers have lighting her eyes.

"We were just kids, Jack. We always seemed so *old*, though."

"I know…"

It's weird to gain the sense of perspective that comes with parenthood—to see your kids ticking off the time like you did, and just as sure they are the most grownup they'll ever be. The ruse of becoming an adult is that you always feel *grown up* at every age; you always feel the most mature you'll ever be. Then one day you realize you completely missed the moment when it was finally true, probably somewhere in your thirties, and you start looking back to find it; to see if you can recognize the final turn from child to adult and warn your children, so they can see it coming—so they can live it up before it catches them. I felt like I'd done a decent job of running away from it, but it didn't seem to help entirely—not when it mattered. Shit always seemed to happen, slowly eating away whatever vestiges of childhood innocence remained.

I've never again slept as well as I did when I was twelve—I've been running from something ever since. Maybe just ghosts, but that doesn't matter when they seem to be gaining on you.

I also knew Tobie wasn't talking about us being kids when we'd met, age eleven, at some sixth-grade dance. She was talking about the summer I'd met Penny Harper and the fall when she'd been there to help me get over her. She'd been there at the exact moment that what I was running from almost caught up to me.

I watched Tobie watching our kids then turned and watched them myself, their bare feet tickled by grass that I could no longer stand to walk on without shoes. I'd been barefoot and carefree once, but where Tobie smiled and saw

164

life and the future, I could only wince and see pending heartbreak. I saw beautiful children playing dangerously close to the precipice of innocence and I wondered what would come along and make them fall, and I wondered who would be there for them, because parents, I knew, could only catch their children for so long. Soon enough they had to learn to pick themselves up or to lean on friends that were closer to the fire and could understand more immediately how it burned.

When we get older, our experience blinds us to the weight and depth of the issues we suffered through as children, and we try to pass along a wisdom that only years can give a frame of reference to. Our kids would brush us away not because they didn't care or thought we didn't understand, but because they knew, deep down, that we'd forgotten what it was like to live life for the first time; what it was like to see first blood welling up over wounds you believed would never, ever heal.

"Jack?" Tobie whispered, her hand reaching out tentatively and touching mine.

"Yeah...?"

"You okay?"

"Yeah. I just... I don't want them to get their hearts broken."

Tobie laughed. Not in a mean or trivializing way, but in a wise way; the kind of gentle grace she's always had. I looked at her and grinned.

"What's so funny?"

"They will, Jack. You know that, right? The problem is, your memory is too long and too deep."

"No... I just remember how it felt."

"That's what I mean. You can't stop everyone from getting hurt, Bells. That was always your problem: you genuinely tried. But you can't take on everyone else's pain, not even for your kids."

"Hmmm…"

I turned back and watched them again. The wrestling game was developing rules even as we watched: tackles were only legal if the run-up started a certain distance away, apparently. There was some disagreement over this, but eventually it was codified when they agreed that a second tackle couldn't be levied until the person tackled was safely away—a three-second count, in fact.

"One! Two! *Three!*" Ophelia cried, eliciting frightened squeals of delight from her brother.

"You know, I think you're looking at the wrong side of it," Tobie said, folding her arms across her magazine. She nodded to herself and squinted.

"What do you mean?"

"Maybe Ophelia's going to help *heal* broken hearts, not suffer them."

"Let's hope so," I allowed. "I was lucky to have you—to have *all* of my friends."

It was true: My friends from high school had been there my whole life and in hindsight, I'm not sure where I would have ended up without them, or with different friends. That thought gave me different levels of anxiety, of course: What if my kids made the wrong friends? What if no one was there to hear them calling out from whatever emptiness pulled them in?

I've always been a worrier, but it was so much easier

when I only had to worry about myself or my friends, who all had other friends to also worry about them, diluting the concern into manageable chunks that all of us, together, could handle. Maybe there, then, is the true meaning of relationships, this fractal web of concern that forms hubs and ribbons and interweaves to the extent that a solid mesh is defined—your group, your posse, your crew. We were the net that caught each other; our bonds of life and the living made it so. The fine line I have to balance now is between pushing my kids in what I believe to be the right direction and letting them screw up and learn from their mistakes all by themselves; letting their own nets catch them and spring them back to their feet.

"Maybe you should call Niz?" Tobie suggested.

"About what?"

"You know…" she shrugged and gave me a half smile. "Penny Harper?"

"I should just ignore her."

"That won't help it go away, Bells. Ignoring her won't make it better."

I didn't want to admit it, but I knew it would fester, just like she said. This was my one chance to finally finish scribing that circle and close the door on the one aspect of my past that still gave me nightmares.

"It feels a lot like inviting a vampire into my home," I mumbled. "Shouldn't you be telling me to ignore her? That she was a lifetime ago and best left forgotten?"

"Is she forgotten, Bells? If it was anyone else, then yes, you're probably right. But you? You always have to see problems through to a happy ending."

"Happy?"

"Well, *an* ending, anyway."

"I just don't know what I can gain, other than ripping open a lot of old wounds."

"Peace of mind. I bet she's not *half* as great as you think you remember."

That may well be true, but oddly it didn't make it any easier. In fact, the thought that Penny Harper would not end up being worth all the importance she had once held—nor twenty years of random thoughts popping into my head about her—made it more frightening: I didn't want to tarnish that summer with her, I wanted it left the way it was, heart-break and all, with the full measure of importance I had given it. It was kind of perfect in its pain, a tiny testament to the power of young love and of friends that had romance and innocence and all the great things of literature woven into its fabric. The thought of it crumbling away under the façade of an annoying middle-aged woman who proved she had once been an annoying teenage girl was too much to bear.

I sighed heavily.

"So call Niz," she suggested again.

"Niz? I can't."

"Why not?"

"Feels too much like high school," I chuckled. "I can't call him out of the blue and ask him about girl trouble."

Tobie snickered happily and shook her head.

"Well, it's the internet." She opened her magazine again. "You can always ignore her later."

"I haven't had my hug yet today, Daddy."

She said it very seriously, as if this oversight had been registered and logged, and had been noted to be a common occurrence. It wasn't. I hug my kids at least once a day. She was parroting back what I always said to them when I got home from work.

I was messing around with my skateboard—one last bastion of childhood I couldn't give up—and I rolled up onto my knees to her eye level and embraced her, and in a wash it struck me almost physically: There is nothing that resonates more deeply, nor is more valuable, than the innocent trust of a child. It inspired me to be a better person, to help make the world as magical and kind as the children believed it to be— that's the power of a parent hugging their child.

My parents didn't do a lot of hugging and I never realized how much it meant to me until I met my friend Kate at college. She was an unrepentant hugger, the kind who would look confused at a hand extended for a shake and bring you in for a hug instead. Then right before Tobie and I got married, something in me snapped. I remember getting in a stupid argument with my parents about something meaningless, and in the end I admitted I only wanted a damn hug from my parents. What I didn't say is that it felt like, when I took the vows and married Tobie, my childhood was really over—all the freewheeling rebellion and rushing into relationships in an effort to grow up were finally out of my system—and I don't think I wanted to look back and be able to

169

say that I never remembered my parents hugging me when I was a kid.

And that's all it took. Now we hug all the time. But I wanted to be sure my kids had the opposite. I wanted my kids to remember that their parents hugged them all the time.

"That's a big hug," I said softly. "You're getting stronger."

She stepped back and squeezed my right bicep. "I won't ever have muscles as big as yours."

"You will if you exercise," I promised.

"Daddy?"

"Yeah?"

"Is your skateboard broken?"

"No. I got new bearings. They make the wheels spin really fast."

"Do you like playing with your skateboard?"

"Sure I do, li'l one."

"Then why don't you play all the time?"

"Aw, you know. I have to go to work."

"Why?"

"To make money."

"So we can buy cake?" she wondered with excitement.

"Sure," I chuckled, resting back on my heels. "Cake and cookies and all that good stuff."

"Thank you, Daddy," she said simply. "Thank you for buying me cake."

"Come here," I said, taking her and hugging her again, mostly because I was afraid I'd cry and she'd see it and she wouldn't understand.

It was one of the most distinct moments I remember from being a parent: to realize that she understand gratitude

170

and sacrifice on a level many adults don't achieve, and she wasn't bitter about it. It just was. I sniffed in deeply and let her go, turning back to my wrenches and wheels before she could see me. I didn't want to explain that sometimes people cry when they're really very happy.

She turned and ran off into the yard, trilling some noise she thought sounded like a train whistle as she rushed to be reunited with a jumble of stuffed animals in a makeshift carriage, attached to her tricycle by a bungee cord.

Tobie burst through the back door and stalked over to me, a strange mix of relief and anger on her face.

"Well, the little monster's napping," she declared.

"He was tired," I agreed.

"He fought it, though. I hate to admit it, but I put on *Elmo* and he dozed off. I left him in his beanbag."

"He'll be fine." I stood up and hugged her and she hugged me back. "TV is better than sleeping pills."

"Well, I wasn't suggesting *pills*," she admonished jokingly. "But I swore I'd never use TV as a parenting device."

"He'll survive. Elmo isn't raising him, just putting him to sleep."

She pulled away and studied my face suspiciously. "You sound… pensive."

"Ophelia just thanked me for buying her cake."

"What does *that* mean?" Tobie chuckled. "It's not her birthday!"

"She asked why I go to work. Cake was her example of why we need money."

Tobie smiled whimsically and studied my face even harder.

"So why do you look so damn sad about it?"

"What happens when the cake runs out...?"

I trailed off and looked at Tobie apologetically. The last thing she needed was me acting all irrational because my six-year-old daughter had thanked me for buying her cake.

"Don't start that again, Bells."

"I just love those kids so much it hurts, Tobie."

"Oh I know, Jack," she lilted. "But let them grow up. Like we did."

"*Not* like I did," I snapped, brushing past her and heading inside.

She didn't follow me, she let me go.

Maybe I do assign too much importance to things and create a weird, rolling existential worldview for myself, but I can't help it and Tobie was used to it. She balanced me by her presence and always has, ever since our school days. She got upset and emotional sometimes, sure, but I brooded. I always played a thing through in my mind until it unraveled— until the cake ran out. I told myself it was prep work for the inevitable, so that when it happened I'd know what to do, like they tell you to go over skate tricks in your head to teach your brain how to function when it matters.

I went inside quietly, holding the screen door as it closed so it wouldn't bang and wake up Fletch. I crept into the kitchen and looked into the living room—our small house was effectively one big room divided into a kitchen and living room by a long counter top, with three tiny bedrooms tacked on over time by various owners. Our master bedroom barely fit a double bed and a dresser, and that's no exaggeration.

172

Fletch was right where Tobie had said, splayed out in a bean bag while Elmo and Mr. Noodle got into some mess or other on TV. He was snoring very lightly, worn out from playing in the yard with his sister: The good sleep of excitement spent. It amazed me to think how many things he was learning new every day—closing synapses to save as memories and experience. No wonder kids need so much sleep: the brain needs time to process all that new data. But I also couldn't help imagining little packets of that data being misfiled or cross-filed or left out altogether, developing into neuroses and ticks and personality. The dark matter used to fill those gaps became as much a part of the experience as the facts. That dark matter had hardened into a strange shadowy emptiness for me.

In my defense, when you've waded out of your depth, the experience stays with you forever. You can feel it all around you, always. You have to acknowledge it so it can't sneak up on you again, and you get used to it; learn to live with it and deflect its advances.

I use childish fun to keep that feeling at bay, like a priest hoisting incense and lighting candles to ward off evil spirits. I think deep-down I figure that if I refuse to play house and take on the trappings of an average adult life, I'll somehow outsmart the end and achieve some level of immortality—I'll never grow old and die if I stayed young and alive. But times like this, when the weight of parenting fell fully on my mind and I understood what I was up against, I felt the edifice crumble; pieces of plaster popped out and tumbled to the ground.

I couldn't save them, I knew that, but maybe I could

teach them to fight. I could teach them to never give in. I could explain to them how a sense of doom always grows from the wiry tendrils of teenage crisis, because I'd felt it; had almost been consumed by it.

I felt tears stinging my eyes and turned away, Fletch's even snores ticking like a pump behind me. He shifted in the bean bag, but the snores continued uninterrupted.

I couldn't stop their eventual fall from innocence, and the recognition of my powerlessness over it froze me. I couldn't stop them from learning that some people are mean on purpose, that people you love die, that average Americans are buried under debt, that all politicians are corrupt and greedy, that alcoholics aren't bad they're just scared, that teachers *do* play favorites, that girls can fill you with unimaginable pain...

And that girls can save your life.

Out front of Now That's Class is a small patio area, mostly for the smokers, but also for people like me who want to take a breather and enjoy the liquid summer nights. It was hot inside—bars always are—and I'd left Gray nursing a beer. He was either too tired to bother getting up, or he wanted to keep his barstool for the show. I didn't see much point in that—the stage was in another room that served as an indoor halfpipe when there was no band, so you couldn't see the band from the bar.

That's right: Now That's Class has an indoor halfpipe. But we were there to see SWMRS, not for skating, and I left Gray after the opener to soak in some moonlight before the main event. The air was still and humid: Perfect for trapping a layer of haze from the smokers, but it didn't bother me. I'm not a smoker, but I never minded the smell of smoke. I guess for me it will always be tethered to memories of nights out with friends, and we forgive a lot of dirt when we're having fun.

I moved over to a corner nominally away from the greatest concentration of cigarettes—you can have too much of a tolerable thing—and watched the cars hum past. It was peaceful and full of life: Quiet conversation among friends punctuated by laughter and raised voices.

"Do you work at the Beachland?" someone asked rhetorically—they already knew the answer—but close enough to me that I turned to see who it was. Penny was smiling at me apologetically, holding her beer glass in two hands close to her lips.

"No," I said with no smile. She shifted her feet, her head to one side.

"They gave you the shirt for being a good customer?"

I glanced down at my clothes, only dimly aware that I'd put on a Beachland T-shirt that morning.

"It was a close-out and I liked it. What are you doing here?"

I met her eyes. I'd assumed our last "chance encounter" had been awkward enough that she wouldn't reprise the conversation, but here she was.

"It's your fault," she decided, stepping over and leaning against the railing beside me. She was wearing a leather miniskirt and knee-high stockings, her black T-shirt a size too big and held tight to her waist with a big knot. Her hair was straight and clean, brushing her shoulders, and her face looked bright and alive, like it hadn't back at the Beachland. She knew what she was doing this time, and she'd dressed for it.

"You keep posting great bands."

I sucked in a long breath.

"I didn't figure you'd find these guys that great. You never really liked music before."

"Well, I dated *you* for a summer—how could I *not* end up liking music?"

"I still don't really like baseball…" I observed.

"I don't follow it as much anymore either," she said quietly. "My dad was the real fan."

And she had to mention her dad. The dick in me wanted

176

to tell her stop trying to use sympathy to disarm me, but the fact is, it worked, mostly because she'd brought her dad up within minutes of us talking both times. His death had obviously left a deep scar. She stood there looking down into her beer, and I imagined she started a lot of conversations about her dad these days. Maybe there was regret in her eyes, too; the things she could have done to make life easier for both of them.

"Did you argue with him a lot?" I assumed. Her head snapped up and she held my gaze, her lips thin, the smile gone.

"No. Not a lot. He only wanted me to be safe."

"Look, I'm sorry—that summer was different for both of us, and I never saw your dad as anything but stern and judgmental. I shouldn't have—"

"He eased up when I had Jason. Like he'd been stressing about keeping me out of trouble, then when it finally happened, it was like it was over and I'd survived and he could relax."

"I can't imagine losing my dad already, Penny. I'm sorry. I shouldn't have said anything."

That mysterious smile again, like she only wanted to be there if things went a certain way, and early signs said they weren't going that way.

"Who are you here with?" I asked hopefully.

"A friend… How was that summer different for you?"

It's all we had to talk about, and I suppose I *had* brought it up.

"It wasn't fun?" she smirked, nudging me with her knee.

"It was great, until it was over," I summarized and unconsciously shuffled out of range of her knee. It was like we were having the same damn conversation all over again. Was she going to apologize again? Try to make me believe it had all been childish whimsy that broke us up? That I'd been *the one* and she was *so sorry*? *Did* she think we were going to get back together? I straightened up and turned to go back to the bar.

"I don't really know anyone up here, Jack," she said.

I stopped moving; acted like I'd only been stretching.

"I'm not here to keep digging up the past. I'm here to get out and have fun, and I figured if anyone knows where the fun's at, it's you."

"Sure," I agreed sourly. "Well where's your friend? Isn't she fun?"

"She's twenty-six and she's only here to get laid."

I narrowed my eyes.

"So not the same friend as before...?"

"No!" Penny laughed, but didn't elaborate.

"And what are *you* here for?"

"I told you..." She met my eyes. "I just wanted to have some fun." Her face cleared and she grinned with a mild epiphany. "Maybe I should bring Jason next time? He's never done anything like this before!"

"Would he enjoy it?" I checked, trying to subtly dissuade her from a "next time."

"Probably not," she admitted.

"Where is he now?"

"At his dad's."

"So you aren't married?" I felt like I knew the answer, but I had to ask anyway. I didn't think she'd be out at bars if she was married, and you didn't use phrases like "at his dad's" if your son only had one home.

"No," she said in a low tone. "We never got married. It's a full-fledged skeleton in my family's closet."

She chuckled without mirth and I could tell she was more serious than kidding around. That meshed more with what I remembered of her dad, he of the mind that he was grooming his daughter to be some lucky man's trophy wife. I didn't feel like I needed to point that out, though. Maybe that was when he eased up on her—when she took herself off the trophy-wife market by having a kid.

"I'm divorced," I admitted, unable to break myself away from the conversation—airing out my own skeleton in exchange for hers. She'd tracked me down twice now and was clearly trying to work through some things. If all I had to do was be an ear and a reminder of her childhood, and that would make her feel better, then I could stand out on the patio with her and talk for a few minutes. It wasn't going to kill me.

"Really?"

"Yeah—we rushed into it. I was… on the rebound, I guess you'd say. She made me feel good when I felt really bad about everything. It wore off pretty quick, though."

"Kids?"

I shook my head slowly. "From the divorce? Nope."

"That's good. It's rough co-parenting."

"Is Jason's dad a good guy?"

"Oh yes—he's great. Talk about a bad breakup, though —there was no repairing *that* mistake."

It was a conversation, but I suddenly had no idea what we were talking about. There were words, and the words

179

formed thoughts, but the thoughts were disjointed because there was no real common ground to tie them together. I wasn't going to share the details of my divorce and I didn't want her to feel obligated to go into her situation. It was the worst kind of small-talk because we should have been able to muster more depth, but we couldn't—or we didn't want to.

"So what does he like? Baseball or music?"

I was trying. I settled back into my former spot and sipped my beer; tried to make her feel like I didn't think this was all a painful waste of my time.

"Jason?" She chuckled. "He's a good kid. He likes computers and video games. Do you have kids with Tobie?"

"Two. Girl and a boy, six and four. Hard to say what they'll like yet."

"Well, they have a good influence, anyway."

"Tobie?" I quipped. "I agree."

She didn't respond and the silence hung heavier than the humid air.

"I wrote that in my diary," she admitted with a wry smirk. "I wrote, 'Jack will be a great dad some day.' It's all I wrote that day."

"You re-read your diary?" I checked, trying to deflect how weird her admission made me feel—now I had to recalibrate everything I thought about what she thought about me.

"Only this year," she laughed, shaking her head and looking away, out into the night and her memories.

"I re-read my old poems," I offered sympathetically. She smiled at me with appreciation.

"Did you ever write any poems about me?"

180

There was a wink in her tone and a glisten in her eyes, like stars flickering through clouds.

"I did."

"Love poems?"

I swear she blushed.

"Not exactly."

Her brow furrowed, and in a wash I remembered that expression and how crazy it drove me when she'd try to reconcile something I'd said with what she thought. I very nearly leaned in and kissed her, because that was my muscle-memory of that expression; that was the thing I did when I saw her brow wrinkle and her nose twitch. She looked over and met my eyes, and I swear she was waiting for me to kiss her—she remembered it, too.

"I better get back before Gray leaves," I said, moving away before she could respond.

"Jack?" she wondered, reaching out and putting her hand on my arm, stopping me. I didn't speak. "I hope you wrote love poems about me. I mean, even if you... burned them or something later."

"I did," I whispered, hoping she couldn't hear me.

"You burned them?"

"I wrote them."

"Jack, I only want to be friends. After all this time, don't you think we've earned that?"

I touched her fingers and let the sensation linger longer than it should have. She squeezed my arm and let go. I had chugged my beer and I felt good, despite the memories of a time long since lost. I held up the bottle and considered its emptiness.

"I better go."

She took the hint and nodded her head and half waved as I wandered off.

She stood by me during the show for a few songs and smiled like we were sharing something. I tried my best to politely ignore her and she drifted away, pairing up with another woman who I assume she'd come with. They both looked kind of lonely, and then the show was over and they were gone.

I got home from Now That's Class and the house was dark and still. After the garage door whirred and shuddered back down, I stood in my driveway and listened to the far-off sound of a train and looked up at the moon. There's a primal part of me that is genuinely amazed by the moon, and at times it seems to have exactly the kind of power our ancient ancestors attributed to it. It also gives me a weird comfort, to think that the old rock has been spinning around the Earth for all of time, unwavering, perfectly happy—I find solace in knowing that I can be stuck, too, and also be happy; that I can follow my course around and around the days, weeks, and years, moving from bed to job to home to shows to bed and back again.

We all have our orbits and paths, I suppose, and we all keep our eyes peeled for comets—some amazing, different thing to break up the long, dark stretches between days that bleed together into long, dark stretches of years.

"I'm home," I said in a soft voice, just in case anyone was listening, then went into the family room to watch TV.

I've never been able to go straight to bed, not for as long as I can remember, no matter how late I get home. To this day I don't have any idea if my parents ever waited up for me, or if they'd only have given me hell if my bed had been empty at two in the morning or something. I'm pretty sure it's the latter, because once they thought my brother hadn't come home—if you knew him, it was a truly laughable idea—and they turned every damn light in the house on and started calling hospitals and shit like that, scaring the hell out of me (we all *knew* the only reason he'd stay out so late is because he was dead). Then my brother walked into the kitchen, rubbing his eyes and asking what was going on. Somehow, they'd missed him curled up in his blankets when they'd gone to check on him.

I listened to a lot of *Coast to Coast AM* growing up when I got home late. There was something about knowing that all those people were also awake and thinking about weird shit that gave me a huge amount of comfort. Other times, I listened to the radio—97X—and kept a scratch pad by my bed to jot down the songs or bands I heard at the bottom of the night and wanted to spin again later. And sometimes I flopped onto the couch and watched TV—old movies or MTV or whatever horror shows the midnight horror hosts had dug up (pun intended). I needed something—anything—to put me to sleep. Something to clear my head and let me drift off.

Sometimes my dad schlepped down to the kitchen and got a drink of water when I came in, but most times it was like I was coming home to an empty house, which is how it felt now with Tobie and the kids in bed. I liked it. I need that downtime—that time when I can pretend no one else is around and I have no one else to care for but myself; a few minutes to unwind and forget the noise of the day.

I poured myself a nightcap—a shot of bourbon—to nudge me into sleep and flipped to MTV. It was basically the same thing as whiskey: mind numbing and addictive, like the next video would be better than the last. It was a reflexive action brought on by Penny, no doubt: MTV is completely worthless these days. In fact, by the time I was sixteen they only showed good videos after midnight—*Headbanger's Ball* or *120 Minutes*—the shit they couldn't show during daylight Top 40 hours. Even then, it had started to pale in comparison to when they first started to broadcast and I'd fallen in love with Stevie Nicks and the Eurythmics. Now there was no reason to even give it a chance so I fired up an ancient copy of H-Street's *Shackle Me Not*, the slap, roll, and grind of wheels a healthy sedative for a troubled mind. Skate videos had a similar twang as AM radio: I felt like I was seeing part of the world I'd never get to see for myself, and discovering that there were people there just like me and my friends.

Or just like me and my friends *had* been—now I bought and watched new skate videos from the vantage point of a wizened old man watching the kids have fun. This was their world now, and all I could do was hope I was ushering my own kids into it the right way.

Probably the biggest thing parents can do is set a good example, and I try hard to do that for my kids. I stopped swearing—mostly—and I don't stay out until two every night, and I don't get drunk. That fabled American night changes for adults; it becomes a hometown street you recognize but no longer belong on.

I envy the youth their wild abandon, but I'd never do anything to stand in its way. Curfews, anti-skate laws, noise ordinances—it's all bullshit designed to try and force the kids inside, and it still doesn't work, it only forces the adults inside, which is probably as it should be. Because growing up works. Getting old and tucking your kids in works. And it should work, I suppose—the parents who forget that are the ones who ruin their kids' lives. Maybe. I still go to shows. I still hang out with Gray and my friends some nights, sometimes into the thinnest hours of morning—but it's not my habit anymore. Now there's homework to help with and dinner to make and sitcoms to watch and skate videos after ten, then I stumble off to bed around one.

Who I am won't change even if how I express it does.

I drifted off into dreams of California and getting to skate all through the winter; of beaches and sunsets and skate shops on every corner; of paradise in the mind of a ne'er-be-good skate rat from Ohio who has a car and a pretty girlfriend and the inside scoop on all the swirls, tops, full pops, and lollies a guy could ever need.

Being a Friday night, Gray had forced me to agree to be back at his house by eight the next morning for breakfast—it was our thing, a holdover from late nights and early mornings at college. Tobie had stirred when I had climbed into bed and I invited her to go, too, with the kids, but she said she'd rather sleep. I didn't blame her, but that's how weekends had always started in college and I needed a reminder that no matter how far we stray, our paths and orbits are still there: with a late night, an early morning, and breakfast.

On the way to Gray's there's a lonely, straight stretch of road that runs parallel to a train track—dangerously close, it seems. In the morning, the sun had yet to burn away the mist, and the air hung thick and orange over the road, the tracks and blacktop fading into distant oblivion. I could have been driving toward a deer or an ax murderer or a cliff that would tip me off the face of the Earth, but I didn't slow down. I knew mornings like this, that spoke of long, hot summer days to come and the memories of pretty girls that burn away like the mist.

I scanned through the albums on my phone and found *Theatre of Pain*—one of the few albums from my pre-adult life that always gets carried forward, burning a spot on every device or format I'd ever owned. I needed to hear "Raise Your Hands To Rock"—to hear Vince Neil singing about being sixteen and having the summertime blues. It's funny that back then, I only heard the anthem to rock-n-roll, but now I heard the other half of that song, the half that realized rock--n-roll was an escape from the weight of years and nostalgia —a monolith that apparently even rock stars, with all the girls and drugs and fast cars, couldn't outrun. It sounds stupid and overblown, I know, but driving back to Gray's that morning I think I truly heard that album for the first time, and I finally understood why it was called *Theatre of Pain*. Sure, the Crüe had grown up rougher than me in my suburban paradise, but when they weren't singing about street fights and drugs and whores there was a certain careless melancholy about the whole thing, about looking back and realizing that the road had been rough, but you'd survived. The drama was a shadowplay, but the cuts and pain had been real.

I think a part of me even back then, when I was sixteen, heard that bleeding edge to the lyrics and responded to the ever-present gloom of real life. It was just a finer point now; a sharper edge that cut more cleanly.

When I stepped onto Gray's porch I raised my fist to knock, then thought the better of it. I didn't want to wake up Deet and the kids, and I wasn't even sure Gray would remember our plans. I sighed heavily and second guessed myself, then caught movement out of the corner of my eye and whirled on what I assume was a squirrel on the porch. Instead, I saw Gray curled up under an old blanket like a hobo, sleeping on his porch swing.

"Gray?" I checked, assuming he'd fallen back to sleep waiting for me. His eyes flickered open and he smiled.

"Jack! You came back!"

"I couldn't miss breakfast. We have to uphold tradition—it's the only way to keep the country in one piece."

"Right you are!" he declared, whipping the blanket off and standing up, ready—as always—for action.

"Did you get up and come down here?" I wondered, vaguely referencing his clothes, which he hadn't changed since last night.

"I got up," he agreed thoughtfully. "But I was always down here."

"Okay…"

"Seriously, Bell—I slept out here last night. It was gorgeous!"

"*What*? You *slept*… on your front *porch*?"

I looked around, my suburban paranoia kicking in. Gray lived in one of the closer suburbs to Cleveland, with houses packed tight and people everywhere.

"Well, it turned out I forgot my keys, and I didn't want to wake Deet, so… Yeah. I grabbed a blanky from the car and settled down."

"Won't she be worried?"

Gray looked at the front door for a few studied seconds, then shuffled over to the front window and tried to peek around the privacy curtains. He tapped the window tentatively then moved over to the front door. A second later it opened and Deet stood there in her fluffy pink bathrobe, smirking with either amusement or stoic boredom.

"Gotta get my keys," Gray said as he ducked past her and into the house.

Deet had changed in the years since college. Her grip on life seemed to have tightened, making her focus on safer cars and better schools and all the things I suppose grownups should lose sleep over. I mean, she was always kind of that way, even in college—always the voice of reason when Gray and I got some crazy idea or other. I got used to it then, but it had gained a new momentum since she'd had kids. So it was weird for me when I went over to Gray's. I felt like she was watching me, waiting to correct me or make an example of me. I'd been getting that look all my life from parents and grownups, but to get it from a friend like that...? It wasn't the first time I'd felt like I'd been left behind while everyone else moved on to adulthood, but to get that look from Deet was the most painful part.

"Hey, Jack."

Always kind. Always polite.

"Hey, Deet—been a while."

"I know! You and Tobie should come over some time with the kids. How is she?"

"Good. She's great."

Emphatic nods that averted disaster.

"Is she still running her own business?"

"Repairing mowers? Yeah, she's doing really well. Almost too much work."

"She should open a real shop. Hire people."

"That would be nice."

Awkward silence because we both knew there was more to it than that, but it couldn't be covered in small talk while Gray hunted down his keys.

Tobie and I had been to a couple of parties that Gray and Deet had thrown—mostly Deet. They were very nice affairs with stacks of hors d'oeuvres and a fridge stuffed with cold beer, but it felt a lot like playing house, like Deet had always had dolls as a kid and now her fantasy had come true—but it's okay to play house as an adult because that's what adults do. Their neighbors came and some friends from the office. Gray invited a couple of faces I remembered from the paper, but I hadn't worked there in years and they were basically strangers again.

189

"Is that new? Did you get more ink?"

Touching my arm as if to prove I wasn't dangerous. Trying to sound colloquial to hide her disapproval. I glanced at my arm.

"Yeah… no, I got that a year ago, at least."

"Oh—I guess you had it covered up."

"Probably."

Now I was uncomfortable because I felt so uncomfortable. This was Deet, the girl who'd been there for me my senior year of college, when things went widdershins and I seriously questioned if life was still worth living. She'd helped me through that—her and Gray and Soulman and Josh. And now we were standing on her suburban porch like a mom and the nervous friend of her only son. It was ridiculous.

I felt like my presence reminded her that we're all a bit unhinged. I reminded her that once a knife cuts, it only takes a nick to bleed you dry. I reminded her that one foolishly bad choice in the darkness can kill you, and because she didn't understand the nature of that emptiness, she feared everything that seemed close to it.

"I miss you guys," I said. "I miss hanging out."

"We've had some fun," she agreed. "But we're better off now."

She smiled her old tilted smile and cocked her head a touch as if waiting for me to disagree. I couldn't, not with all the evidence before me, but I don't think she understood that my prime motivator in life has always been finding the time and money to hang out with my friends. Only my friends were scattered across the country now, so I held on to whatever scraps I could find; whatever reminded me of who I

190

was. Because without my friends—without any fun—I was quite certain the emptiness would take over.

I smirked and nodded—of course we were better off.

She chuckled and shrugged, and Gray tumbled down the stairs behind her, chased by his kids. Two boys. One still small enough to be swooped up and kissed, the other a bit too big now but still open to a hug.

He slid past her onto the porch, swinging back and kissing her cheek as he moved by.

"Let's walk," he said to me and headed toward the sidewalk, so I fell in step beside him.

I hope I said bye to Deet as we left. I don't recall—I just wanted to get out of there. Seeing people my age acting like moms and dads freaks me out.

What freaks me out more is that I probably act like a dad more than I let on.

"Okay, Bell, let's cut to the chase," Gray said after a minute or so of silence.

The nice thing about Gray's neighborhood is that you can walk places, and those places are local businesses. The world was starting to wake up from Friday night, but it still seemed slow and hungover—drivers hunched over their wheels, unwilling to go anywhere that took them away from their beds. Even the birds seemed suspicious of the sunlight.

It was a nice morning for a walk, anyway, and I liked being out in the weather. We don't get many mornings on this planet, and you have to be sure to make some of them count.

"What do you mean?"

"That girl last night? That was Penny again? The ex

from when you were a kid…?"

"Yeah…" I agreed slowly; suspiciously.

"Damn…"

I wasn't sure how to interpret his declaration—it could have been amazement or commiseration or recognition of her outfit—so I waited for him to expound upon it. We ended up shuffling to the end of his street, where we got stuck waiting to cross at the light. There was a little diner across the street that we'd gone to a few times and I assumed we were heading there now.

"So what's the real story there, Bell? With Penny? I've know you for a while and I've seen you with a few girls, but I don't know what this is."

"It's nothing. She broke my heart when we were sixteen, and now she's trying to apologize."

"She tracked you down twenty years later so she could fabricate chance meetings at bars—twice—so could say she was sorry?"

I didn't respond. The light changed and we crossed. I wasn't mad and he knew it, but he wasn't going to let it drop and I knew that, too. I held my tongue, though—making him work for it. We were seated and waiting on coffee before he spoke again.

"You remember Crystal?" he wondered. "Long hair, down to her ass?"

I chuckled. "I remember that wasn't her real name. Was she *actually* a fan of Crystal Gayle or—?"

"Did you know that she friended me online a year or so ago?" he went on.

I sighed and closed my menu, not anticipating having a

192

chance to look it over. I always got biscuits and sausage gravy (with a side of home fries), so it didn't really matter.

"No."

"You know why?" he asked rhetorically. "Because it didn't matter. Because I haven't thought of her since college, and then when I did think of her, I didn't care. I didn't mention her and I didn't friend her because it wasn't important."

"I get it, Gray."

I nodded evenly and held his gaze. It amused me when he tried the tough-love angle, and sometimes I think he did it to amuse himself, like that old movie running in his head: Everything he said seemed *just right*, like a script. My smirk faded as it occurred to me that maybe everything he said seemed like that because he was… well… just right.

"Penny was my perfect girl—I told you all this."

"Yeah, yeah—the American dream and the Fourth of July and fireworks and her dad hated you. I knew a girl like that, too. Her name was Marlene Litchfield—we called her Leena. Leena the Savage. Just to be dumb. She was perfect—but then I grew up."

"Oh—so now I'm acting like a child because I don't want to pretend the past doesn't matter, because I'm older and have two cars and a house in the 'burbs?"

"Two *kids* and a house in the 'burbs," he corrected.

The waitress brought us coffee and gave us the stink-eye, but we ordered and Gray said something that got her to laugh. I felt bad because I knew exactly what Gray was driving at: There was more to Penny, of course. And he was right —if any of my other exes suddenly friended me, I'd crack a few jokes about them and ignore the request. Except for

193

three, I realized: Penny Harper, Ally McShay, and Hannah Blakely, a girl from college. That sobered me up. I almost mentioned Hannah to try and make my point because he already knew all about her, but I knew that would open up a second front on this conversation, one that would lead to our friend Kate and the cuts on her arms and my talks with her outside, after night had fallen and hidden our faces from each other, and how that all eventually wound back to Penny Harper.

But I wasn't ready to tell Gray about all that. Not even Kate knew the exact names and situations, and we *had* ostensibly talked about it. Only Tobie knew everything, because Tobie had been there, right beside me…

"Look, Gray, this is just one of those things. We were two kids and we thought we were in love. I was her first boyfriend and she was my longest girlfriend, and the first girl… I don't know… I just don't forget things. Not big things, like her. I *can't*. It's how I am. I'm the guy who stops on the trail every so often and looks back through the woods to see how far I've come."

He nodded sagely and sat up straight. He believed me because it all made sense, and it made sense because it was all true, what I'd said. There was a hole in the story, sure, but I'd got really good at talking around it so that people didn't even know it was there.

"Yeah… Shit…" he mused. "I remember when we met at that party freshman year. You remember that first party in college? You seemed like you needed a friend." He laughed and gazed out the window. "Like you needed a friend, but like you wanted to be left alone. I had to know why a guy like that was at a damn party."

"Y'know, Gray…? That's why I hang out with you."

He looked back at me with a quizzical this-should-be-good look.

"Because you always try to understand people."

He smirked and narrowed his eyes.

"I don't really care how I got here," he admitted.

I knew he didn't mean the diner. He meant it didn't matter to him that he'd slept on his front porch—he didn't see the beauty and value of that simple act. How it symbolized not only his concern for Deet and not waking her, but also his lack of concern for the little rules that end up turning life into a chore. And it showed his unwavering faith in humanity that nothing would happen to him—how the chance that he may not have survived had no meaning after he'd already proved that he would.

Or maybe it showed how oblivious he was. Maybe it showed that he didn't learn anything from the past and so only scratched the surface of life, seeing nothing of the depth below. Maybe it proved that he didn't have any sense of resonance, and when he was old and infirm, he'd be lying in his bed wondering how he got there, to the end of his life, and he wouldn't be able to remember. And I think that would be worse: To forget a life lived because your drive to the future hadn't let you admit how much it all meant, until the future ran out and the past had faded away, like the trail and the woods behind you that you never looked at again.

"Still," he prodded lightly, either curious or trying to kickstart the conversation. "It's gotta be weird, her turning up like that? *Twice.*"

"Yeah… I didn't expect to see her in person *again*, that's for sure."

"Do you think she's trying to… you know… have one last fling?"

"The thought crossed my mind, but there's a couple of problems…"

"Do tell."

And like that, we were back to our old college selves, talking about girls and shows to try and overcome that fuzzy, heavy-headed feeling of not enough sleep and too much activity.

"Well one, I'm not that vain."

"But you have aged well, if I may say so."

"And two, it wouldn't matter in the least if she did. I have way too much to lose for one night with Penny fucking Harper."

"You said 'fucking'," Gray pointed out.

"It was a curse."

"It was Freudian."

"You know, just because something *can* be interpreted sexually does not mean it's Freudian."

Gray had duped me again, with banal talk that skirted the edges of something serious, like a ridiculous nursery rhyme that's actually a biting political commentary.

Gray had always done that for me, but on my way back home to Tobie and the kids, I realized I needed to talk to Tobie more. That breakfast had seemed like the right thing to do last night and after a few hours of sleep, but really, I should have recognized that we weren't in college anymore and Gray lacked the insight to truly help out. That sounds like I think it was his fault—a character flaw or something—but it wasn't. He lacked the insight because he lacked the history.

I needed the people who had been there through everything with me, and at least respected that mutual past enough to remember what it meant, even if it didn't mean as much to them as it did to me.

I got home and started a game of tag with the kids and Tobie, and then we went to the park and played a game of hot lava. We ate lunch outside on a picnic blanket, then we went home and the kids fell asleep and Tobie drifted off to see about getting herself a better web site. I found an old Twisted Sister concert from 1984 I'd got on DVD—a concert I had originally taped off MTV back when it was still new. We'd watch that shitty old VHS with its burbles and static skips whenever Niz slept over, so I'd replaced it somewhere along the line because that's how I am, and because I knew I'd need to sit and watch it again some day, as if for the first time.

My life seems like a complex, wired network of friends and relatives and places and events, and those touchstones—those DVDs and songs and photographs, and the detritus from the top of my childhood dresser—are the solder spots that allow the energy to flow through and around me, and keep me going. I have to find and cherish those touchstones otherwise the past is meaningless and the unknowable, empty future I'm floating in is all I have. Without the touchstones, there are no blue-hot tracks of lightning through the network—no power, no substance, no comfort. Without the touchstones there is only the emptiness.

197

I don't remember everything, just the things that mattered most—and *those* things I hoard. The only things I throw away are the things I didn't even know I had in the first place. It doesn't cause me any grief when I find some old trinket in a box and can't remember why I kept it. But the memories tied to those objects I find and *do* remember...? I need those triggers to exist and inform the future.

It just hadn't occurred to me before that a human being could be a touchstone.

And an anchor.

The days of summer had boiled into a stretch of weeks by the start of August, leaving in their wake stripes of crisp, browned grass and cracked-earth mud plates in the beds of dry creeks. The cicadas whirred and ticked off time in their own rhythms, and the steady wail of the crickets became like a ringing in my ears that had faded to a background noise.

Everything slowly grinds to a halt in the dog days: too fat, tired, and sweaty to move. The only escape was the mall or a friend's basement or the soft embrace of the night, when the sun rested and a minuscule stirring of the air, as if by accident, brought a momentary coolness that the sun's burning eye covered up.

By August, Penny and I had eased ourselves into a summer rut of leisure. The honeymoon period of our first month together—when we were still getting to learn each other's ways—had given over to a month of expectations: we knew where each other would be, who we'd be with, what we wanted to do, and how to make it fun. I only worked about twenty hours a week, but my shift was typically five-to-nine at night, and since Penny still had a curfew, I often hung out with Niz and Sammy after work and Penny all day before I had to leave. It worked out perfectly: Penny and I spent all day bumming around the park or the mall or catching a matinee, then I went out skating with the boys at night, after the sunlit day-heat had been replaced by a heavy blanket of humid moonlight.

"So you called her that night? And she *talked* to you?" Niz checked one night, having suddenly rediscovered how amazed he was that Penny and I were dating—probably because we had been going out so long and he wanted to know how that worked.

"Yeah… that's sort of how you go about getting a date, Niz. And if you call her again, you get another date."

Niz was concentrating on prying a pebble from the treads of his sneakers; I wasn't even sure he was fully processing what I was saying. He'd become obsessed with the idea that pebbles in his treads were throwing off his ability to land tricks, but it was really nothing more than a good excuse to sit on the curb and take a break.

"You got a *date*?"

"Niz, would ya listen to yourself? You act like you forgot the whole fucking summer!"

He stopped prodding and cut me a look. "No need to swear, young man."

"Fuck you."

He raised his eyebrows.

"Don't."

Cooler heads prevailed—perhaps due to the hour and the rumors that this particular skate spot was haunted by a skinny old guy who chased people off with a rake—and Niz didn't respond to my slur.

"So it's pretty serious, huh?" he asked. "I mean, it *is*."

"Yeah, I guess."

I hadn't really thought about it in terms of seriousness; of weeks together. Summer has a way of making time stretch into meaningless measures. Days and months merged into a

200

single block of time lit by the sun. Summer was a second long or a year long, depending on how you looked at it.

"It is," Niz stated again. "Like, two months serious."

"Sure."

"No offense, dude, but it won't last much longer."

"What the fuck does *that* mean?"

"Jesus, Bells—watch a movie! Read a book! Summers like this are always the setup for a heartbreak. Plus, I mean, you're sixteen."

"Fuck you. This isn't some kind of *math* formula. And it's not like you're talking from *experience*."

Me, Niz, and Sammy—none of us had really had a steady date before, not like this. Tobie was close for me, but since we'd been hanging out for years anyway, it didn't feel a lot different when we were dating. But Penny—she was a stranger, a new girl in the circle, and that held its own mystery and magic. The idea that was she was becoming a regular—maybe some day a new spoke in our crazy little wheel—scared us all, I think, in a way I hadn't expected. What Niz was really saying was that he wanted us to go back to the way we were before—before serious shit, like high school and girlfriends. Your whole life you couldn't wait for either of those things, and now that it was here, I think we were scared.

"What about you and Jess?" I prodded. I didn't want to think about me and Penny breaking up, and I didn't want to fight with Niz.

"Jess?" he mumbled, intent on his shoe. He finally gave up with a huff and slapped his foot back down. "Jess is fucking *great*, Bells."

"What the hell? I thought you liked her?"

"Yeah, and that's the problem."

"Nah—she's just playing it cool."

Niz smirked wryly at me, his eyes lit with a strange orange glow from the reflected streetlights.

"You think you're so smart," he decided, not in a mean way. He was stating something that had suddenly occurred to him, is all. "I mean, you've been there now. The hot girlfriend. The American dream…"

"Now you sound like Sammy," I complained, cutting him off before he got back around to talking about the end of the summer. "But tell me: Why is liking Jess a problem? Seriously—just ask her out. But, y'know, make sure she *knows* you're asking her *out*."

Niz nodded sagely and stood up.

"I hear ya, Bells—I do."

I looked up at him and my eye caught sight of a car rolling toward us. I shielded my eyes against the headlights—slow-moving cars coming up on skaters were either cops or jocks, and I didn't feel like dealing with either of them right now.

"Niz," I stated simply; dryly.

We'd been bumming around long enough that he immediately understood my tone and started to run past me, away from the direction I was looking, without even a look back. I jumped to my feet and grabbed my board, backing after him, and the car fired up. I waited for the pop of the red-and-blue lights, but the car revved and swarmed closer, the muffler rumbling with menace—a detail that made me stop and narrow my eyes.

"Bells!" Niz shouted in a stage whisper.

"S'alright," I said as the car roared up beside me and screeched to a stop, the engine trundling. It was a yellow Camaro. The driver's side window was down and I saw Timmy "The Toad" Toderman grinning ear-to-ear. He sported a thin, adolescent mustache over a broad smile and he was an inch or two shorter than average height, but built like a brick—mostly we bonded in shop class over Mötley Crüe, Ratt, and Ozzy.

"Scared you *shitless*, Jack!" he declared.

"*Jesus*—sorta," I admitted.

Niz had got a good head start on me. He'd stopped running and now he flopped his board down and rolled back over to us.

"I finally got it!" Toad said excitedly.

I knew he'd been saving for a Camaro—his uncle's, I believe—but it had always seemed like a typical kid fantasy, the kind of thing all kids said they were going to do when they were old enough to drive. But here we were—here *the Toad* was, heading into his senior year—in a shining hunk of American steel that proved hard work did pay off. I whistled lightly.

"C'mon!" he said. "Get in! I'll be your chauffeur for the evening."

Niz looked a bit concerned, but only because he didn't know Timmy that well and he didn't know if we should trust him to drive us around. The Toad was more of a motorhead first and a skater second—which was unfortunate, because he was one of the best skaters in town—so I knew him more from the art and shop classes I took than from skating with him. The stoners and motorheads were another stripe in my wide prism of friends that Niz didn't meet much on their own turf—such as in the frame of high-octane-fueled American steel—and he wasn't sure how he fit in.

"It's cool," I said to him. "Toad works at the hardware store with me and Tagger—he got us the jobs."

I whipped around to the passenger side and opened the door, kicking the seat up so Niz could climb in the back.

"He's worked hard for this car."

Niz nodded once and climbed into the back seat. I popped it back and sat down, afraid to touch anything. Niz mumbled something about how nice it was. The interior was cherry red leather that creaked with a sound like money—or maybe it was pleather, I don't know, but it smelled brand new and everything seemed shiny in the dash lights and the low glow of the streetlights.

"This is awesome," I said.

The Toad grinned, popped the clutch, and we sprang forward into the night like a pouncing tiger, the tires chirping once before settling into the asphalt. He headed out to Niles Road, which ran along the western edge of the suburbs and divided the township from the city. The speed limit was 55, and he took every bit of it, topping 70 (maybe 80?) on the straightaways—I think he wanted to do more, but I think he was also afraid of breaking his new toy on the first day he had it. The windows were down and the roaring wind was magnificent—even Niz started laughing maniacally—and we seemed like the only things in the universe, chasing the white cones of his headlights on the road in front of us. I almost suggested we go to Tobie's but I didn't want the ride to end. He took us all the way out to the county JVS and turned around in the wide-open parking lot, his tires squealing and filling the car with acrid smoke, then we were gone, the smoke a memory behind us, and we were barreling back into town, back to the stop light at the end of Niles, back down to 35 MPH, a turtle's pace in the wide America night.

"So where to?" he asked gleefully, grinning over at me, the engine purring at a red light.

"Let's go get Sammy," I said, turning and cricking my neck to see Niz. He was staring out the window into the dark sky and nodded slowly without a word.

"Where's he live?"

"Right by Tagger."

And I know he didn't speed through town, but I swear we got to Sammy's house faster than we'd ever got there before. Maybe it was an illusion created by the fact that my car could barely limp to Sammy's without breaking down.

Sammy was out piddling around in the driveway with Tagger—they'd bonded over the bumper-sticker fiasco and had started hanging out more. It was easier for Sammy to hang out near his house, anyway, and he had the added bonus of learning tricks from the world-famous Tagger. When we pulled up, Tagger looked like he was expecting us—or *someone*—and Sammy looked suspicious. Of course, Sammy always looked suspicious—it's why most God-fearing people in school gave him a wide berth.

"Samuel!" I declared, hopping out and running over to him, grabbing his hand and pumping it furiously. "Nice to meet you, my good man. Now let's go!"

"Go?"

205

Tagger didn't need a second invitation. He scooted over to the car without a thought and popped the seat.

"You three in back," he stated.

"But…"

"Sophomores," he observed, pulling rank—even though we'd be juniors in September, he was still a damn graduate.

I grudgingly accepted and clambered in, Sammy getting wise to the antics and climbing in behind me, which left me sitting on the bump between seats, because apparently the back seat of a Camaro is basically two more bucket seats, not a bench.

"This is bullshit," I decided. Tagger grinned in a decidedly saccharin manner, and his expression more than anything shut me up.

"Does everyone know the story of Mr. Toad and the Mythical Camaro?" I checked sarcastically. "He's been talking about this damn car since we were in the back of German class my freshman year—"

"Frau Spahr!" the Toad cried.

"—and now it's his, and we're all invited to help him break it in."

"Take it down Niles," Tagger suggested. He knew the Toad about as well as I did, maybe better.

"Already did."

"Do it again!" Tagger rebutted, and in a curl of smoke from the tires, we were off again.

This time we stopped for a while in the JVS parking lot—Tagger knew of a bitchin' curb or something—and spent some time messing around. Tagger was fun to watch—way better than me or Niz, and a bit better than Sammy and

206

the Toad—and eventually we all sat on the curb watching him. Tagger tried to show us how "easy" some variation of a kickflip was, but I could barely see what the board was doing, let alone his feet, so it was like watching a strange spectral thing twirling in front of us, mesmerizing us with its repetition. Then it was all of us sitting out there on the curb in the moon-shadow of Timmy Toderman's Camaro, shooting the shit.

"Little Kings, man," Tagger was explaining. "It's *soft* and has more alcohol than shitty light beer."

"So why not just go with King Cobra?" Sammy weighed in. "I mean, if you're looking for the most alcohol per dollar?"

"Because it tastes like shit...?" Tagger surmised rhetorically, and we nodded as if this was, indeed, a sage opinion.

Niz and I weren't immune to the allure of underage drinking, but we weren't as knowledgeable as Sammy and, apparently, Tagger. Beer—and one particularly unfortunate incident involving peach Schnapps—was not our go-to vice, not when there were building sites to loot for cast-off lumber that could be turned into skate ramps. Tagger seemed to sense this mild disconnect, and I don't know if he thought we were into harder things or what, but he sat silent for a second, then his expression fell.

"Say, Timmy..." (It was weird he used his real name) "Dude, I got fired today."

I was stunned. My first real job was at a hardware store out past the high school—a tri-state chain, not a local mom-n-pop. I was in the lumber department. The Toad had got me and Tagger jobs there—he worked in housewares; it was how he'd paid for the Camaro. I probably wouldn't have lasted long if it hadn't been for him, because the store manager seemed to have a pretty dim view of teenagers, especially ones that weren't all buttoned-up. Not that the Toad was all buttoned-up, per se, but he took work seriously and our manager could tell I didn't.

The manager, Mr. Perry—*aka* Perry the Prick—was a short, round man who looked like he'd been pulled out of central casting to play the part in a cliché movie. He always seemed exasperated, and for some reason he took to coaching me in particular, like he could fill some gap in my upbringing he thought my parents had failed to fill. I didn't have the heart to tell him that my parents would think he was an assed-up busy body. He was mostly concerned with me and Tagger being friends—it was apparent rather quickly that he thought Tagger was no good and he regretted taking the Toad's word about him. I think Perry the Prick saw me as his salvation: his proof that he was still a good judge of character. Or maybe he was trying to be political with the Toad and keep one of his recommendations on so he didn't lose one of his best employees.

"What did you do?" the Toad wondered.

He didn't sound surprised and he was probably thinking through his own politics, and how he could distance himself from Tagger without turning his back on his friend.

Tagger looked at me and grinned mischievously.

"It was that day he made us run to the other store, Bells. That dick at that store saw what we did and snitched."

In the store Tagger was relatively soft spoken, but also not too concerned about impressing authority figures. They made him pull back his long hair in a ponytail, and he had a

208

scraggle of whiskers along his jawline that looked enough like a light beard that they didn't make him shave it.

"What... Did you do?" the Toad asked evenly.

Sammy was grinning and moved in for a good story.

"Perry the Prick asked me and Tagger to drive out to another store," I explained, "to pick up something for a customer and bring it back to our store. It sounded like a bullshit chore to me."

"It was," Tagger agreed. "He was hoping for an excuse to fire me—and you. Why else make both of us go?"

"Right—but *you* drove. Sorry about that, man."

He waved me off. He hadn't liked the job anyway, and getting fired was the best way to go out with a bang.

"What did you *do*?" the Toad repeated.

Sammy scooted closer.

"The store was way down Route 4, where it's like four lanes and a turn lane," Tagger replied. "We were in a left-turn lane with a grass median beside us. The store we had to pick up the shit from was *right fucking there*—if we made that left turn, we'd be there in twenty seconds. But there was a traffic jam because the lights were all fucked up and nobody could get anywhere. Three cars managed to turn left on each light, and there were like ten cars in front of us, so we'd be sitting there a while, but we only had *five* minutes to get to the store on time. And Perry the *Prick* had told us like twenty times what time we had to be there."

"We knew he was going to use it as an excuse to fire us," I interjected. "So I was like, 'Just go left now'. The traffic was totally blocked, but we could turn *across* the median and drive over the sidewalk, right into the parking lot."

"No way!" Sammy gasped.

"Yeah!" Tagger said enthusiastically, getting caught up in his own tale now. "Well, my car's a piece of shit anyway, so I didn't care. I just cut the wheel hard to the left and gunned it. We plowed over the median and across the other lanes, then slammed up the curb and parked. We hopped out of the car and bolted for the store with three minutes to spare, by their clock."

"I guess the Prick didn't like being shown up," I concluded.

"So he fired my ass for endangering lives or some bullshit. He didn't fire you?" Tagger added to me.

"Not yet," I said slowly, a pit dropping in my stomach at the thought of having to go to work the next day. I wasn't sure how my parents would feel about me being fired.

Tagger looked almost proud. He always seemed confident to me. Not in an arrogant way, but in that casual way certain teenagers have when they figure out the world doesn't owe them anything so it shouldn't expect anything in return. I don't want to say I looked up to him—he was definitely a bad seed—but I did like his style. Or at least his flourish—his take-no-shit/give-no-shits attitude. Everything seemed to make sense to Tagger, and whatever didn't make sense was scrapped—like some kind of weird American form of Zen. I wanted to be more like him—less concerned about what people may be thinking of me and more aware that live-and-let-live is a two-way credo, not something you only said to cover your own ass.

"Well," the Toad decided. "I guess you deserved it, then."

"Sure," Tagger agreed diplomatically. "I guess so."

"That's *awesome*," Sammy emoted.

"Not really," the Toad sighed, but he didn't seem truly upset, just disappointed, like it was his fault Tagger had got hired, so he felt like it was his fault he'd got fired. Niz looked over at Timmy with a newfound respect, I think, but he didn't say anything either way.

"You still with Penny Harper?" Tagger suddenly asked me, changing the subject to something less disagreeable.

"Yeah. I mean, I guess we're steady now."

"Penny *Harper*?" the Toad cut in. "You're *steady* with *Penny Harper*?"

"Unbelievable, right?" Niz joked and the Toad nodded emphatically.

I glanced at Tagger and he winked at me—he actually fucking winked—and I smirked at how easily he'd deflected the conversation.

"Dude... Jack... Why didn't you *tell* me?" the Toad wondered, mildly offended.

"I'm sure I did," I mumbled, which I knew wasn't true.

The Toad was definitely somewhere past a school friend, but not quite a close friend. We saw each other at work from time to time, and I'd slept over our friend Dave's house once with him, and we'd snuck out into an icy February night for some mischief or other, but outside of school and running into each other at skate spots, we didn't really hang out a lot.

"No... You never mentioned that," he responded. "Girl-friend, huh?"

211

"Yeah, I guess."

"You *guess*?" he wondered. "You don't *know*?"

"But you hang out, right?" Tagger asked.

"Like, *hang out*?" I checked.

"Yeah, man! Like, *hanging out*. Do you *make out*, y'-know?"

"Sure, yeah… we kiss…"

"Did ya feel her up?"

I glanced at him, suddenly wishing we hadn't taken this path to get over the story of Tagger being fired. Tagger didn't seem like the best person to talk to about girls—one look at his grin and I imagined lots of questions coming about the size of her tits and what color panties she wore, and I didn't want to deal with it.

"Uhhh…"

Tagger returned my glance and his shit-eating grin faded.

"Okay, so when you guys hang out with her friends, does she hang all over you? Give you little kisses and all that kind of shit?"

"I don't know," I fumbled. "I mean, we don't really hang out with her friends."

"Ever?"

"No. I mean, she's on a softball team and most of her friends are sporty types. Like, all of them. So I don't know, we just have more fun alone. She's not really into parties or anything."

"What about *your* friends?" he wondered, looking at Niz and Sammy. They shrugged and looked away, giving me the lead on how Penny was within our circle.

"*My* friends?" I spat out.

212

"Look, if you don't hang out with *her* friends and she doesn't hang out with *yours*, then I don't know, man. She's like your secret girlfriend…"

He trailed off, not wanting to finish the thought because he really didn't have to.

"She's not a secret," I mumbled. "We just want to be alone when we're together, I guess."

"She is kinda stuck up, though…?" Tagger observed.

I glanced over at the Toad, but he was watching us curiously, letting the conversation play out on its own.

"She *isn't* stuck up!" I defended. I cut Tagger a look—the exact opposite of a friendly wink—and he held my gaze.

"She never hangs out with anyone—except you," he stated.

"She's got really strict parents—"

"But they let her hang out with *you*? No, man—she uses her *parents* as an *excuse* to not go out."

He nodded, still holding my gaze, waiting for me to dispute him, but I honestly couldn't, not entirely.

"She must really like you," he concluded diplomatically, finishing with a broad smile.

"I guess."

It was a weird compliment—if it was even meant as one—but I took it anyway.

Tagger looked away and began picking up pebbles from the gutter and tossing them absently into the parking lot. The Toad sucked in a deep breath and lay down on the sidewalk to watch the stars. Niz and Sammy and I exchanged glances, not sure what to say or do: Timmy had the car and Tagger, being the oldest and most mysterious, always had the floor.

213

"Do you like *her*, though?" he wondered. "*You're* not stuck up—"

"Thanks…? But she's not stuck up!"

"She kinda is," Sammy chimed in. "She's only hung out with us—what?—once? For the fireworks?"

I mumbled something about her parents again.

"Whatever, man—she must be a good piece of ass, I guess."

"No, it's not like that…" I trailed off, glancing at the Toad to see how he would react. He didn't. He lay there and gazed up into the darkness.

"It's the honeymoon," the Toad finally decided, as if sensing my stare. "Leave 'em alone—they're getting to know each other."

Tagger nodded and looked away again—it was a fact he couldn't accept because he knew it was way past the honeymoon period for me and Penny.

"So it's *you*, then," Tagger observed, his brow furrowed as if he'd finally figured out something that had been bothering him for a while. "You're keeping her from *us*."

We'd all been there, with a new girlfriend who was the only person in the world you wanted to hang out with, so he was willing to accept that it was possible.

"Yeah, that's it," the Toad intoned solemnly, with an almost bored lilt. "We're not good enough for her."

"Shit, guys—that's not it!" I protested. "*Jesus*!"

I was over discussing my relationship with Penny… in the parking lot of the JVS… with a bunch of guys who thought she was stuck up because we didn't hang out and drink Little Kings with them. That had life-changing argu-

214

ment written all over it, and it was Tagger, so I knew who'd win, no matter what. I didn't care about Sammy or Niz—they'd still hang out with me—but the Toad didn't need to be a part of that shit. If I lost the motorheads, art class would be rough.

"Forget it," I decided and stood up. "It's the honeymoon, like Toad said. I keep trying to get her to hang out with you guys..."

"It's cool," Tagger admitted. "I get it, man—we barely know each other."

It was a good insight, but my eyes flickered warily to Sammy and Niz. Sammy might have looked a bit curious—even hurt—but he didn't say anything.

"Maybe we should get back?" I said.

"Sure," the Toad agreed pointedly. "I gotta *work* tomorrow."

"Yeah—I'm beat," Tagger added.

I guess that was his way of apologizing—or going along with us or whatever. He didn't have to agree with me, after all—he could have called me a pussy and said we should go find some beers or something, but he let it slide. Sammy and Niz shared a glance, but neither of them said anything else, so we headed home.

That moment sort of broke the evening, anyway, as talk of girls so often does. It was the kind of conversation that made you realize how insignificant you are, and then everything starts to remind you of that fact: either you have a girl and you realize you could lose her, or you don't have a girl and you realize you may well die alone. Or at least not have a date to Prom.

215

The adolescent male is not designed to weather girl trouble, no matter what the movies tell you. He is defined by his ability to talk to girls without stuttering; his ability to catch a stray glance and return a smile; his chances to make a pretty girl laugh. Every fiber of his being hums along those chords, waiting for the missed note; the careless strum. Some guys deal with it with bluster—macho posing and general douchebaggery. Others get quiet, stay still, and hope upon hope that they can stand in the canoe without tipping it.

All of us had been there, I guess. Niz, I knew, was worrying about Jess and how she felt about him, and Tagger seemed to have his own underlying issues, like his comments about Penny were some kind of passive-aggressive warning based on his recent experiences. I wanted to ask him about it, to see if I could pin him down, but it suddenly didn't seem right. As he said, we barely knew each other, and taking him to task over his own girl troubles and how they related to me and Penny didn't seem like the right move.

Still, that moment stuck with me and made me want, more than ever, to get Penny to break out of her shell and hang out with us like a normal teenager. It was something I could overlook when I was with her because I got everything I needed out of our relationship, but knowing that it bugged everyone else—even a slight acquaintance like Tagger—made me rethink it in a way I didn't like. It made me feel like I was in that canoe, gripping the sides and preparing to stand, and I knew that if I rocked it too hard, I may fall out, or overturn it altogether and spill Penny into the drink, too.

It was a canoe I didn't want to rock.

We got quiet as the Toad drove us home at a reasonable

216

speed, and that gave me some solace—I was glad to know I was among friends who knew when to let things rest. No douchebag comments, no loud brags and hideous taunts, no demands that we roll up on Penny and force her to come out with us.

We rolled down the windows and floated quietly through the vast American night, with the summer air buffeting our hair, each lost in his own thoughts and reasons, the buzz of the hours before having worn off or worn thin, or both.

"Jack, you're a good kid," Perry the Prick said.

"Thanks."

"I'm afraid you just choose to buddy-up with the wrong kids."

"Buddy-up?"

"Tagger was let go. He wasn't a good kid like you."

"Why was he fired?"

I knew, but I wanted to hear the Prick admit it was bull-shit.

"That's not for me to say. I just want you to think long and hard about who you're choosing to buddy-up with, okay? If you pick the wrong friends, they'll get you into trouble. It may seem like fun now, but when you're older and you look back, I'll bet you'll wish you'd had better friends."

"You don't even *know* my friends!" I snapped defen-sively.

He pulled in a deep breath and nodded as if I had made his point for him, which only confused me. I knew Tagger was a bad kid—anyone could see he had a high potential for a long rap sheet—but that didn't mean I had to be a jerk to him. And really, what "bad" had he done that I'd witnessed? Skipped a traffic jam? Slapped some stickers on cop cars? Ogled hot, young housewives while they shopped for bath-room cabinets? It's not like we smoked pot in the break room or something.

"This is a good job, Jack, and I think you have a bright

218

future here. You just need to keep your head screwed on straight, okay?"

"Yeah… okay…" I acquiesced.

"Okay. Good. Now I need you to straighten up the lumber bins, okay?"

"Yeah. Sure."

I got up and slunk out of the office and went straight back to the lumber department, at the back of the store. The girls at the customer service desk watched me as I walked past—I could feel their eyes on me. They had their own little clique going on, although the Toad always seemed to talk to them and get along with them.

"Clean up in aisle nine," a dull voice intoned over the intercom.

I glanced back at the front office and grinned privately, then cut across to housewares and over to aisle nine where the Toad stood waiting for me, nominally straightening a shelf of air fresheners. "Clean up in aisle nine" was our code to meet up somewhere between housewares and lumber.

"Man, I didn't get you this job so you could get fired!" he squawked immediately.

"Relax—I didn't get fired."

"Ellie said you did…"

"Ellie?"

"Cute girl at the front desk…?"

I was momentarily perplexed by how that narrowed it down—they were *all* cute girls at the front desk.

"Look, Perry hated Tagger, Jack—don't take it personally. *I'm* not."

He'd been at the hardware store for a while now—even

219

had his face on the wall of fame by the break room—and he knew how things went down.

"I better go fix the lumber or the Prick really *will* fire me. But Timmy…?"

"Yeah?"

"I think I'm going to quit this job. It's only a matter of time."

"That's cool."

The Toad nodded with something like relief.

The next time I saw Penny she seemed like a different person. She'd cut her hair, even with her jawline, like it had been back in math class when I'd first seen her, and it gave her face an excessively cute roundness that I'd forgotten all about. I reached out and touched the ends by her left ear, smirking, as if making sure it was real.

"You dyed it," I observed.

That was, perhaps, the bigger change: Gone was the dim blondness that shone in the sun—the dark-blond-on-blonder-highlights replaced with a uniform nut-brown color. I'd never seen her like that before, with plain brown hair.

"It's my natural color," she said flatly. "The blond was the dye. I didn't like it anymore. Never really liked it."

"Oh."

"My dad always said it looked better blond…" she laughed nervously, and I thought it was a weird thing for him to say to her, but I didn't want to point that out. I could tell she was tired of hearing my opinions of her parents' actions.

"It's cool," I accepted. "I think it's nice. And if it pisses off your dad, then that's even better!"

I don't know why I was trying to play it cool. I loved it. I loved the way it framed her cheeks and drew you to her eyes, and she looked much better with dark hair and dark skin and dark eyes, but it seemed like she was trying to force me to say something, like she needed my blessing, and I've never responded well to that kind of emotional ploy. She didn't need me—or her dad or *any*one—to tell her that what she did was okay, and I wasn't going to bolster that kind of thinking by playing along. If *she* liked it, that's all that mattered.

"Is that all that matters, Jack?" she wondered quietly.

"What?"

"That my dad hates it?"

"No, no—of course not. I said I liked it!"

"You said it was *nice*."

I huffed and shook my head—I wanted to backtrack and go along with her game to avoid this dead end, but now no matter what I said she wouldn't believe me.

"Look, I *like* it, okay? But what does it matter what *I* think, anyway?"

"Jack!" she begged in a whisper and I swear she was close to tears. "I always wanted it like this!"

"It's *cool*," I repeated, frustrated with the whole thing already—with my inadequate initial response and for painting myself into a corner so that I couldn't respond well now.

I reached out and took her into my arms—her hair still smelled like the salon—and hugged her, but she only half-heartedly touched my back then pulled away. I smiled, hop-

221

ing it would serve as consolation and apology.

"Wanna go for a drive?" I suggested and she let me lead her to my car.

Of all the nights in my life I wish I had back, the night after Penny got her hair cut has to be near the top of the list. She withdrew in defense, and before I knew it, I'd forgotten her hair and didn't understand her mood, and there is nothing more egotistical and dumb that a guy can do than forget why he pissed off his girlfriend.

As I drove, Penny put a tape in—Mötley Crüe for some reason, as if she was trying to make amends—and I started thinking of elaborate ways I could force us to hang out with each other's friends, finally settling on the most obvious solution of simply taking her to Niz's and hanging out. I felt like she'd only seen a glimmer of Niz and Sammy and the gang at July Fourth—it hadn't *truly* been hanging out, not in the way friends hang out when they don't have to be at least somewhat respectable. I still saw Niz and Sammy and the gang plenty that summer, but only when Penny was unavailable, and I didn't like it that way; I wanted us all to hang out together. Looking back, it was like Tagger had said: I'd had two lives, one with my friends and another with her, and I think that's how she'd wanted it.

But life shouldn't be secret because secrets take work, and work destroys fun. She didn't want to share me, and I went along with it because, truth be told, I didn't want to share her. I think I knew that what we had was fragile gold, and I was as afraid of the dynamic my friends would create that could drive us apart.

The stupid thing is, I imagined this secret me—the new

me, the me with Penny—was somehow the *better* me, the more grown up me: The me that had a job and a steady girlfriend and a car. The old me that went skating and sat around watching shitty horror movies seemed like something I should slowly wean myself of—not in an obvious way; not in a stop-hanging-out sort of way. I'd suggest different movies, maybe, or that we find somewhere to skate that was more isolated and less likely to cause trouble.

She didn't want to go to Niz's, she said, because she wanted to be with me, but the look in her eyes seemed more cagey than that. I could tell she was still mad about something.

I looked over at her, her hair wavering in the wind from the open car window. She smiled at me as if she knew what I was thinking, and that it was all okay, so I kept driving.

I drove out to the JVS, maybe trying in some unconscious way to bring my two lives together, only Penny didn't like it as much as the guys had. Or maybe she did but she was being obstinate in her own way, to get back at me for being obstinate in mine.

"What are we doing out here, Jack?" she wondered quietly, shifting in her seat.

"I don't know…" I admitted. "We came out here the other night—me and the guys—and it was quiet. I thought we could see if the stars out here were different from the ones at the park."

I smiled warmly, but she furrowed her brow. In the dim parking-lot lights she looked like a silent-film heroine in soft focus, only without all the eye makeup and black lipstick. Her expression looked unsure, like she didn't really know who I was.

"They're the same stars, Jack."

"I know. I was kidding."

She turned away and gazed out the window, maybe checking to be sure.

"Wanna sit on the hood…?"

It was the tried-and-true refrain of a thousand love songs: Those long, hot summer nights spent finding somewhere quiet to make out; an investment of time and emotion that ultimately doesn't pan out. I guess I thought our kisses would make us forget whatever it was that seemed to be hanging over us. Penny always smelled so nice—vaguely of orange peels and fancy shampoo—and I wanted to hear her talking to me in a hushed voice, not to be private but because we were so physically close to each other that she didn't need to speak loudly.

"No," she said thoughtfully. "Let's go back."

I sighed; I hadn't realized I'd been holding my breath. But instead of apologizing or trying to find out what she was thinking, I tried to simply appease her.

"Sure," I shrugged, turning the key and starting the engine. "Back where? What do you want to do? We could see what Niz and Jess are up to—I think they said they're hanging out."

It was worth another shot, and I couldn't think of anything else to do.

"No…"

I pulled out of the lot, back toward town. It had always been nice driving around with Penny. Sometimes we talked, sometimes we stayed quiet, but it always seemed like fun.

Truth be told, I didn't want to hang out with Niz and Jess either—not if they thought Penny was stuck up. I know she seemed standoffish because she never wanted to hang out with people, but I think she was one of those rare, genuine, lone-wolf types: someone who only likes to hang out with one or two people at a time. All of my friends—and her friends—were more of the group-hang types, so it wasn't ever going to work out for her.

"That's cool," I decided.

She looked over and smiled—the first warm smile she'd given me since I'd headed out to the JVS—and I reached over and touched her hand.

"So… what?"

"I don't know," she admitted. "I feel like we've seen all the movies and I don't feel like ice cream again."

"How about a burger? We could go to Big Boy…?"

"Don't your friends hang out at Big Boy?"

I glanced at her; she was smiling sweetly at me.

"Sometimes. Not *all* the time."

"Let's go back to my house. We can rent a movie."

"You just said we've seen all the movies… And your dad hates me. It's always awkward."

I reached out at a stoplight and moved her hair back over her ear. It looked good in the soft glow of the streetlights and was the perfect length to tuck over her ear and leave her delicate neck exposed. I leaned over and tried to kiss her neck below the ear, but she pulled back.

"Maybe we should call it a night, Jack. I'm tired."

I didn't mean to look panicked, but I'm sure I did. It was the first time we'd not agreed on *some*thing to do—*any*thing

225

to do—so we could hang out more. She smiled and put her hand on my arm.

"We can hang out tomorrow," she promised.

"Sure," I agreed. "There's always tomorrow."

That night was a schism of sorts, and looking back, it all started with God damn Tagger and his fucking "secret girlfriend" bullshit, because I started to feel like Spider-Man after that night, like I had a secret identity beneath the skate-rat veneer; like I was something special and amazing, but only when I was with Penny.

Penny was real, and I loved her. I loved her with the passion only a sixteen-year-old boy can muster. I loved her because she existed in that time and place when I first steadied my footing and took a few slumbering steps toward manhood. I loved her because she uncovered the best parts of me—the serious parts, the thoughtful parts, the parts that would hold me up.

I loved her for every future moment she came to represent, and I loved her because she seemed to be changing, too; growing and becoming stronger, more independent. I loved her because she let me help her along and because she always turned back to me and smiled and took my hand as she pulled me into the future.

In that way, I built a pedestal for Penny and I put her on it.

Penny became gold spun from summer sunlight, and together we were building something memorable, something that would outlast all my other thoughts and dreams.

what eludes us in those long summer days

It's easy to take certain things for granted—not obvious things, like health and youth, because deep-down we all realize those things will come to an end. It's the subtle things we take for granted, like the way a summer evening feels when you're sixteen. There's a glow and warmth to a teenage summer that never happens again: a strange mix of hope, promise, and the first inklings of nostalgia—that subtly we take for granted; that twinge that pulls us back to the summers of our childhood, when everything seemed to be laid out before us simply because there wasn't enough road yet to look back on. What eludes us in those long summer days is that the past gets constantly further away—the road a dwindling arrow to a point beyond our line of vision, even as the final stop in the distant future begins to take on a vague shape and form. We take for granted that the road before us will always be longer than the road behind because we can't imagine it any other way, and that solace allows us to bask in the long evenings and see nothing more in a sunset than the promise of a new day.

"You seem preoccupied," Tobie said.

Summer was almost over now and I hadn't hung out alone with Tobie for weeks. I'd started dissing all of my friends to be with Penny more, breaking the cadence of time with Penny, then work, then Niz and Sammy and whoever was around. I'd get off work and go back to Penny's house—her dad notwithstanding—and if Penny couldn't hang out, I went home.

Niz and Sammy still thought it was funny to give me a hard time about my secret girlfriend, and it was wearing thin. I misinterpreted the fact that they missed me. I saw it as jealousy of me and Penny, and I was done being reminded that Penny didn't like to hang out with people.

"Yeah, it's Penny."

We were sitting on Tobie's back deck, watching the sun set over the fields and the encroaching darkness lap toward us like an ocean. Penny and her family were on vacation for two weeks, so I'd spent all day moping at home then went over to Tobie's after work.

"What about her?"

"I don't know… Nothing. It seems like we've gone on all the dates we can think of, so now we just sit around at her house. I can *feel* her dad hating me."

Penny's softball league had ended not long after July Fourth and it had broken up our usual rut of evenings in the park and ice cream, and we had never really replaced it as our go-to date. It's weird that we only got bored after we had more time to do other things, but our new-found freedom had resulted in a sort of social panic—with so many options, we didn't know what to do and we froze, renting movies and watching them in her basement, sometimes with her brother and his friend (if her dad let them).

I'd started to feel claustrophobic in Penny's basement—it held none of the excitement that me, Niz, and Sammy usually explored as we cruised between skate spots—but it was a penalty I was willing to suffer to be with her.

228

"Are you guys going to Homecoming?" Tobie asked hopefully.

"Yeah, of course," I said.

That much was true. Penny was a planner, and even though school hadn't started yet, she was already thinking ahead to the end of September. We'd even settled on a color for her dress—or rather, she'd told me the color and I hadn't argued.

"She's wearing pink."

Tobie chuckled. "So... a pink tie for you, huh?"

I smirked in agreement. "It's my own fault. I introduced her to the Psychedelic Furs, then we rented *Pretty in Pink* one night."

"Smooth, Beltane," Tobie sighed happily. "Well, I wouldn't worry about her acting weird if she picked out a dress for Homecoming already."

"I didn't say she was acting weird," I snapped.

"Oh."

"What?"

"Nothing," Tobie replied defensively. "I just... she seems to like the idea of being with you."

"Yeah..." I said suspiciously.

"You really shouldn't worry."

"You're saying that like I *should* worry."

"You're *acting* worried," Tobie retorted in a level tone. "I'm telling you she wouldn't be planning Homecoming if you had to worry."

I sighed heavily.

"What are you listening to these days, Jack?" Tobie wondered, changing the subject before we got too far off track—

she knew very well how to get me refocused.

"Mötley Crüe, actually. I finally got their new album."

"Jesus, Jack…" she drawled. "I was hoping you'd outgrow them."

"Come *on*! Nikki Sixx is a vastly under-appreciated songwriter—do you know how many hit songs that man has written?"

"Please don't list them."

I remained silent, but believe me, in my head I was listing them all. When I was sixteen, the Crüe still held an edginess that slowly wore off with the close of the eighties, and my palate still hadn't become refined enough to be able to fully distinguish metal from punk from no-wave.

"I don't know, Tobie," I admitted out loud. "*Theatre of Pain* is a great album. A *classic*."

"Is that what you've been listening to?"

"Yeah… I mean, the new one's really good… but, man, that album takes me back…"

Tobie chuckled.

"I remember how excited you were when it came out. When was that? Like, eighth grade?"

"Sure…" I agreed. "Seems like forever ago."

We were silent again. Tobie shifted her weight in her chair and somewhere we heard some fireworks going off— the rattle and pop of July Fourth always echoed through all of summer.

"And what does Penny think of Mötley Crüe?"

"Oh, she like them now."

"Poor girl."

"Well, she's basically an empty vessel."

"*What*?" Tobie blared, sitting up. I couldn't see her well in the gloaming, but I knew she was somewhat upset, for real.

"What? What did I say?"

"An empty *vessel*?"

"She is! She hasn't really listened to *any* music! She has really strict parents!"

"That doesn't make her an empty vessel, Jack." She shook her head and sighed and sat back again. "You never said that to her, did you?"

"No…"

I sat up now and looked at Tobie, and something in my expression made her laugh. She covered her eyes in dismay but couldn't help herself from laughing, then took a deep breath and looked at me, her face writ with pity and education.

"Penny may be new to the *wild* life you and Niz and Sammy lead, but that doesn't make her *empty* for God's sake, and she *certainly* doesn't need *you* to do anything about it. She can figure out what she likes all by herself."

I slumped back into my chair with a huff. Of course I knew that, and of course I didn't think any of that—I'd been talking *music* for Christ's sake—but if *Tobie* had suspected that I thought I was doing some great service for poor, sheltered Penny, then…

"Is that why we broke up, Tobie?"

"Hmmm…?" she mused, not following my logic.

"Did I say stupid shit like that to you?"

She chuckled lightly and touched my hand.

"No, Bells. Well yes, you did, but that's not why we

broke up." She gazed off thoughtfully for a few seconds, framing some kind of thesis. "Let me ask you this: If you had to choose between Penny and me, right now, who would you rather date?"

It was a trap and I knew it, and I didn't like it.

"I can't answer that," I replied stiltedly.

"Exactly. You're being polite, Bells, but we all know you'd pick Penny."

"We *all*? 'We all' who?"

She was right, of course—I would have picked Penny—but I didn't understand why that mattered. I didn't realize then that the way I'd been avoiding my friends had been noticed, and my friends didn't like it. But being my friends, they didn't say anything because they thought I was happy.

"You guys are a cute couple. Kinda weird—but y'know, opposites attract."

"I don't think we're *that* opposite."

"Well, she's an *empty vessel,*" Tobie emphasized.

"Zippit, Malloy!" I growled and squeezed her knee, tickling her and sending her into an involuntarily gasp of laughter.

"Bells!" she shrieked and punched my arm. "Cut it out!"

"That actually kinda hurt," I said, rubbing the spot.

"Well, yeah," Tobie agreed. "So... *what*?"

"You're awfully agitated tonight," I commented.

"It's *hot*," she sighed. "And we don't have A-C."

I turned and glanced back her house, at the wide-open patio doors that led to her kitchen, and beyond that to the family room where her mom and dad were watching TV and, most certainly, hearing every word of our conversation.

"Are your parents still up?" I whispered.

"Yes!" she whispered back with mock drama, her eyes wide in the darkness and her smile all glee. "So keep it down!"

I watched her for a second, really seeing her for the first time, it seemed, as a friend. As a *good* friend. That *is* why we'd broken up after all, because we'd both felt it getting weird. We'd both felt like us dating had been a squeeze play we'd been forced into by everyone we knew, and it had scared us. It had scared us because it wasn't comfortable, because it created a whole other side to our relationship that wasn't freewheeling. It made me want to impress her, not just hang out with her, and we'd both realized that right then, we needed to hang out with each other more than impress each other. Still, for some reason I had to hear it again, from her. I had to make sure, in some indirect way, that it wasn't happening to me and Penny; I need reassurance that what Penny and I had was different, lasting.

"So why did we *really* break up, Tobie?" I whispered.

Her expression faltered and fell; her right eyebrow quivered up in mild shock. She had no idea why I was bringing it up, and I wasn't about to explain that I wanted to make sure whatever had broken up me and Tobie didn't break up me and Penny.

"We discussed this, Jack," she whispered back, almost timidly. "We *agreed*…"

"No, no—I know. But I mean, was there anything I did? *Anything*?"

"No…" she breathed.

233

"I really like Penny, and if I ever said anything stupid to you or made you feel bad or acted like a jerk—"

"Jack," she begged, touching my hand again. "No... It just didn't *feel* right."

"I know. It didn't. But you'd tell me, wouldn't you? If I was an idiot?"

She chuckled and looked down at her lap, brushing off phantom dust and shaking her head slowly. Then she looked back over at me and took in a deep breath, her eyes twinkling mischievously.

"You *are* an idiot, Bells."

"Thanks," I breathed and settled back in the chair, gazing up at the sky. Somewhere under those same stars Penny was on vacation, and I wondered if she was thinking about me.

"You really like her that much?" Tobie asked in a more normal tone of voice, but I could tell by the way it sounded that she'd settled back, too, her head pulled back to look up at the stars.

"She's pretty great."

"Did you ever talk to her before? In school?"

"No. Nope. She was the hot girl in math class who sat at the front and always knew the answers. I tried to play it *so cool* when we ran into each other that day, like I wasn't sure I recognized her." I chuckled at the memory; it already seemed like a hundred years ago.

"Well she seems really nice."

"I'm afraid she'll forget me on vacation," I admitted. "Or figure out I'm not as cool as she is."

"That won't happen, Bells."

I rolled my head to the side and looked at Tobie, and she looked over and smiled back.

"Hey, what about you?"

"Me?"

"Niz said there was some guy at the pool or something…?"

It was dark, but I think she blushed. "Oh *stop*. We went out *once*."

"And?"

"And nothing. It was okay."

"Did he call?"

"Yeah."

"And?"

She laughed in disbelief. "And… *Nothing*. That's it."

"Prom still got you down?" I guessed.

"*Prom*?" she spat. "Richie *Dolovar*? No! Can't a girl just *hang out* and not be dating or pining over anyone?"

"Sure, I guess," I said.

"Good," she decided. "Because that's how it is and that's how I want it. I like being an *empty vessel*."

"Oh, Christ! Leave it alone!" I joked with a sigh.

"Want some lemonade?" she wondered casually.

"Sure."

And she left me there to look at the stars and ponder the ways of women.

"I don't know why I've never been here before," Shaggy said in an impressed tone as he looked around. "It's nice."

We were at the venerable Grog Shop, Cleveland's crown jewel of the bar-band circuit, tucked at the end of Coventry Road. We'd got there early and sat on barstools like a trio of bullfrogs, nursing beers and talking at each other through the mirror behind the bar. I'd started with a Guinness on tap and was transfixed by the foam as it settled, cascading through the brown liquid like snow swirls on the highway.

"Best club in town," I intoned.

The stage lights popped on and Shaggy hopped off his stool.

"Sit down, man," I said to him. "They're just checking them. We'll be standing for the show."

"I'm okay," he said, looking around again and sipping his beer.

The Grog wasn't big by any stretch of the imagination, but apart from a single booth off to the side, there was only the bar to sit at, and a big open floor in between it and the stage. The stage itself was small, and no matter where you stood, you were close, which was perfect, especially for this show.

Bleached was co-headlining with Beach Slang. I've often told people I have an unhealthy relationship with bands, especially the ones I obsess over—and I was obsessed with Bleached, from their weirdly original old-school vibe

236

mashed up with straight-ahead punk, to their lyrics and the way they presented themselves in interviews and online. But those certain bands, they become like friends to me. I look to them for comfort and commiseration, and to live vicariously through them. Bleached seemed like people I would have hung out with in high school.

Beach Slang was a close second to Bleached for me these days, and to have them on the same bill seemed like a Heaven-sent chance that absolutely could not be passed up. I'd wanted to share the joy so much that I'd grabbed three tickets and forced Shaggy and Gray to come with me. Well, Gray and I forced Shaggy to come—Gray was usually up for anything, as long as Deet wasn't working or something. Shaggy, steadily trending toward the most adult of us, wasn't sure he should be out on a work night. He looked vaguely nervous holding his beer bottle, taking sips instead of swigs, like a teenager so self-conscious of being cool that he looked scared.

I looked at Gray and shook my head, motioning my concern at what we were going to do with this guy.

"He's had a long day," Gray explained. "He had to cart home four cases of mislabeled beer."

"It *was* a long day," he agreed emphatically. "I had to figure out what the hell happened and ream the guy responsible. I only caught it by accident."

"Isn't it your job to catch it, though?" I checked.

He laughed. "No." And sipped his beer. "I do more office work now. It was *his* job. So this band—all girls, right?"

"Yeah… Not the drummer, though."

"Is that why we came?"

"No, *Shaggy*, we came because their music is amazing. And because Beach Slang—a *dude*—is on the same bill."

"Uh-huh," he agreed sarcastically.

"See, Gray, that's the problem, right there. If a guy likes a band with a girl in it—or all girls—everyone assumes it's because of the girls. It feels a lot like sexism somewhere in all that."

"Now Bell," Gray opined wisely, showing Shaggy how to swig from a bottle. "You have to admit it looks bad. These girls are twenty years younger than you."

"Bullshit," I spat. "They're barely younger than us. And so *what*? What the *hell* is wrong with people when there's a girl in the *God damn band*?"

"You do like a lot of bands with girls," Gray said evenly, goading me into our ritualistic barroom argument about something nonsensical; winding me up because it entertained him, and always had. We'd had countless nights exactly like this through college, and after college, and even now, when the stars aligned. I'm not sure why he did it or why I put up with it or, more to the point, why I still fell for it.

"Like, I can't relate to a song because a girl wrote it?" I wondered. "That's really fucking limiting. Love hurts the same for both sexes. Crushes hold just as much weight. And going out and having a *good fucking time* is not gender-specific, despite that whole 'girls night out' thing. Bleached reminds me what it was like to be young and in love and getting my heart broken."

"That sounds horrible," Shaggy cut in. "I'd rather forget all my troubles, especially past troubles. Huh…" he mused. "Speaking of past troubles and girls twenty years younger

238

than you" (I rolled my eyes) "whatever happened with that chick from high school?"

I furrowed my brow, then nodded, then yawned. Maybe Shaggy was right about coming out on work nights.

"Penny," I said. "Yeah, I friended her."

"I know *that*," he said, mildly confused. He glanced at Gray and added, "Hadn't he friended her when we went bowling? I mean, whatever *happened* with her? Why were you so wound up about her friending you?"

"I don't know…" I took a moment to drain half my Guinness—a truly chuggable beer—and put my glass down right as the bartender delivered my bag of chips. I let Shaggy snake a couple, though he claimed not to "get" them. Shaggy liked to point out that he didn't get things, usually when it came to bands, like, "I don't *get* Johnny Cash." I wasn't sure how you couldn't get chips, but I let him have it.

"Penny was my American dream, Shaggy," I decided, not sure I wanted him to know I'd run into her a couple of times since then. Shaggy was a friend, but I wasn't sure how close a friend he was.

"Oh shit—gather 'round, kids," Gray mumbled mockingly and gave me a beaming no-offense smile.

"Seriously, though… It was summer a hundred years ago —we were sixteen. I'd just got my license. She was vibrant and tan and athletic, and her parents hated me. Her dad, anyway. Which only made it more romantic."

"We've all been there," Shaggy agreed dismally. With what appeared to be considerable effort he managed to hoist his bottle high enough to take his last sip. "I think it's the car that does it—did you have your own car?"

239

"Yeah… a piece of shit my brother didn't want. Fucking Malibu sedan. Shit brown."

"Oohh!" Shaggy cried happily. "I *loved* my crappy high-school car! But yeah—I think if you have your own car, daddy assumes you're not coming back with his daughter."

"Is that what *you* think now?"

"My daughter isn't dating," he said dismissively, so I let it drop. "And this Penny girl… hot?"

"She's *still* hot," Gray agreed. "We've ran into her a couple of times." His eyes flickered over to me like he'd said too much. I shrugged: We had, it was true.

"Oh, I like where this is going…" Shaggy grinned, waking up fully for the first time all night. He slipped his empty bottle onto the bar and motioned for another one. "Let's start with the summer-of-love a hundred years ago, though."

"You'll be disappointed," Gray observed. "Bell here spent a long night of the soul in college telling me about his first time, and her name wasn't Penny."

"Is nothing sacred with you anymore?" I asked him pointedly.

"Fuck you, man!" he joked. "You're the one writing a damn *book* about it!"

"Whatever. So long story short, we dated all summer and she dumped me when we went back to school, and it fucked me up. So… there's that."

"Well, shit," Shaggy said quietly. "That there's exactly why everyone loves *Grease*. You ready for that shot?"

"Sure."

Shaggy ordered it when the bartender brought his beer (Gray waved off another round because he was still nursing

240

his first beer) and we drank to summer loves. I'd cut the story really short, and I think they both knew it. I could also tell that Gray was wondering what I wasn't saying about her; what I'd kept hidden.

I don't think Gray is wired for broken hearts the same way as I am. I'm sure he'd been hurt, but Gray had been right before when he was making fun of me for falling off the deep end when I got serious about a girl. I put a lot of weight into relationships—sexual or not—and he knew that, but I don't think he understood what it means to try and crawl out from under that weight when things collapse. That's why I'd never talked about her before: She was the shadow and the weight, and talking about her only shone light into corners I'd forgotten were there.

I'd learned to leave her out of my stories because some people—like Gray—don't want to talk about it anyway. That's why my high school friends had meant so much to me—Niz and Sammy and Jess and Tobie. They'd always been there to pull me back out, especially Tobie, and it takes a very special person to be able to do that; to recognize a danger they don't personally feel and may never experience; to pull a man out of a paddling pool because you know his weakness and you know how little it will take him to drown.

I looked at Gray and finished off my Guinness—he had a curious expression, debating what to say. Gray never diced words when he spoke, but he did wait until he *understood* before he spoke, so he wouldn't misspeak. He had been there once for me the year we graduated from college—he and Deet had pulled me back that time—but to them it had been a single, understandable plunge. They didn't understand the

241

history. They didn't understand that people like me, we're held together by tides and lunacy, and that's not something you can ever really explain to someone who isn't wired the same way.

Shaggy either missed the whole undercurrent or was willfully glossing over it—and maybe that was exactly the right thing to do—because he raised his eyebrows comically and looked over his glasses at me expectantly.

"Aaaand…? So…? *Still* hot…?"

I couldn't help but laugh. "That's what's fucked up. She doesn't look like she's aged a damn day."

"She looks sixteen?" Shaggy checked.

"Basically…"

I pulled my phone out and showed him her profile picture. Shaggy took my phone and looked at the picture over his glasses like he was ninety-five years old or something. He nodded as if accepting a painful truth and handed the phone back.

"She's just posting old pictures, man."

"With her kid? And her friends who look like they're forty?"

"I don't know…"

"She's a textbook milf," Gray said seriously. "I've seen her in person. How old's her kid now?"

"Sixteen."

"Shotgun wedding?" Shaggy asked rhetorically.

"No wedding."

Shaggy raised his eyebrows even further.

"She ran into you here?"

He looked around hopefully.

"Nah—at the Beachland, and then again in Lakewood."

"No shit? Only twice?"

"*Only?*"

"That *could* be coincidence. Baby steps," Shaggy surmised. "Testing the water. Nose to the wind. Three times and she's after you."

"You're so damn wise," I replied sarcastically.

"But enough about this," Gray suddenly boomed, choosing that the best direction was misdirection. I think that's why I liked him: He didn't coddle emotions, he bulldozed them. "I didn't come here to talk about ghosts. I came to watch three hot chicks play rock-n-roll."

"You're such an asshole. Truly," I observed, smiling privately.

"Oh no, I want to talk about ghosts," Shaggy rebuked. "I came hear to drink and to hear Jack's ghost stories."

"Why *mine*?"

"I know all of *his*," he stated, cocking his head at Gray. "But yours always seem more complex."

"I don't think we should talk about ghosts," Gray said very studiously, his tone even and quiet.

I looked at him and his eyes softened at me, telling me he understood as much as he could, and he knew not to force me down that path if I didn't want to go. If she'd never come up before all this, he inferred that it was because I didn't like to talk about her. Then his eyes widened a barely discernible amount, but enough to say he'd seen... well... a ghost. I turned slowly and followed his gaze, looking back toward the door.

"Jack?" Penny asked—her tone said she was honestly

amazed, but her posture said she was acting. She pulled her hair back over her ear—embarrassed, she'd have you believe—then fixed me with a resolute smile.

"Penny." It was a word, and I simply said it. "I guess you know this place, then?"

I couldn't blame her—everyone knows the Grog—but it still seemed like a stretch. I hadn't posted this show online on purpose, but I had checked in when we got there—although the Grog wasn't exactly down the street from Akron.

"I guess," she allowed.

"Quite a haul from Akron, though."

"I was dropping Jason off at his dad's for the weekend. He lives in Cleveland Heights."

"Oh."

It was an honest enough excuse: She had been in the area when she saw my post, so why not come over and say hi?

"This is three times now," I pointed out, but I did so more for Shaggy and Gray than for Penny. She knew damn well how many times it had been.

"Hi, Gray," she added nicely. Gray waved. Shaggy was staring, beer raised but not drunk.

"That's Shaggy, a friend of ours. Shaggy, this is Penny, a girl I knew a hundred years ago."

Moments like that tell you how good a friend is, and Shaggy was, for all intents and purposes, still a relative stranger by that count. He could make an ass of himself right then and there, and embarrass me and Penny, and I'd never want to hang out with him again. Or he could play it cool, like a friend would.

"Hi, Penny," he said and shook her hand. "Nice to meet you. College friend?"

He was totally cool. Shaggy was a stranger to me no more.

"High school," she corrected.

"That *was* a hundred years ago!" he joked, catching my eye with an understanding look. "It's amazing that you're still in touch!"

"Yeah," she agreed with something like an apology in her glance at me.

"Did you come here alone?" I wondered, not seeing anyone hovering nearby.

"Yeah."

And I hated her for that fact because I felt like she'd come alone on purpose, to gain my sympathy, to remove her excuse to leave me alone.

"I feel like we didn't get to hang out before," she explained. "I mean, not really."

Her eyes flicked over to Gray and Shaggy but she didn't apologize for insinuating that they were unwelcome. The only reason they didn't take the hint was because they were waiting for *my* signal, not hers.

"Sure," I accepted, motioning for her to sit on the stool Shaggy had vacated. "But Bleached is my favorite band in the world, and Beach Slang is one of my others... I came to see *them*."

"Oh, I won't bother you," she said, sitting down nervously—and she did look nervous. I think she was getting my hint now; maybe rethinking her whole plan.

"Let's go check out Mac's Backs," Gray said to Shaggy,

245

looking at his watch. It was still a while before the opener would go on and Coventry had a long line of great stores, anchored by Mac's Backs, a massive indie bookstore stuffed with hard-to-find titles and more than willing to promote local authors.

"I'll be here," I said as they drained their beers and wandered off. Then, to her: "So why do you keep looking me up, Penny?"

I was done with being polite. Shaggy was absolutely right: Three times was no coincidence. And Tobie was right, too: for once in my life, I needed to be direct and worry more about my own feelings than someone else's.

"I told you: I don't know anyone in town—"

The look in her eyes said she didn't believe that herself.

"Do you think we're going to get back together or something?"

"No!" she gasped. "*God* no!"

She had a look of horror; panic. She squirmed on the barstool, subconsciously deciding if she should leave. It seemed like she was being honest. She was wearing a lightweight hoodie with jeans and sneakers—she looked like the last thing on her mind was a night out. It made me wonder if the last time, at Now That's Class, had been a coincidence, not a plan—out with her friend but not intending to try and meet up with me until the last minute, when they couldn't think of anything better to do. The bartender hovered and I nodded at Penny.

"Whatever you want, Penny." I said evenly.

She ordered a beer and looked at me, her smile thin and soft, her eyes rounds ohs of apology.

"I've just been feeling that summer lately, y'know?"

"Because your kid turned sixteen," I concluded rhetorically with a nod—I'd heard this story before.

"Maybe." She narrowed her eyes. "The day I looked you up online was the day my dad died—"

"Look, I know I'm going to sound like a dick, Penny, but you keep coming to shows and telling me your dad died. It feels a lot like you're just trying to gain my sympathy, and I'm not sure why. I don't know what you want from me."

She misted up and turned away; sucked in a deep breath before she looked back at me with a big smile.

"I know," she agreed. "I know... Maybe I figured if I looked you up, he'd come back to life to yell at me one last time." She chuckled and waggled her head to dismiss her own foolish notions.

We all tend half-formed memories with slender threads to the past that tighten and tug in unexpected ways. There was a thread there for her, between me and her dad, and between me and that summer, and between that summer and her dad. Those threads had all tightened at once, knotting together and pulling her toward something she could no longer identify; something she could maybe never identify—a complex emotion wrapped around independence, young love, and family bonds. What she needed to know is if I could cut that knot out and release her dad—or her regrets now that her dad was gone—because the tug was too hard and the pull was confusing her. It was like that for me, too: So many threads over the last two decades had wormed their way into the webbing of that summer.

247

"He really hated me?" I asked quietly, hoping I'd tugged the right line; hoping the knot would unwind and let her move on.

"Believe it or not, I think you loosened him up that summer."

I snuffed an ironic laugh through my nose.

"I guess it seemed... I don't know..." She was genuinely struggling to put it all together. "That summer was the first time I felt his grip relax. He *was* strict. He ruled over my mom her whole life, and then you came along and said that maybe it didn't have to be that way."

She shook her head slowly and gazed down into her beer bottle as if checking for wasps at an outdoor picnic.

"That definitely scared him, but I *loved* him, Jack... I *did*... and I didn't want to hurt him."

"Okay," I accepted.

She looked up, confusion flickering across her face.

"Okay," I repeated. "That makes sense. I get it."

Nope, I didn't sound motivational. I sounded sarcastic.

"I'm sorry—but we keep having the same conversation, Penny."

She gave me a thoughtful smirk. I ignored it.

"July Fourth?" I suggested, assuming that would be the next thing she brought up.

Her smiled solidified and turned golden; her eyes sparkled—that knot was tied to the middle of that summer for her as well as for me. It's where the threads pulled tight and the web became a cloth. I sighed and felt my mood shift into a more sympathetic gear—July Fourth was the one day we could agree on. That memory was the same for both of us.

248

And I started to re-imagine the nature of that knot, with its vast tendrils spinning off into the rest of my life. I had forgotten the brightness that day had given me—a brightness she had always carried. Penny had reminded me of it that night at the Beachland, twenty years later, almost to the day—if nothing else, I owed her thanks for that.

"Why did you break up with me, Penny?"

It seemed like the right time to ask. It seemed like she'd be ready to admit that her dad had forced us apart. Maybe that was the knot she needed me to cut; maybe she needed to admit his part in ruining our relationship, his part in destroying the future we were building.

"I mean, for real," I added, trying to make it seem like curiosity. "I figured you either suddenly hated me like you said you did, and I had no idea why that had happened, or your dad made you break up with me—"

"I *did* hate you," she cut in softly. "I *thought* I hated you. My dad and I, we had a *huge* argument—I think he was triggered by me going to Homecoming—and it all came out and I *hated* you for *constantly* trying to get me to disobey my parents."

"*What*?" I squeaked. "I *never*—!"

"You *did*," she stated firmly. "You didn't *mean* to, but you *did*. You made me feel *dumb* for always doing what I was told, and you never seemed to *care* when I finally stood up for myself. And you made me *jealous*, with all your friends! I felt like our lives would *never* be in sync, and you'd just keep *pushing* me…"

I went cold.

All this time I'd been convinced she'd never really hated

249

me—that I'd lost her and everything that summer because of her dad, because that was the only thing that made sense to me. That I'd let her sideline my friendships only to have her snatched away by forces I couldn't control; that the summer had been for nothing because love had lost against the unfeeling will of the universe. But this? This wasn't like that at all—not entirely. Sure, you could say her dad was to blame on some level, but he wouldn't have been a problem if I'd been less... dismissive of him; more aware of the struggles she was going through as she tried to break free.

It might never have happened if I'd only been more understanding. My mood melted. I looked into her eyes and I saw the remorse and I couldn't keep up any semblance of anger toward her.

"Jesus, Penny... Why didn't you just *say*...?"

She smiled nostalgically.

"Because I knew your friends didn't like me. I knew they'd win."

"What do you mean, didn't *like* you? They *loved* you!"

"They were *nice* to me, Jack—it's not the same thing."

"They always wished you'd hang out with us..."

She thought for a second, reconsidering, gazing off into the mirror behind the bar. She took a slow sip of her beer and shrugged.

"I was sixteen, Jack. It was easier to be angry at you."

"I really thought I loved you," I admitted. "It really hurt when you broke up with me."

She reached out and put her hand on my arm. "It was a shitty thing to do—I know that now. I think I knew it then. That's why I avoided you... I wasn't lying when I said I

250

looked you up so I could apologize. I *am* sorry. I *was* sorry…"

I looked away, pretended to read the labels on the bottles behind the bar.

"I didn't know I made you feel like that."

"I tried to tell you…"

"And now?" I wondered, looking at her again. "Why wouldn't you *still* hate me?"

"Because now I know that you made me a better parent, Jack. Because now I understand what you meant about cutting loose and having fun and bending the rules. Because I realized when my dad died, I think *he* finally understood, too. You helped *him* relax. He died from complications of a lot of things. He was in-and-out most of the last week."

She started to get misty again. I touched her hand and she wiped her eyes, sniffing heavily.

"He told me… Right before… He said I made him a better person by standing up to him. He said I should let Jason do the same to me…"

She stopped and composed herself, gazing into the mirror behind the bar again. Around us the crowd was tightening —it really was a great double bill and it was going to sell out —and it was easy for us to lose our conversation in the background noise. We sat silently for several minutes, her nursing her beer and me spinning my shot glass.

"You did that, Jack," she finally said. I had to lean in to hear her, and she subtly leaned in, too, our shoulders touching, our heads cocked toward each other. "Well, you *started* it. And I couldn't stand the thought of you believing I still hated you—that I ever *really* hated you. Not after what he said when he died."

251

Her voice cracked and she looked away quickly, dabbing her eyes.

"I'm sorry, Penny…"

I was still trying to process what she'd said. I was still trying to believe it had all been her dad's fault, even as it sank in that it wasn't true. Maybe it had turned out better for everyone—maybe *everything* turns out better if you look at it through the right lens—and I could feel my thoughts racing, churning through all those threads, re-weaving all those strands, all those days strung together by silvery tendrils to that one summer, a hundred years ago.

"It's been a rough year," she admitted with a heavy sniff. "I needed that perfect summer back, and only you could prove that it had been real."

She turned back to me and held my gaze, a sincere smile touching her lips.

I didn't speak. I couldn't speak.

It was weird: Everything had eventually played out like I'd always hoped, with Penny apologizing, but the victory was Pyrrhic at best—she may have regretted saying she hated me back then, but she'd had a good reason to say it. I couldn't help but wonder how many girls I'd blamed for a break up, and how often it had actually been me. Maybe it had always been me.

"Jack…?" she wondered softly.

The bar was loud and in the din I almost didn't hear her. I met her eyes again. The smile was gone. She looked concerned, maybe in the midst of her own revelation. Maybe she'd assumed that I'd had all my friends—all my wild nights out on the town—and I hadn't really cared that she

252

broke up with me. Maybe that's what had helped her sleep all these years, if she was telling the truth when she said that summer had been special; had been long in her memory. Maybe she'd convinced herself that it hurt *her* more when it ended, and that I'd quickly forgotten all about her. And maybe now she was understanding that it wasn't true—her own Pyrrhic victory.

"It was real," I said sincerely.

She slipped off the barstool and reached out to hug me, so I stood up and took her into my arms and she hugged me tight and I awkwardly hugged her back. She held on for what seemed like too long, but I didn't mind. I'd got that chance, after all, for another hug from Penny Harper—a real hug, a hug that meant something—and it felt like the warm embrace of that summer a hundred years ago; the soft dusk of a windless night and a purple sunset.

She finally let go and sat back down, clearing her head and putting on a bright face in the hopes her mood would follow. I sat down, too, and watched her dab her eyes again then suck down a few chugs of her beer.

The pedestal I had put her on all those summers ago finally crumbled, and she was suddenly just someone else I used to know, or never really knew. Because who are we at sixteen? Are we the people we become, or are we gross caterpillars inching toward our cocoons? I'd always wondered where she'd ended up, and now here she was, sitting beside me: Dr. Harper, a middle-aged woman way more put-together than I was, but still with her own demons nipping at her heels.

And our demons bound us together and I wondered if

253

we'd ever truly be free of them.

"What was the best part of being sixteen?" I asked her.

"Of that summer?" she checked rhetorically, understanding that we needed to move the conversation into less volatile waters. She cocked her head and gazed at the ceiling for a second or two. "Honestly? Mötley Crüe."

"*What*?" I gasped, my shock completely sincere. "Are you *serious*?"

"Hundred percent!" she laughed. "Donny and I—Jason's dad—met at their show."

"Well no wonder he knocked you up!" I joked, immediately thinking that was probably a step too far.

She leaned in and nudged me playfully with her elbow, grinning happily.

"Stop—he wasn't like that. Neither was I—that's why it worked out." She turned and eyed me curiously. "What about you? What was the best part of being sixteen?"

"Oh, driving, for sure. The *shit* we got up to with my car!"

"I image you still get up to shit," she suggested with a sidelong look, the curse word not sounding entirely comfortable on her tongue.

"Well, nah, not anymore," I admitted. "I have a job and kids…"

"Pardon me," Gray suddenly interrupted, having muscled his way back over to us. Shaggy lingered a bit further back and waved at me with a paperback he'd bought. "Are we talking about the shit Jack got up to?"

Penny swung around on her stool to face him better, and I swung around, too.

254

"Not exactly," Penny replied suspiciously. "But I'm all ears."

"Jack is a bad influence," he said very seriously; I rolled my eyes at Penny to suggest that Gray was always full of crap. "Drags me out to bars, drinks too much, leaves me for dead on my front porch—"

"Hey! That was your fault!"

"—takes me to tattoo parlors…"

She glanced at my arms and asked, "Full sleeve?"

"Yeah."

"How long ago did you get it?"

I shrugged. "Five years…? I needed a good job to pay for it—they're expensive."

"So… no high-powered sales career in the cards for you anymore?"

"Shit!" Gray blurted. "No high-powered sales career for this guy *ever*!"

Shaggy finally moved close enough to hear us, but he didn't interject.

"I like my job," I said quietly. "They leave me alone."

"So you're still pretty wild?" Penny checked.

"Was I ever *really* wild?" I asked her.

"Wilder than me."

She shrugged as if it were a simple statement of fact, and I guess it was, but it sort of iced the conversation. Gray looked at me and I tried to subtly motion that I had no idea what to say, then Penny turned on her stool and smiled broadly at me, her eyes flicking to Gray and Shaggy.

"I think I'll go home, Jack," she said, standing up straight and tall, smoothing her hair with her fingers. She might have been about to cry—I couldn't tell and I didn't want to ask.

"It's okay, Penny—you came all this way and you paid the cover. They're one of my favorite bands—*two* of my favorite bands. You should *definitely* check 'em out."

"I couldn't have stayed long anyway," she admitted. "I have to go into work tomorrow—early."

"Sure."

I wasn't going to try and talk her into staying. She glanced at Gray and Shaggy again, then gave me another quick hug.

"Next time, Jack, okay?"

I'm not sure I even answered her.

Suddenly it felt a lot like I'd lost her all over again.

Tobie had been right, even though she hadn't really said anything. And Tagger had been right, too, I guess. Everyone had been right, all the way back to Sammy when I first met Penny Harper. Everyone had been right, except me.

She'd been acting different since we got back to school—clutching her books to avoid taking my hand, or turning the other way down a crowded hall as if she hadn't noticed me. I knew she was friends with the sporty types— the softball players and soccer girls—but I didn't think that was all that mattered. There was something that drained out of her as the summer golds turned toward autumn browns; she seemed to lack the energy to deal with me. Her expression had more accusation than apology in it. I tried to make jokes about it. Penny tried to smile. I tried to pretend nothing was wrong.

I learned that we refuse to see the things that matter when they matter most—the things that could save us or change us or make it all worthwhile.

I dove blindly into things when I should have stopped to look, and I stayed under when I should have come up for air, convinced in my youthful slumber that nothing could ever hurt me. But I learned. I learned that falling off a skateboard is one kind of pain, girls can cause another kind of pain, and the pain of facing an uncertain future is something altogether *other.*

"I don't really like you, Jack."

257

That's exactly what she said. I'll never forget it. The sibilance and inflection of her voice still spins in my dreams at night, echoing from a long, dark past that never truly goes away. It can't. Some cuts are real, but others are deep, and that *other* pain is deeper still.

There was a phone in my bedroom—back in the old days, when kids had phones attached to wires attached to walls. I sat with my back to my closed door and talked to Penny in hushed tones so we couldn't be overheard. She did the same—talking quietly in her quiet house, her dad no doubt lingering within earshot, just in case. I'm sure I heard him speaking to her in the background at least once.

"What does that mean?" I asked.

"I don't want to see you anymore."

I tried to convince her to meet me in her front yard—a subconscious attempt to reignite our romance by using the same conditions as when we'd first met. But she wouldn't have it. She was crying and she hung up softly to stop me talking. I slammed the phone down, then picked it up and slammed it down again. I stopped breathing. I was dizzy. My eyes welled with tears. I went cold. I blinked.

"What about Homecoming?" I'd asked, trying to use it as an excuse to tough it out; to buy us some more time—time for me to fix it. But she put an end to that idea.

"I'm not going," she'd said. "Not with *you*."

I punched my door.

"Okay up there, Jacky?" my mom called out.

"Fine!" I yelled, but it was enough to make me move. I didn't like the sound in my voice and I didn't want anyone to ask me about it.

I grabbed my car keys and bolted. My mom may have said something from the kitchen, but I didn't hear her. I had my very own shitty old car and I didn't have to sit around and listen to anyone anymore.

Outside it was finally cooling off—late summer to early fall didn't change much during the day, but the nights were a lot cooler. There were crickets and darkness and moths picked out by my headlights as I gunned it past her house and over the hill. Somewhere my ghost still stood there, bathed in early summer sunlight, his heart pitter-pattering as she pulled an errant strand of hair over her ear. I blew past without looking. The streets were wide, wider than I'd ever need, and I powered down the hill, all the way to the stop sign at the bottom, then cut right, into the park, past the gates that said they would be closed at dusk but never were, over a speed bump and into the lower lot, way back out of sight, down by the Roots—somewhere I could hide.

The Roots was a washed-out creek bed that had left a tangle of roots behind deep enough to crawl under and sit. An old secret hideout discovered on some grade-school field trip with Tobie when were little kids. I scrambled in—it was tougher now that I was bigger, but I made it—and sat staring up through the wooden bones of an ancient rib cage. It looked like the hardened lines of a blown-ink tree against the black paper of the sky.

Then I cried—real, uncontrollable sobs, pausing only for dry heaves. I felt sick with how fucking foolish I'd been to believe that a girl like Penny Harper actually liked me, hating myself for going along with it long enough for all her friends to laugh at me, to whisper behind their binders in school and giggle as Penny walked away from me.

Just like everyone had told me she'd do—a stuck-up pretty girl with no time for dregs like me.

It all made sense now. No one really liked me and they probably all sided with Penny, anyway. That old loser Jack —learned to drive but still rides a skateboard. Listens to shitty loud music. You know him? The guy who sits in the back of class and only participates long enough to be sarcastic? The guy who takes study hall and art instead of honors credit? The guy who hangs out with the stoners in the one-hundred wing?

"It's not going to work out," they'd all said, maybe not in so many words, but it wasn't the time to quibble over details. "*No one really likes you, Jack.*"

Now it was all so God damn obvious, and I'd missed it. She didn't like me—she said so, like it was the most obvious thing in the world. She never had. *No one* ever had. They hadn't been trying to do *me* any favors, they'd been trying to save *Penny*. They were all fucking liars, every last one of them. I couldn't imagine how I'd got it so horribly wrong. No one understood me—I drifted among my groups of friends like an untethered kite, and they let me drift because no one really wanted me around for too long. Not like Penny had wanted me around—or like I *thought* she had.

Penny liked long walks and holding hands. She liked animated movies and butter on her popcorn. She liked the Reds. She liked buying ice creams and going to the park to eat them.

I loved the way she looked, hunched over her ice-cream cone in my car while I drove us to the park, trying to suck the drips off before they fell, her hair shining in the sunlight, lapping against the breeze from the open window, her legs flexed and tan in her favorite bleached denim shorts. It sounds like a God damn music video, I know, but it wasn't like that at all—or it was, but not in the way video directors pervert the image. She was young and carefree, unconcerned about impressing anyone. She was *comfortable* in my company, and nothing put a fine point on that like the contorted, goofy faces and postures she made when trying to juggle two ice cream cones and not get drips anywhere.

"You're driving slow on purpose!" she accused me once.

"You're fun to watch."

"Jack!" She paused long enough from saving her ice cream to grin at me. "Turn it up?"

Despite Tobie's doubts, Penny *had* come around to Mötley Crüe, and that's why *Theatre of Pain* will forever be burned in my mind. No matter how old I am, I will always feel that summer when I hear that album—all the sunlight; all the nightscapes. The strains and riffs of *Theatre of Pain* are etched so deeply in the synapses of my brain that when I die, they could spool the curves and curlicues therein on some kind of macabre reel-to-reel tape deck and play back the whole album—every chord; every drum fill; every solo; every shriek, plead, and moan. And if they could record the pictures that went with them, they'd see Penny Harper: Penny licking her ice cream; Penny grinning against the blazing sun; Penny skipping in her tight white shorts; Penny's perfectly tanned arms reaching out to me.

The crickets whirred in the darkness like a migraine.

Eventually the tears and dry heaves ran their course and

261

I realized I was sweating, despite the air beneath the roots, along the dry creek bed, breathing coolly against my skin. My shirt was soaked, my shorts were uncomfortable.

Now there was nothing. The crumbled façade of a certain future had left behind a void that cannot be explained, only experienced. It was a dark clarity that felt right and decisive—a whim that seemed like a well-planned strategy. That emptiness seduces you into thinking it has substance and meaning, and when something that meaningful is nothing, the static feedback it creates whines into a long, low note that sings into the deepest part of your brain and teases out your demons as solace.

Out there, somewhere, up the hill a piece, was the overlook where I felt like we'd spent the whole summer. We always sat up there and ate our ice cream, then lay there on the hillside on a big pink blanket I kept in the trunk of my car, and we watched the airy wisps of cloud float across the blue background, or else we gazed into the steely blue madness of an August summer sky and imagined all that space, leading off into forever.

The air was always thick and humid, but we never minded, and we got so tan. She usually rolled her T-shirt up over her belly and tucked it under her bra so her stomach tanned, too, and it about drove me mad. Sometimes I'd roll onto my side and put my hand on her stomach and I'd feel her breathing and look into her smiling eyes. Once I even dared kiss her navel; her fingers slowly playing with the hair on the back of my head. Then I kissed her neck and her cheek and her lips—her kisses were deep without desperation; long without being bashful; tender without being sad.

The crickets in the darkness merged with the whine and buzz of the static trying to fill that void. Things began to make more sense. The tears on my cheeks hardened to salt ruins.

There was really nothing more to life than summer and Penny Harper, and as summer had rolled back into school, I could see now that I'd lost them both. No, not just both—*every*thing. Niz had Jess now, Sammy had some girl or other, Tobie barely even looked at me… Penny was all I'd had left, and now she was gone, too. Like those clouds that skidded over the summer sky above us and evaporated, the world had burned too hot to hold something so light and free.

Another week of school. Another week of her avoiding me. Another week of waiting for the weekend. Outside of school, Penny had been the same as always. We went to the movies on weekends and hung out at the arcade. That was one of the things I really loved about Penny: She was very prim and proper to look at, but she wasn't hung up on money and she actually enjoyed video games—the arcade was usually her idea, perhaps because it was the safest vice she could think of that her parents still wouldn't approve of.

I'd played it all off as nerves, like she was afraid the teachers would get the wrong impression if we were seen together in school, but I think I knew we were done, just like it always is in the movies: a slow fade, a dissolve, a head turning pointedly away. That's why it hurt so much: I couldn't believe I'd actually fallen for something so cliché as a summer romance with a girl who should never have said "Hi" to me in the first place. I'd given her my summer—I'd given her *everything*—and she'd left me with nothing.

The hollow sound from the void hummed around me. I could hear it, like the rush of false waves in a seashell. It seemed alive; it seemed beautiful; it seemed warm and comforting, away from the static. It was wide and unknown, but I knew that I could have it forever. The cicadas whirred and scratched as lightning bugs danced like tiny orange stars. It all looked so deeply gorgeous, and I understood that the only way to keep it forever—to keep the summer and the feelings and Penny and the lightning bugs—was to pack it away into that void; to fill the empty spaces with memories then fall into it. To keep it pristine, the moment had to last forever before it was gone for good.

The only way to keep it was to implode.

I held the knife above my wrist, barely denting the flesh it rested on, my teeth set in a grimace. A pocket knife I'd bought in Gatlinburg, Tennessee, in another summer that would never happen again. It was supposed to be scrimshaw carved by a real Indian warrior. I wondered passingly if a cut-bone knife could cut bone.

I pressed harder, stretching the skin on either side of the blade. It looked like a tiny tent. Like when I used to go camping with my parents and brother and I'd lay on my back and look up at the tent over me, at the way the crossbeam seemed to push against the roof, as if we were upside down and I was floating above it, making hundreds of tiny creases, just like my skin; just like I was floating now.

It seemed easy to let it all go: the regret, the loss, the errant pain of being alive. The idea of the noise cutting out and the formless void taking over—the weightless float of nothingness—was the only option that made sense; the only way to move worry away, to wipe my debts, to make sure no one ever hurt me again.

If I touched those creases the rain would come in.

Camping was another endless summer that would never happened again, preserved in the fading remnants of childish memory. A past so long ago I wasn't even sure it had happened—proof that nothing ever lasted so there was no use trying to hold on to it. The darkness beyond the roots looked like a black velvet sheet stretched over me; the roots hung like a loom for a funeral shroud.

I didn't realize I was still pushing on the blade until the skin gave way in a flash of pain. My head snapped down; I closed my eyes; my mouth curled in agony. I was vaguely aware that I wanted people to know I had meant it. But first, the pain: tiny, but oh so sharp and spreading.

It fuzzed out into jagged edges as I closed my eyes and held the knife still. I felt the numbness descend and I began to float, to lose myself in that great nothingness that wanted nothing from me. I didn't have to be like anyone else in the void, I didn't have to try and fit in, I didn't have to be good at school or better on my skateboard or act my age—I could simply float, free of the noise, free of the pressure, nothing but an echo on a pond.

This was the easiest way to be: If no one wanted me around then I would be around no one. I could disappear into the dark and never have to worry about anything ever again. The static would end, the hum would fade into silence, the knife point would stop its chattering. Everything would stop. Everything would be at peace.

"Bells?"

"Fuck off!" I yelled, not even sure I was talking to anyone. I dropped the knife and looked down at my wrist.

"*Jack*? What are you doing?"

"Go away."

I had never felt *carpe diem* so intensely as when that knife was tenting the skin against my wrist. Nothing had existed beyond that second; nothing else had mattered. Everything before it had led unswervingly to that pinpoint moment, leaving nothing behind, and nothing after it was real—life quivering for balance on the point of a needle.

I wanted that moment back. I wanted to feel alive. I wanted to be alone again.

She scrambled in under the roots and sat beside me. The static cleared, scuttled like a fog of gnats parted by a chill wind. The hum of blood in my ears faded. The world telescoped back out from the void and seemed wide in a way I wasn't sure was real. Everything seemed vivid in the moonlit shadows, full of sound and color—a thousand tiny orange stars winking in the black universe above me.

"Am I dead?" I whispered, tears pricking my eyes.

I really didn't know, and I couldn't imagine why else she'd be there. I felt her touch my wrist and flinched back from her, hiding the cut in my lap.

"No," she said in a very small voice.

I could hear the tears, the fear, the hollow buzz in her own head as she tried to think what to do. She sounded afraid to talk; afraid of upsetting the balance.

"She hates me, Tobie," I explained. "Everyone hates me. It's all gone."

The tears came back. My wrist pulsed with a dull drumbeat of pain: sharp then dull; sharp, dull.

I cried against her shoulder. She put her hand on my head. She didn't stroke my hair or coo or say anything stupid. She just sat there, with me. She sat in silence like a rock for my strength and let me cry, and when I was done, she let me speak first.

"She said she didn't like me."

"She's confused, Bells."

"Why *would* anyone like me! Look at me! A fucking *loser*!"

It felt like I was Spider-Man waking up one day and realizing the spider bite had worn off, that he was just a regular guy, after all. It was like asking me to leave that new life behind and go back to my old ways, hanging out with my skate-rat friends and watching shitty horror movies on TV. I didn't want to be me again. I wanted my secret identity back. I wanted Penny and everything Penny had done for me. The future was a big place and I was convinced I couldn't face it without her.

"How could we go out for *eleven weeks* and now she doesn't *like* me?"

"*I* like you, Jack. And *Niz* likes you. And *Jess*. And *Sammy*."

I caught her eyes in the moonlight, glistening but no longer wet. There was a strength there I knew I didn't have in myself and I knew that she was letting it go, falling apart inside so she could hold it out to me—a lifeline for a dying friend; a searchlight in the night. It should have hurt more, I remember thinking: My ex-girlfriend finding me in the woods should have added salt to the wound. But it didn't. It felt right.

"What did I do, Tobie? What did I *do*?"

She eyed my pocket knife curiously, waiting to knock it out of my hand if I tried to pick it up. She sighed heavily and shifted her weight, then she smiled decisively. It seemed strange for her lips to curl like that; I no longer understood the gesture, but I liked the way it made me feel.

"I mean, you said she'd never had a boyfriend before, and now she's surrounded by all her friends again—her *school* friends. She freaked out. She's an idiot."

"Maybe..."

"Jack," she said seriously. "You didn't *do* anything, okay?"

"Yeah..."

She dug a tissue out of her pocket and took my left hand, her face drawn with apology and fear. She looked at my wrist for a second, nodded, pressed the tissue on the cut— small as it was, it still sent sparklers of pain into my arm. But I didn't pull away and I didn't cry out. I gritted my teeth and sucked in a breath and she met my eyes and she smiled and I think I smiled back. My head was pounding. My nose was stuffed. My eyes felt too big to grin.

"D'ya wanna go for ice cream?" she asked.

"No," I said definitively.

She pulled back, a heartbeat away, and I felt my soul chase hers, take her hand, beg her for mercy.

"How about that Chinese place?" I suggested dimly. "Feel like an egg roll?"

"I don't care, Bells," she whispered, a single tear betraying her as it tumbled off her cheek. "I just want to be somewhere else with you."

Her dad had driven her to the park. As we came out of the woods he got out of their car and walked over to us. He didn't say anything. He put his hand on my shoulder and squeezed it once, his smile stern but sympathetic—a stoic look that almost made me ask if he'd ever done anything like this before.

"Look at the fireflies, Jack!" Tobie whispered as she gently turned me around to look into the darkness we'd emerged from. The treeline over the creek was full of orange lights—thousands of fireflies stretched in either direction, pulsating in oddly choreographed waves of light and darkness.

I didn't speak. Under cover of night, I let a few more tears slip down my cheeks: It was the most beautiful thing I'd ever seen; the most indescribable display I have ever witnessed—ripples of light wavering back and forth into the distance and the darkness. And I realized I could have missed it—could have missed everything worth living for—if Tobie hadn't arrived.

Red and blue washes of color suddenly ruined the image, and a bright white light swept over us. We turned back to the street and I saw Tobie's dad standing with his hands up.

"I'm sorry, officer," he said. "It's my fault. I heard about these fireflies—have you seen them?—and the gate was open, so we came in."

"Park closes at dusk," a voice stated, but the white spotlight went out, then the red and blue color vanished. The cop turned on his flashlight and walked over to us.

"It's my fault," Tobie's dad said again. "I told them—"

The flashlight cut off.

"It is pretty amazing, isn't it?" the cop agreed with a light laugh. "Only reason I even came out here again was to take another look. Ever seen anything like it?"

Tobie's dad slowly lowered his hands. "No, sir. Never."

"They've been like that all week. I looked it up. I guess if there are enough lightning bugs, they'll do this—get in sync like that."

"Really?"

"Yup."

There was a pregnant silence but I wasn't about to say anything. Tobie had surreptitiously slipped her hand into mine. I didn't think the cop was entirely buying it, but he probably couldn't come up with a better explanation for what we'd been doing there.

"Well, I hate to break it up, but y'all better move along now. Park's closed."

"Yes, of course," Tobie's dad said and glanced over at us.

"Jack will take me home," Tobie said weakly.

"Okay, honey—not too late. It's a school night."

He looked over at the cop and they shared a knowing smile—*Kids, y'know?*—and Tobie and I hurried to my car. The cop sat there while we pulled out, then looped in behind us and chased us out of the park. Tobie's dad tooted his horn twice as I turned down my street, and I tooted back.

Before we went in to explain to my parents about Penny—I guess they'd assumed something and called Tobie after I ran out of the house, to see if I was with her—Tobie

270

took my hand again and pulled me around to her, then she took me in her arms and gave me a deep hug. Like a drowning sailor clutching a life preserver, I hugged her back. She cried softly against my chest, and I cried for her, for the pain I'd caused her, but she never said anything about it.

She pulled back and wiped away her tears as if they were foolish and said, "So... You wanna go to Homecoming with me?"

"You don't have a date?"

She shook her head.

"Well... I don't know... Do you have a pink dress to match my tie?"

She smiled broadly and coughed out a relieved laugh, then pulled me in for another quick hug and pecked a kiss on my cheek.

"I'll find one, Jack," she said. "For you."

You know that feeling you get when you get home after a long day at work or a long trip away from home? That feeling of thorough *comfort*? The knowledge that you're in a safe place and you know where everything is and what it means? That you know how to deal with it, and it knows how to deal with you? Well *that* feeling is the feeling I get whenever I see Tobie. And not just when I get home, but whenever I *see* her, wherever we are. When she visits me at work for lunch or when she meets me with the kids at the bookstore—or when she came to visit me when I worked at a toy store in high school. Even then, even when I was a teenager, Tobie always felt like home.

Even when I was sixteen and alone in the woods at night.

Thing is, I didn't recognize it then. Hindsight didn't kick in on that until after college, after we'd been apart for years, when I finally went back for her and took her on a trip to New Orleans. Standing in the sunset looking west over the Mississippi River, I realized for the first time—*really* realized, deep down where it sticks—that as long as I had Tobie to go back to, I'd be home, no matter where my feet stood.

That's why I married her. I couldn't risk never seeing her again.

That's why I grinned privately at her now, standing against the darkness with her hand raised over her eyes like a sailor spying land.

"You didn't *hear* that?" she whispered.

We were in the back yard—the kids tucked away in their beds—poking the dying embers of a campfire before we went to bed, too. We always did our cookouts more like camp-outs, with a real fire and over-charred hotdogs on sticks. And we told stories around the fire with the kids—tales of Mr. Bones the skeleton, who was always trying to make friends with the regular humans in town. We each took turns spinning out a bit of the story, and the kids always took it somewhere amazing, free of the constraints of logic and plots and continuity.

"I didn't hear anything," I replied.

"Sshh!" she demanded.

"How do you know what a skunk *sounds* like, anyway? Are you able to glean size and coloration from—"

"Sshh!"

There were certainly skunks in our neighborhood, and deer and even foxes. We didn't live anywhere rural—just one of the suburbs the next county over from Cleveland—but I guess it was rural enough. I honestly didn't know how she could hear anything over the bugs in the first place—we were heading into deep summer and the insects whirred and chitted all night.

"Come sit back down, Tobe—we have a fence. Even if there is one out there, it can't get to us."

"Don't they climb like cats?"

"No clue."

"It's a hot night," she said, coming back over and sitting down next to me, as if the air temperature changed the climbing ability of skunks.

273

We'd scored a couple of those low-slung Adirondack chairs, and it was easy to sit back and relax in them. I reached over and took her hand in mine and she squeezed it. I could feel her smile even without a glance at her, but I looked anyway so I could see her face in the firelight; see her eyes sparkling more than the flames.

"So... Was she there last night?"

"Yeah, she showed up. I'm going to have to stop posting shows."

Tobie nodded thoughtfully. She wasn't worried for herself, but I could tell she was getting sick of it for me.

"You could defriend her, y'know?" Tobie suggested.

"Yeah..." I mused. "But I don't know. It seems mean. She seemed... lonely last night."

"Lonely...?"

"Not like she was trying to hook up or anything. I think she's having a midlife crisis. Or something. If I can help her, y'know... I don't know..."

Tobie emitted a doubtful grunt but said nothing. Her fingers stroked my palm and I could hear her breathing evenly.

"You've always been too nice," she finally decided. "This is Penny Harper, Jack. She doesn't deserve nice, just because her damn dad died and her kid is suddenly not a kid anymore. What does she even *want*? Like, what does she *talk* about?"

"I don't know. She basically just makes fun of me."

"Makes *fun* of you...?"

"I mean, not really. She sounds like her dad, to be honest, asking me passive-aggressive questions intended to make me rethink my life and grow up."

274

Tobie laughed an honest, full laugh and even kicked her legs up a little.

"She doesn't know who she's dealing with!"

"Yeah," I agreed. "I don't know—she wants to feel like she's sixteen again. It's not doing me any harm…"

"But it is, Bells. It *is* doing you harm."

"Not really…"

She was silent, letting her words settle in and worm their way deeper. She was right, of course, and I also had to wonder if part of me liked it—if part of me was enjoying the fact that, after everything, Penny still needed me for something. But that thought only made me feel used, and like a bubble popping in a tar pit, all of the nice evaporated.

"You don't want her there," Tobie stated.

"No."

Had we still been in high school, Tobie would have argued more, but by now, I knew exactly what she was going to say, so she may as well have said it—and she knew that, too, and that's exactly why she *didn't* say it.

"Does it hurt for you, too, Tobe?" I asked softly.

"Does what hurt?"

"Getting further away from it all. Knowing that every day is another day further away from… I don't know… being so *alive*?"

"I miss it," she said thoughtfully. "But I think the way *you* miss it is what made you get that poetry degree."

I grinned to myself—that's why I loved her. That's how she thought about the void, the thing that I felt waiting to swallow me whole: she considered it inspiration. My muse. And maybe it was. God knows the bands and books I enjoy most harvest that same fertile ground of nostalgic regret and loss.

"I'm not trying to get the past back," I explained. "I like the past right where it is."

"I know. You just keeping going along like you always have. That's why it works. It bothers you, but you don't let it stop you."

"*We* keeping going along," I corrected lightly. "Gray doesn't think it's even worth thinking about."

"Well, that's Gray. And he's probably wrong."

The fire crackled and popped, sending sparks up into the darkness on ribbons of heat. I twined my fingers through Tobie's and squeezed her hand. We'd sat together many times, holding hands, at all points in our long lives together, since middle school, weathering the ups and downs, staying constant and ready. I watched the orange light play over the trees and fencing, dancing like strange shadowy demons around us.

"Did you ever break anyone's heart like that?" she asked thoughtfully.

"No..." I considered. "Well, there was one girl, right after I got to college. I think I broke her heart."

"What was her name?"

"Hannah."

"How have I never heard of her before...?"

I shrugged. How do some people, some stories, stay buried until the right wash of time digs them back up?

"I don't know... I felt pretty bad about breaking up with her. When I came home for Christmas, I wanted to forget the whole thing and just... *hang out* again. I guess I forgot her."

"You don't forget people, though, Jack."

I imagined Hannah out there, somewhere, laughing as she always had, completely full of humor. Hannah had been so grounded and *happy*. She'd skipped along a yellow-brick road while I'd tested my weight on a thin bridge over the void that wobbled a bit too much.

Hunter S. Thompson always talked about *doom* and an impending sense of doom, and I always assumed it was an exaggerated comic point he was making about being paranoid and high, and maybe that is all it was, or maybe what he really meant by "doom" is those weird, visceral feelings you get in the middle of the night, when you wake up from an innocent dream about hiking or skateboarding, deeply convinced that some big, evil, nameless fear is about to kick in the door and murder everyone in the house.

That *doom* is that great, unknowable thing: the *void*. It's the future, but it has substance and personality, like it's already written through with characters and regret. When the empty future takes shape in those moments of crisis—or you *think* it's taking shape—that's when you have to run and hide. But knowledge is power and certainty is the mark of insanity: to be certain of your knowledge of the form of the void is a weight too great. The pylons crack; the structure collapses. All you can do is pray that you make it out of the rubble alive, looking back over your shoulder—you hear it creaking constantly, like weak trees in the night swaying in a hard wind.

That's what it really is, that *doom*: it's the shapeless knowledge that out there, somewhere, is something that could take it all away, everything I love and care about, because I'd seen it firsthand, once upon a time. I'd felt its hot wind on my face; felt its pull; felt it the way we feel that soft squeak in our hearts at moments of real terror.

You can't explain that amorphous pull to someone else; that tingling like the hackles on your neck rising because someone across the room is staring at you.

With some of us, that doom runs deeper and flows more constantly, into a bottomless well you know but cannot touch; cannot explain. It's the long silence between years, stretched taught like a rubber band waiting to snap. It's the cold depths between the stars. It's the memory that you came too close once and that you can't say for sure you'll never come that close again. It's the low, thrumming sound of a distant, inner voice reminding you that if something upsets the order, you'll fall—you'll fall because there will be no one there to catch you. It's the knowledge that eventually you'll be all alone in the woods at night and you don't trust yourself enough to find out what will happen.

"So… Hannah?" Tobie prodded lightly, sensing my thoughts heading into the wrong alley.

"Yeah," I intoned.

"Why didn't it work out?"

"I don't know. She was kind, funny, pretty…"

I trailed off again. Tobie had always had a way of asking me things that made me realize something else entirely. Not in a passive-aggressive way, not like that at all. It was almost like she was working things out, too—trying to get to the core of the issue. And her line of thinking so closely matched my own internal monologue that I reached her conclusions as if they had been my own thoughts all along. I glanced at her.

"I was away from home, with absolutely none of my friends—not even any acquaintances—and we hit it off. Then I met other people, and she didn't like them that much, but they were more like *my* kind of people, y'know? Like how our crew was in high school?"

"Is this Gray and Deet?"

"Yeah... Him, and Kate and Sugar. Deet wasn't around yet."

Tobie nodded. The fire crackled and popped.

"I felt really bad about Hannah. *Really* bad. I haven't thought of her for years. She must have moved dorms or something, because after we came back from Christmas, I don't remember ever seeing her again. I just wandered off with my new friends and forgot all about her."

We were silently for several seconds. If she'd had a point she wasn't going to make it explicitly; she smiled slyly, her eyes glowing like embers in the firelight.

"What about Ally? Senior year?" she wondered, slightly changing the subject, but I could see what she was doing now: She was proving to me that I was no mere victim when it came to heartbreak—I'd broken my share of hearts, too, and maybe that should give me insight and perspective into dealing with Penny. "Where does she fit on the heartbreak scale?"

"She was a whole different heartbreak. We broke each other's hearts, so that was fair."

"I liked Ally," Tobie mused. "I kinda wish I'd met Hannah."

I looked over and fixed my gaze on her until she couldn't help but look at me.

"What?"

"You do know it's weird, right? Talking with your husband about all his exes, like you wish they were still around?"

"I don't think we get the luxury of that cliché," she decided with a grin and a squeeze of my hand. "I was there for most of your heartbreaks—probably *caused* a few of them—and I like to hear the way you remember things." She narrowed her eyes and nodded slightly. "It actually makes me feel good to know that you cared—that you didn't throw girls away, even the ones that hurt you. If you ever ditched me, I'd like to think you still thought fondly of me, or at least of our time together."

I looked back into the fire and sighed. There was so much static tied to the memory of Penny Harper—a rough interference pattern created by crossed waves of negative and positive. So I tried to think of her fondly, for Tobie's sake. She was summer and golden sunlight and warmth and promise. She was freshly cut grass and crickets at night and fireworks on the Fourth of July. She was softball and baseball and ice cream and movies and independence. She was smart and charming and beautiful and untouchable.

And when she broke up with me, I lost all of that. I lost that summer and the entire world that came with it, swallowed in shadows with sharp edges that hadn't existed when I'd been a kid.

"Maybe you should write a book about all of this?" Tobie suggested with total clarity.

"A book...?"

"Isn't that what therapists say? You should write it all

280

down, to get it off your chest and confront it or something?"

"So now you're my therapist?"

"Well isn't that what a good friend should be?"

"I'm not *your* therapist," I denied sullenly.

"Pfft," she disclaimed. "Who's the one who told me to start my own small-engine repair business?"

I shrugged. "That's not therapy, it's smart."

"Who got me through the first days of motherhood?"

I looked at her.

"Who got me through high school, Jack?"

"Not me."

"I love her dearly, Bells, but it wasn't Jess. It was you. You made me feel like I mattered. Like I was special. *That's* therapy. That's all you need from your truest friends."

She was right, of course—she was always right—and in her calm, no-nonsense way she'd told me what I needed to hear without saying it out loud; without cheapening it by making it obvious. I knew how lucky I was to have her, and I knew what would happen if I ever lost her. I'd tried to break away from her after high school, as if to prove that I could stand tall on my own—more so, I think, than I felt the need to break away from my parents. I even married another girl right out of college, but nothing ever worked until I went back for Tobie Malloy.

There is a distinct moment I recall when I saw her again for the first time after we'd been apart for six years: I felt the weight of that emptiness suddenly lift—I *physically* felt it. It was a real sensation, and I hadn't even fully understood what that weight meant until it was palpably lighter. It made me realize how far down I'd spiraled emotionally—how close to

281

the edge I'd been standing. Just *seeing* her pulled me back. Just knowing she was in the world and happy to see me made everything seem right.

"So this book, Doctor Malloy—"

"Doctor *Beltane*," she corrected.

"Where do I begin?"

"You always told me the best stories start in the middle."

I nodded sagely.

"But you weren't in the middle…"

"Then you'll have to keep writing until you find me."

"I never lost you, Tobie, you know that. I wouldn't be here without you."

She smiled with something like sorrow and pride and looked away, lost in her own private thoughts for a moment.

"Do you mind that you married a child?" I wondered out loud. "That the father of your children still rides a skateboard and reads comic books?"

"What's my choice, Jack?" she asked rhetorically, smiling that same private smile again. "A business man in a fancy suit with a mistress? No thank you."

Her eyebrow twitched and she smiled warmly, looking very much like a woman who shouldn't be with me; like the kind of woman your basic high-powered businessman should be lavishing with gifts and spa getaways. But looks can be deceiving, and I knew that, too. Tobie wasn't trying to make me feel better when she balked at the idea of a more successful, more adult husband. It's what made us work—what had always made us work, since we first started hanging out: We were different enough to make strangers wonder and keep each other curious. In that prism of friendship, we were complimentary colors.

"I know who I married, and that's why I married him," she added succinctly.

I stared at her, my eyes stinging but dry. That phrase still rang in my ears, said without forethought but echoing into a truth so deep it hurt: *I wouldn't be here without you.*

"I know what you've been thinking about, Jack," she said quietly.

I looked away, afraid she'd see the emotion on my face, as if she didn't know it was there. She reached over and touched my arm, running her fingers slowly across my wrist. I turned back and looked into her eyes.

"We've never talked about it," she said softly. "Not once, not in all these years. It scared me too much back then, Jack. I didn't want to think about it. It still scares me."

I squeezed her hand tightly.

"I felt so grown up that summer, with my license and my first real job, and when she broke up with me, it felt like everything I had—like, *every*thing—was suddenly gone."

I stopped and breathed out slowly.

"Now I see our kids and I think: I *did* lose everything that summer. I lost my *innocence*. I learned how fragile life is…"

"Jack…" she said quietly, meeting my eyes again; two shining lights in the darkness around us. The summer bugs whirred and clicked, and somewhere a dog barked, probably at Tobie's skunk—a lonely, distant sound that made me shiver.

"It terrifies me, Tobie, because I can't say for sure I'd be sitting here if it wasn't for you. I saw what's inside of me that night. It didn't feel like an impulse, it felt like a *plan*, and it seemed *right*. And what if our *kids* think like that? What if they're friends aren't as good—?"

"They will be," Tobie promised. "We'll raise them to pick good friends, like *our* parents did."

I thought about that for a minute, sitting there, holding her hand. Gone were the golden summers of high school and the reckless abandon of dating pretty girls who wanted to be with you despite what their fathers said. Gone was the easy excuse of youth to blame for bad behavior and poor decision making. This was my life now: there were no take-backs, no do-overs, no time to reset and try again.

"I know I can't stop our kids from getting hurt, Tobie. But you know, that's all I pray for...? I pray that their fall from innocence is more gentle than mine was."

She snuffed softly.

"Our job is to keep them happy for as long as possible, Jack. That's it."

The only thing I feared now was a life cut short, by whatever means and for whatever reason. Car crash, disease, murder, suicide—there is no good way to die too soon. I learned that because of a girlfriend who died alone on a state route in a crumpled mass of steel. I'd seen it in the aftermath of a drugged-out friend who'd died on the train tracks. I'd dangled over the lip of the void myself—had dipped my toes in, like a kid at a paddling pool—and it had only made me love life more than ever.

But there's no way to communicate that sense of relief to someone who hasn't also looked hard into nothing and seen... nothing.

"And how do I keep them happy? How are they happy when I get moody and yell at them for stupid fucking reasons?"

"But they don't remember being yelled at," she defended. "They remember you teaching them to ride a skateboard. They remember how excited you are when Spider-Man gets into trouble. They remember your stories about concerts and hanging out with Gray. They remember sucking whiskey off your pinky because they asked to try it. They remember the *fun*, Jack. You've taught them that life should be *fun*, no matter how hard it is. And that's what *I* remember, too. You are always looking for *fun* and you only ever get upset when the good times end."

"And they always end..."

"And then you find more fun."

Tobie and I gelled because we both recognized that there's way more to life than paying bills and making rules—all those spaces in between what you have to do to keep a house and stay alive shouldn't be filled with work, but joy. *Life* is what happens between responsibility, and the people who forget to live it are the ones who end up old and grumpy long before they have earned the right to be either.

I can see how some people may say that conclusion led me down a path of perpetual immaturity—and I'm sure there are ex-girlfriends out there who would heartily agree—but the only exhibit I need to hold up in my defense is Tobie, the girl I married, the girl who always taught me how to balance responsibility with fun and not self-destruct in the process.

There was a point I was trying to make and I furrowed my brow as my mind fingered around it, trying to nudge it out into the light so I could study it. Maybe having fun allowed me to ignore reality, until reality couldn't be ignored—and maybe that's why I always fell so hard. I looked away, out into the street, pretending the answers were out there somewhere.

"Maybe that's why I can't unfriend Penny. If I do that, I'm admitting the fun ended."

"Well… She won't find you at your *next* show," Tobie decided, sitting up and letting go of my hand. She didn't need to respond to my comment—her silence on the matter was neither her agreeing nor disagreeing, she was simply indicating that it was time to move on to something else. She squirmed to the edge of her seat, grinning. It was the look of someone who can't wait any longer for you to open the gift they got you.

"Chvrches?" I checked. "If she drives to Columbus to find me, I think I'd give her a kiss for the effort."

"No…" she drawled playfully. "Your next show is in Philly."

"*Philly…?*" I asked, absolutely confused. Philadelphia was at least seven hours away, and I had no intention of driving that far for anyone.

"Lush?"

I sat up straight, searching her eyes for any whiff of a cruel joke.

"We're going to see *Lush*?"

Lush is one of my favorite bands of all time. They were from England and I'd only managed to see them once, at a festival the summer after we graduated high school, but festival sets don't entirely count. I'd always lamented never seeing them headline, and they'd recently reunited for a short tour. The closest town to us was Philadelphia, way over on the east side of Pennsylvania, and Pennsylvania was a long state to drive across from Cleveland, so I'd moped around for days, cursing my rotten luck.

"*You're* going to see Lush," she corrected. "With Niz and Jolly."

"*What*?"

"Well, Jolly lives in Philly now, and Niz wasn't hard to convince to take a roadtrip. He's driving here, then you're driving there."

"Are you fucking *serious*?"

She nodded emphatically.

"But you're coming, right?"

"Jack," she stated. "We have kids…"

I cut her off with a hug.

"You want to relive your past?" she wondered rhetorically, whispering in my ear, knowing it wasn't true. "I'd rather you relive it with Niz."

"Me, too," I agreed. "Niz and you."

"You get me every day."

"Thank God."

And I hugged her harder.

Pennsylvania is a very green state. I swear the whole thing is nothing but a massive forest, with Pittsburgh at one end and Philadelphia at the other. Niz said it reminded him of driving through Kentucky, on the way to Lake Cumberland and his parents' houseboat—an ornery old tub that spent as much time broken down as running. In high school, we took several roadtrips to the houseboat, and the drive there and back—several hours each way—was as much fun as the weekend on the lake. And Niz was right: All those trees in Pennsylvania, with only a highway proving that humanity existed, was a lot like those drives through Kentucky. There were moments when I thought we would run out gas before we saw a filling station, let alone some place to grab a bite to eat. It's weird how long distances with the same background can do that to you: we were never truly in danger of running out of gas, but at a certain point—say, three hours in —you become convinced that what you've been seeing for so long is all that's left of the world.

At least the company was good. Niz knew all of my stories, which only made them easier to tell. He was most recently living outside of Indianapolis, doing some kind of science or something, and after a night hanging out with me and Tobie and our kids, he had the old glimmer in his eyes that seemed like summer and mischief all over again.

We spent the first hour of the trip to Philly reminiscing— the verbal tour of our usual highlights: closest calls, worst skate injuries, best lunchtime escapades, memorable mall moments. Then he looked at me slyly and said, "I think humans relive the old times to prove to each other that they haven't been replaced by robots," and that set us off on a long tangent of science, science-fiction, amateur philosophy, and a dash of futurism. That's how it usually went with us. We'd once spent hours convincing each other that time didn't exist... then we hit the streets and rustled up trouble at the local skate spots.

Niz had the math and I had the daydreams, and since we both existed largely in between those extremes, it all worked out; we fed off each other and provided what we each needed to stay balanced. Without me, Niz would have probably ended up a painfully shy nerd, and without him, I probably would have ended up in jail or on drugs or both.

Niz was the long con and I was the short grift.

In high school once, Niz had caught me hanging out in a forgotten nook of the art wing with the stoners, who were all smoking cigarettes. The look on his face had been a weird mix of shock and temptation, like he thought he knew me better and was trying to figure out if he should be offended. He played it off well enough, but as we walked back to wherever he'd needed me to go, he said, "I didn't figure you for a smoker."

"I wasn't smoking," I said. "I cough too much and look really uncool."

He pretended to laugh, then explained, "I really don't care if you do. It's just not healthy and very addictive."

"Don't worry, *dad*. I know, and I don't. The only time I've ever smoked was with you."

"*When*?" he charged.

"That time we invented that card game—"

"Oh shit! And we figured out how to climb up on my roof, and sat there playing cards on the skylight and smoking…?"

That's how Niz was: Tiny life lessons tucked away in a history of comic mischief… We'd been about twelve years old when we first tried a cigarette. I probably convinced him we could get up on the roof to smoke, and he probably made sure we did it without falling.

It was that kind of long history that got to the point of absurdity for people who didn't know us well, since they often had no idea what we were talking about. It's why when Niz said, "Wanna stop for a smoke?" somewhere in the middle of Pennsylvania, I knew that all he really meant was that he wanted to take a break; find somewhere to grab a Coke and stretch our legs.

Oblique references in unwritten languages: that's how old friends communicate.

We managed to find a gas station with a convenience store attached and rolled onto the pumps. There was one other car off to the side, with a guy leaning against the hood and drinking Coke out of a bottle. It was hot outside, like summer back home—not Cleveland home, but further south in Cincinnati, where I grew up and got into trouble with Niz and the gang. Summers south of Columbus are heavy, wet seasons, not from rainfall but from humidity.

The guy at his car raised his bottle to us and I gave him a nod and a lazy peace sign: *Fucking hot* his bottle said, *I hear ya,* I replied.

"Jesus," Niz breathed. "We used to run around in this shit, all damn day."

I figured out the gas tank and got the pump going and Niz wandered into the store. After filling up I pulled the car off the pump, into a wide gravel space in front of a garage bay that looked like it hadn't been opened in two decades. Weeds poked out of the corners and the single light post looked ready to fall if a mosquito full of blood landed on it.

"Where ya headed?" the guy at his car asked as I walked past him, toward the store.

"Philly. You?"

"Nah—we're from around here. Just came down for some gas and a Coke."

He must have seen me glance surreptitiously around for the "we" and chuckled.

"She's in the can changing the baby. Figures he'd need changing as soon as we left the house."

"Ain't that always the way?" I offered.

Then I was beyond the reach of comfortable small talk and we left it at that. When I reached the door, I saw a woman carrying a baby coming out so I held the door for her and smiled, then held my hand up to the guy and went inside. Niz was at the counter paying for a couple of hotdogs and Cokes—and no doubt trying to figure out the money that would get him the least amount of silver change back—so I snuck into the bathroom. I grabbed a pack of peppermint gum on the way out—probably used Niz's discarded penny to make my own change better—then went out and found Niz sitting on the curb outside the door, holding a hotdog out to me.

"Best there is," he declared.

291

I took the food and leaned back against the wall, then slid down it to a sitting position. He handed me a Coke once I'd landed. I looked over at the guy with his wife, but they were gone already. I raised my Coke to him anyway.

We sat in silence for a few minutes, chewing on our hotdogs and wallowing in the heat. I half expected Sammy to roll up on his skateboard and tell us about some new spot he'd found, but Sammy was somewhere in Idaho living the good life. I hadn't seen him in years, and I suddenly missed him very much. Not only the lack of his presence, but in that weird way where you realize the other person may not miss you as much as you miss them; the way that said he'd grown up more than I had. Sammy—now Sam—had left it all behind and I was struggling to catch up to him.

"This is full lollies," I declared.

"Absolutely," Niz agreed. "Huh… Weird to think there was a time that was our *last* time hanging out with the infamous Tagger."

I squinted my eyes against the past, as if I could pinpoint the moment and determine if I'd realized then that it was the last time. I came up empty.

"Did he go to college?" I wondered instead.

Tagger had been around that summer of Penny Harper, and then we never really saw him again. I hadn't ever fully parsed what it meant that he had already graduated high school by the time we met him.

"Yeah… I mean, he told me once he was going to some art school or something. Maybe community college?"

"Wonder where he is now? Did you ever even know his real name?"

292

Niz chuckled. "Nope."

"That's fucked up. I wonder why he latched onto us?"

"Well, I didn't get the impression he'd ever had many friends. Plus, he lived right by Sammy."

"I guess. What about the Toad?"

"He's a God damn *attorney* now."

"No shit?"

It's weird how someone who flicks through your life like an errant sparrow can end up having such a great impact. Out of my whole life, Tagger was in it for maybe a week's worth of total time, but there we were, talking about him twenty years later. It was Tagger who tried to tell me about Penny first, and I wouldn't listen, and again later, and I still wouldn't listen. Maybe that's why he'd stayed in my memory, even though we'd only ever hung out maybe six or seven times.

"He warned me about Penny Harper," I mused. "You all did."

"Bells," Niz replied in his let's-talk tone of voice. "You are the only man I know who can be happily married for ten years, to the girl he's basically dated for a quarter century, and still have girl trouble."

"*Girl* trouble?"

"Penny Harper, Bells?"

Niz turned more fully to me so he could read my face better.

"What does she have to do with this trip?" he asked.

I'm sure Tobie had told him *some*thing to convince him to go on it.

"What does *any*thing have to do with this trip?"

"When Tobie called, she say you needed a break—an old fashioned high-school roadtrip. Why would you need a break from Penny Harper…?"

"She's basically stalking me at this point."

"Seriously?"

"Yeah… She keeps showing up at concerts I go to. It's why I stopped posting them online in advance." I laughed lightly. "The irony is, that's exactly why I used to post them in advance: I always hoped someone would take the hint and show up."

"Just not her?"

"Well no, she was not my first choice."

Niz let the conversation settle and finished off his Coke, looking at the empty bottle as if waiting for magic to refill it. When nothing happened, he put it down between his feet. It felt a lot like that summer, sitting outside a convenience store with Niz, and I knew Tobie was right: that's what this trip was really about. It wasn't about getting away from Penny Harper, it was about getting back to the things that were still good from that summer. It was about immersing myself in the old days with the right people.

I smiled to myself and shook my head: Tobie never plotted against me, but she very often plotted in *favor* of me. She knew it was the only way to get me to go along with it, if it all seemed like a wild coincidence and a freewheeling ride.

"I didn't figure you were *that* big of a Lush fan," I admitted, casting him a sidelong look.

"Oh, it didn't take much for her to convince me. I've been jonesing for a roadtrip."

"How's life, Niz?"

"Life's good, Bells—you know that. Life's always good."

"Yeah," I considered. "Yeah, it is."

He turned and held my gaze, willing me to explain why, out of all the girls, Penny was the one who still freaked Tobie out. I wasn't sure I could tell him, not entirely. And now that it had all come to a head of sorts, I knew that I hadn't *ever* been haunted by the girl—not the girl, it turned out, but the *season*. The first summer I could drive; when I first understood that I didn't have to be dependent on anyone but myself; when I first learned that independence also meant I held the power of life and death in my hands.

"Were you in touch with her?" Niz assumed. "Before...?"

"Oh, hell no," I stated. Niz's face visibly relaxed. "I'd never even looked her up until she found me. Remember the counter man? He's always watching."

"Is the heat getting to you, man?"

I laughed softly and shook my head.

"That summer? When I'd just got my license and started dating Penny and we went on that Coke run with Tagger...? Remember the bum that told us the counter man is always watching?"

A shit-eating grin split his face at the memory.

"Holy crap! I haven't thought about that guy since then!"

"Well I have," I admitted. "There was something really *deep* in what he said, and it always stuck with me. There *is* always a counter man watching—*some*one watching, anyway. I'll be at work and I'll see some VP or something and I'll think, 'There's the counter man, always watching'."

"Jesus, Bells... if you ever got laid off, you'll end up just like that bum."

"It's philosophy, Niz."

"If you say so."

He finished off his hotdog. Mine was already gone. I held out my hand for his trash, then got up and tossed it in the trashcan and sat back down. I was sweating full-on now, just from being outside. I actually liked it. One thing I'd never got used to in Cleveland is the mild summers; it felt good to be back in the heat.

Niz looked over when I shook my head. He saw me smiling.

"What?"

"Maybe the counter man isn't bad, though."

"Do you think the counter man is watching us now?"

"Maybe *Tobie* is my counter man."

"Jesus..." Niz breathed. "Convenience stores really bring out the deep shit, y'know?"

I laughed. "Isn't that why we always headed there? To talk philosophy with bums?"

"That summer may have been the highlight of our careers," Niz considered. He looked up into the sky, thinking. "That first taste of real freedom was *so sweet*."

"That's why Penny breaking up with me has haunted me for so long," I admitted. "You asked, and that's it. I got that first, sweet taste of freedom, and when Penny dumped me, I thought it all got taken away with her."

"You were late for school the next day and Tobie was freaking out," Niz recalled. "She thought you were suicidal or something."

He laughed nervously. I looked at him and sighed.

I still couldn't say it out loud. It was the one thing I was still trying to hide, as if after all these years Niz would suddenly think differently of me. Niz nodded and punched my arm—he let it go without forcing me to say anything more.

"She *is* your counter man, and it's *not* a bad thing. I'm glad we did this. I wish Sammy was here, though."

"Maybe she misses Jess...?" I suddenly thought. "This *is* pretty great. I should see if I can get her and Jess in the same room again. Get *all* of us in the same room..."

"Maybe you need to renew your vows—your wedding was the last time we all managed to get together. Jesus, we were *tight*, though."

"C'mon," I said, standing up. "Let's get to Jolly's and have our kicks. This shit is bringing me down."

Niz stood up beside me and we sauntered back to the car in silence.

"I'm glad we survived," he said as we got back in.

"Me, too," I agreed and started the engine.

There is nothing better than a night with friends. It has to be night, and it has to be friends—people who have no reason to hang out with you other than wanting to hang out with you, at a time when there's no good reason to still be up. It's why campfires and front porches were invented.

We got to Jolly's right at dinner time, when the summer evenings start to stretch and it feels like you've managed to squeeze a few extra hours out of the day. He gave us big bear hugs and opened the front door wide. The guy hadn't changed a lot—"Jolly" Roger didn't get his nickname for nothing—and his laugh was exactly as overblown and genuine as I'd recalled. Tobie once summed it up that he laughed with his whole face, but as he bent over howling at something Niz had said, I realized he laughed with his whole damn body. And it reminded me why we all liked the guy so much: He made you feel happy.

"I'm glad Tobie orchestrated this," he sighed when he'd calmed down. "How long's it been?"

"Ten years," I said without hesitation. "My wedding."

He actually looked too sober to laugh and scratched the back of his head like he'd just broken his mom's favorite vase and didn't know how to tell her.

"Damn… We're old."

"That's a state of mind," Niz decided.

"Old enough to drink, anyway," I added, and Jolly's face broke into a smile.

"And that's what my front porch is *for*!" he said, grabbing my backpack and walking toward the stairs. "I'll show you guys your rooms first."

Jolly lived in a small house—what the realtors call "modest"—that was roughly twice the size of my house. It was all hardwood and modern rustic and it made me wish I had both the space and the money to really give Tobie and the kids a good home. Jolly had no kids and a good job. He had two spare rooms, so Niz and I got our own beds and no one had to sleep on the couch—my house didn't even have enough room for my own family without the kids sharing a bunk bed, and that setup wasn't going to last much longer.

"John went to visit his parents," Jolly explained as we eyed the pictures on the walls. "His dad's having surgery."

"Nothing serious…?" Niz assumed, otherwise Jolly would have gone, too.

"No—carpal tunnel. But with his mom gone, his dad'll need help for a day or two."

"You still call him your roommate?" I asked with a smirk; Jolly smirked back.

"Only to you guys. It still seems weird," he admitted. "No one in high school knew. Old habits…" He shrugged an apology.

Jolly had been with John almost as long as me and Tobie had been married. He'd told Tobie first that he was gay—actually, he'd told her back in high school, which explained a lot about why he kept going along with her plans to set me up with girls—but she'd told him *he* had to tell *me*. It took him another couple of years, by which time I'd figured it out, so now we just laughed about his "roommate" and I ribbed him about having secrets with my wife.

"Anyway—you guys can play punchies for the better bed," he said.

"Which one's the better bed?" I asked, ducking my head into the rooms he'd motioned to, which had equal amenities to my sight.

"We'll know tomorrow morning," Jolly chortled, so I snatched my bag from him and tossed it into the nearest room.

Jolly lived in Scranton, the town made famous by *The Office*, but it honestly seemed a bit more worn out in person

299

than on TV. The same realtors that would call Jolly's house "modest" would call Scranton "charming"—and it was, in its way. It reminded me of the town I went to college in—the way everything seemed like it needed to be scrubbed and aired out—and I found my thoughts drifting back to the hills and rivers of southeastern Ohio.

We settled in and sat on the front porch and listened-more-than-watched a local intramural softball game in the field across the street. The park even had big field lights for night games that popped on around 8:30, right at the seventh inning stretch. Jolly figured it was a church league, other-wise the noise would have it shut down. They were always done by ten, anyway, he added—he wasn't even sure they played a full nine innings all the time.

We sat in the summer gloaming—the purple time when the light is liquid and darkness is coming down—and ate meat and cheese and veggies on his porch, drinking craft beer and bourbon. Jolly had kinda gone yuppie, so we talked about the things we had in common, which was high school and the things those memories led to.

I also found myself talking about Gray and my college friends a lot, too, and started to become self-conscious about it because I knew, deep down, I was trying to equate the two: Two parallels lives and groups of friends who never came to-gether like they should have. I realized I wanted to be shar-ing this moment with all of them, and Tobie most of all, and I started getting jiggy about how middle age is the final turn toward home plate—all those moments that will one day be memories start to gain more weight because of the finite na-ture of time, not so much for the events themselves.

Jolly said something about Senior Prom and I laughed, then realized the other two weren't laughing.

"What?"

"Who was the asshole that punched you at Prom?"

"Oh... uhhh... Greg Wilson?"

"Greg!" Jolly shouted, snapping his fingers. "That was fucked up, Bells."

"It was King of Hearts, though. Not Prom."

"Whatever... Man, I wouldn't have hung out with *any*-one if it wasn't for you guys."

"That's bullshit," I protested. "Your were a soccer star! Hero of the football team!"

"Nah—they never really liked me. I was like the wormy cousin your mom forces you to be nice to. I could kick a field goal in a pinch, and that's the only reason they didn't bother me. Greg, though—*Greg*! Jesus, that guy hated you!"

"You know, we got in a fight later on the golf course in the middle of the night?"

Jolly laughed. "I remember. Tobie was *pissed*. She expected it from *Sammy*... Say, where is Samuel?"

"Idaho?" Niz guessed rhetorically. "Too far away to join our merry caravan, anyway."

"That's too bad," Jolly said. "You three were inseparable."

"No time, no money, and too much distance," I opined, counting it off on my fingers. "That's what kills youth."

Jolly gave me a quizzical look and an odd twist of a smile, then a subtle nod of agreement. It was like I'd struck a chord with him that he'd never even realized was there to strike, and he was trying to figure out why what I'd said held so much resonance.

"I miss this," he finally decided, and raised his glass for a toast. "We can't wait ten years again between visits."

"Hear, hear!" I agreed, and we clinked glasses. "We can't let life get in the way of *fun*!"

"But isn't *life* fun?" Niz argued with a wink in his voice.

"Life is the shit you have to do to stay alive," I explained. "Fun is the stuff you do in between."

"Don't bring me down, man," Niz warned.

"Don't quote ELO!" Jolly and I yelled at the same time, and he laughed with his whole body, and I couldn't help but laugh as well.

Jolly's cellphone rang and he checked the caller then stood up.

"It's John..."

He disappeared into the house, leaving me and Niz to our beers on the porch and the ping of an aluminum bat across the way. It only took Niz a few seconds to pick up the thread of our conversation from the gas station.

"So... Penny Harper...?"

I glanced at my beer and realized that maybe we were buzzed enough to talk about; that maybe he'd sensed the same thing.

"Oh, you know..."

"Do I? I know you got pretty serious with her—we barely saw you all summer. And I got it—she was pretty, she was smart..."

He trailed off and let it drop, putting the ball firmly in my court. Either I came clean, or we let this awkward silence extend into small talk, and then we'd go to bed early so we could avoid the conversation the small talk was trying to

302

hide. It wasn't fair to him and, to be honest, it wasn't fair to Tobie.

"Shit, Niz—no one knows the whole the story. Except Tobie."

"I don't mean to pry."

There was another long stretch of silence punctuated by a home run on the field—the cheering wasn't as loud as I'd expected. I guess the crowd wasn't that big for church-league games—only a few spouses, and all in good fun. That made me think of Tobie again, and I felt a weird twist of re-gret that she didn't think, somehow, that talking to her was enough for me. I knew that twist: It was my gut telling me to trust Tobie, no matter if I understood her motivations or not. I sucked in a breath and spoke.

"I think I tried to kill myself when I was sixteen, Niz."

He slowly put his beer down and looked over at me, but I couldn't face him. I talked at the softball game across the street because they couldn't hear me anyway, willing the tears away and trying to prove that it wasn't such a big deal.

"End of summer... Because of Penny Harper... I think Tobie saved my life."

Even now I couldn't be sure—I had to believe I would have pulled back even if Tobie hadn't been there. And I would have. I *know* I would have. My eyes got even more watery and I looked away from him—never in my whole life had I accepted that night so directly. I'd never spoken those words out loud to anyone, not even to Tobie, not like that. Never had I admitted what I'd been thinking, what had been my endgame. It's like I'd been willfully unable to put it all together—pretending the scattered pieces of a jigsaw puzzle didn't form a single picture. It hurt to put it into plain English; to make it more real than it had felt since the tip of the knife had broken my skin. My eyes burned and my breath got stuck in my throat.

I finally faced him. He looked like he'd seen a ghost, and I couldn't tell if he felt horrified or guilty for making me spill the beans, or was simply considering in hindsight how close he'd come to experiencing something so horrific.

"Well I'm glad you didn't," he whispered. "Senior year would have been very different without you. And very boring."

"Save me the *It's A Wonderful Life* moral, Niz," I tried to joke.

What welled to surface was the same feeling of inadequacy that had brought me to that point in the first place: I felt unworthy of Niz's sympathy or Tobie's plans. I hadn't done it, after all, and I'd barely even *tried*, and I'd never tried it again—I wasn't sent to see a shrink, I didn't end up in the hospital, and no one else ever even knew, until now.

"I'm serious," he replied. "I only have good stories because of hanging out with you."

"Bullshit," I dismissed. "You were there, too, Niz—you were there for my whole life."

He nodded thoughtfully.

"No—it's true, Bells. You and Sammy—you ran with some guys that I never would have talked to, and we always had a great time. Like, you were outsiders by *choice*. And you *liked* it. It helped me out of my shell."

He saw my twisted expression of disbelief. We'd never been anything but equals in my eyes, egging each other on,

304

but it made me wonder again how life would have been different for me without him. If he hadn't been there to rein in the hijinks, how much trouble would me and Sammy have got into?

"I don't think it was by choice," I decided. "I used to wonder if I listened to Ozzy because he shared my worldview, or if listening to Ozzy *formed* my worldview. The other night, Tobie said, 'Jack, if you didn't already share his worldview, he would have scared you too much to listen to him'."

"That girl's a genius."

We clinked bottles in a toast to Tobie.

"There's a reason I still listen to *Diary of a Madman*, Niz. It comforts me to know I'm not the only one who wonders if they're insane, who wants all the fucking *pressure* of our fucking *society* to just leave him the *fuck* alone. Yeah, sure, I was an outsider, but that doesn't mean I *wanted* to be an outsider. It's just how I *am*."

"Okay—but he was also a millionaire drug addict when he said that shit, Bells. He didn't have to care."

"Doesn't matter. Cuz think about it, man—the albums I've carried through my whole life, from middle school to now, tell a story: *Theatre of Pain*, *Diary of a Madman*, *The Last In Line*… That's how I think, *all* the fucking time."

I held up a hand to stop him interrupting.

"I'm fine with where I am—I love my life. I love Tobie. I love my kids. But I *still* feel like an outsider. It's like, I want to be part of the world, but not on their terms, and that's not how it works, and it drives me fucking *nuts*."

"And what does any of that have to do with Penny Harper?" he wondered almost casually.

"What kind of scientist are you again?" I asked flippantly. He smirked.

"I did take some psychology classes, if that's what you're wondering—but I'm not a psychologist."

I shrugged. "I guess she makes me feel like a loser for being the way I am. I mean, when I saw her again—a fucking *doctor*, all put together. And what am I? Sitting there with my fucking sleeve tattoos, still riding my damn skateboard—?"

"You're not a loser," he said seriously. "*I'm* a doctor. *I* don't make you feel like a loser."

"You have a *doctorate*," I replied, as if that made a difference. "You're a scientist."

"Some may say that's more 'doctor' than being a doctor."

There was a grin in his tone and when I looked at him he smiled, daring me to argue.

"Niz, are you saying you're more of a doctor than my GP? That's pretty arrogant."

"No," he replied evenly, grinning at my sarcasm. "I'm saying that you don't think *I* make you feel like a loser, so it has to be the *person* not the title. Bells... she *always* made you feel like a loser. I knew it. Tobie knew it. Tagger saw it—"

I cut him a look and he snapped his mouth shut. He raised his eyebrows slightly, waiting for me to rebuke him.

"Y'know, it sounds stupid, but I think that Ozzy album keeps me afloat."

"That does sound stupid," he agreed. "Or at least delusional."

"I'm serious, Niz."

"I always worried about you, Bells, you know that?"

I looked at him sidelong and frowned, and he nodded dourly.

"You worry too much. You try too hard to make other people happy. Keep your music and your skateboards and your comic books and your horror movies, Bells. Be an outsider. Fuck society. Make your*self* happy. Hop in a damn car and drive to Philly with your friends and see your favorite fucking band *in person*."

I sighed heavily and chuckled. "You sound like Ozzy."

He held up his beer and I clinked bottles with him again.

"I sound like *Tobie*," he corrected. "What I *don't* sound like is Penny Harper. Look, I know you don't want to hear it, so I'm only going to say it once, and I should have said it to you back then: You don't need her in your life. She's a nice person, but she's not right for you. She never was. She only brings you down, man. And people who bring you down *aren't* your friends, Bells."

I let it settle in—let the words rumble around my head for a bit before I spoke—and Niz let me sit quietly. He watched the game across the street and sucked on his beer, giving me all the time and space I needed.

"You're right," I finally admitted. "I felt like I wasn't good enough for her, and I've always felt like I wasn't good enough for anyone. That's what it's *always* been about. Tobie deserves better than me. My *kids* deserve better than me. At some point, they'll figure that out."

"No," he stated emphatically.

"I can't help it, Niz. Life isn't all summer nights and skating with my friends. I can't stand the thought of it all

307

going away, and I'm terrified my kids will think the same way. It's all too big, too unknowable. Sometimes I just want to get it over with."

"Get what over with?"

"Life. Dying. *Every*thing."

"Shit, Bells—that sounds pretty natural. It's called a midlife crisis. And you fear for your kids—of course you do. That's what makes you a good dad. And all that other shit happened a long time ago."

"But it was there *then*, Niz, and it never goes away."

"Did you ever...? Did you ever try again?" he asked quietly.

"No," I answered truthfully. "Right after I started college, I thought for a while I should get myself institutionalized. I just felt *off*."

I smiled at him. "It might be there, Niz, but I'm only talking about it now because *you* brought it up."

He nodded slowly and sipped his beer, then grinned devilishly. "So you're saying this all *my* fault?"

I chuckled, letting him lighten the mood. I could still hear Jolly on the phone inside his house, but it sounded like he was starting to wrap up.

"You know what's funny?" I wondered. "Penny Harper coming back around didn't bring up the past like I thought it would. It actually made me feel *good* about that summer. It *was* a pretty great time."

"Yeah..." He gazed off across the street, his eyes narrowing. "Sometimes you just have to let go and live with the regret."

It was like a bubble popping. For years I'd thought it

308

was Penny and the woods and what had happened that summer when I was sixteen that had been haunting me—and it *was* that, but that wasn't *all*. It was also my denial; my inability to come to terms with what I'd done and who I was.

But Niz hadn't seemed like he was talking about me.

"Jess?" I asked softly.

He nodded but he didn't speak.

"Thanks, Niz," I whispered.

He grinned.

I swigged my beer and sat back, listening to the game under the lights across the street. The echoes of Penny's softball games were not lost on me, and for the first time I let them resonate cleanly, no longer the sounds of loneliness and fear, but the sounds of beautiful summers past, spending time with my friends.

Jolly stopped short on his porch, smirking as he slid his phone back into his pocket. The screen door slammed behind him.

"Looks like I just missed something," he observed. Niz and I shared an apologetic grin.

"Not really," I said. "We were just tying up a conversation from the car ride."

"It's okay," he deflected, waving away the thought. "I always did come in at the end of the action."

"Ah—that's not true, Jolly!" I protested; Niz shook his head in agreement with me.

"It is—it's fine, though. Let's go for a walk," he said. "See what Scranton has to offer three bums on a summer night."

We got up and he led us off his porch and onto the sidewalk.

"John was calling about his dad, by the way," he offered. "All good news—his dad's fine."

"That's good to hear," Niz replied.

"Say, is there a convenience store around here?" I wondered.

"Sure," Jolly said, and turned us around to head the other direction. "I figured you'd want to hit the local park and scout for skate spots…?"

"Nah," Niz said. "I didn't bring my board."

"Man, who forced *you* to grow up?"

"You don't have to be *forced* to grow up, Jolly," I pointed out. "Life's been doing that to us since grade school. But that doesn't mean you have to lose your *soul*."

People change but I honestly felt like I hadn't, not in the fundamental ways that mattered. I'd married my best friend since middle school and I still wanted to hang out with my friends.

Niz cut me a knowing grin.

"And what's *your* soul, Bells?" Jolly asked.

"A court jester."

I didn't even have to think about it. I was the classic fool.

My heroes are all skaters and musicians, and I've never been good at either. All I can do is write about what I saw, what I felt, what I experienced. I guess that's a talent, it's just not the talent I wish I had. Hell, I'd settle for a wicked kick-flip and the ability to hold down three chords in a bar band... but maybe not if I had to trade-in being able to string together words and sentences into something that captures the past in amber, so I can read it all again when I'm ninety and trying to remember.

We riffed about the differences between growing up and being responsible all the way to the convenience store, laughing at ourselves. They decided that Tobie had allowed me to stay young, or immature. I pointed out that I was the only one with kids, but that only produced another string of burns about them letting *anyone* have kids these days.

It was nice, but I have to admit that it felt kind of hollow. Not because the company was bad or because it wasn't fun to be jawing down the street with Jolly and Niz, but because I knew it was missing that inexplicable *something* that makes a teenage summer night infinitely different from a mid-dle-aged summer night. Maybe it was nothing more than the nagging threat that now, if things got out of hand, we'd go to jail, and we had families and jobs and kids on the line. Or maybe it was the subconscious knowledge that the future was suddenly shorter than the past, a thought that bumped against our fun like a fish under ice.

But we ignored it. We sucked down frozen Cokes and laughed too loudly in the harsh white lights of an all-night mart, watching the cars and people come and go, and it felt a lot like being sixteen, and that's what we focused on. *That's* what I needed: those little reminders of who I was and where I'd come from—the little things Gray tried to ignore.

And the next day turned out like the vacation day we'd

311

never had back then—we did what we wanted and we had the money (or credit, anyway) to back it up. We went and saw the Liberty Bell like a bunch of tourists, and Jolly tracked down the most real of the "real" Philly cheesesteaks, and we took our own walking tour of Philly, and we ended up at a bar across from the venue where Lush was playing, drinking bourbon at a table next to the roadies. Somehow that made it real: I couldn't believe that I was there and that I was going to see Lush.

Music has always been a huge part of my life—not in creating it, but in sharing it. I use it to make friends, I use it as the soundtrack to movies that only play in my head, I use it for escape and comfort and wisdom. I filled up my first credit card buying music. I'd figured out how to game the mail-order music clubs before I could drive. I can pinpoint exact moments of my life only because I can remember, distinctly, the song that was playing. I impressed bullies, met girls, and found myself through music. By the time I left for college I had amassed so many albums that I had a tagging system for them because people were always borrowing them—I had to treat my collection like a lending library.

But out of all the bands I've heard and loved and collected, only a handful have risen to that truly obsessive level in my mind—that level that Bleached had risen to, where my relationship to the music feels more like a real, human friendship. It's an indescribable *gut* feeling I get with those select bands, and Lush was one of them. A *big* one.

I was almost physically sick with excitement and anticipation and fear at the thought of seeing them live—and I wish I was exaggerating.

To me, Lush had become almost legendary over the years, like the gods and goddesses of myth—they represented, somehow, those halcyon days of youth, from senior year of high school through college graduation. Seeing them on the album liner notes filled me with the joy of paging through an old photo album—and with the melancholy twinge of time gone by. Because they had also become a very real reminder of how quickly good things can end, and how catastrophically: The band had called it quits not because of artistic differences or some other celebrity bullshit—they'd come to a screeching halt when their drummer killed himself, right as their career was peaking.

I remember. I was living in an apartment in Lakewood, working at a coffeeshop, and I suddenly couldn't bear to face my favorite band. Their last album had only come out a few months before the drummer's death and I'd not had the chance to buy it yet, and then I just couldn't. It wasn't a conscious choice, but I think, in hindsight, it was too much. The resonance I feel with those certain bands rang through me: My friend was dead, and it hit too close to home. I wanted to cover the mirrors and drape veils over their pictures to avoid any chance of seeing something that might hurt me or drive me insane.

And it scared me because if a guy who had it all—by my estimation—could still hurt so much that he'd take his own life, I wasn't sure how that played out for a college graduate with no motivation to slump into the American Dream, who had a young wife and no meaningful job and limited prospects.

Years later, I looked them up and found out that Miki

Berenyi, their lead singer, worked in an office for a magazine or something. It only deepened my depression: She'd almost escaped into the dream, at least using my measures of success, only to be tugged back to Earth in a violent way that broke her wings and left her with a life that mirrored my own pathetic existence, sulking through the cubical hell of a shitty office. I know that probably said more about my mindset than hers, but it still nauseated me.

So to have them back now and to know the dream was still alive... it filled me with an equal measure of hope for the future and regret for the past, and it felt like the warm embrace of long-lost friends home for the holidays.

Tobie was exactly right: I *needed* to see Lush, for so many more reasons than because it was a show by a band I liked. It wasn't just a show, not to me. It was everything. It was a roadtrip, it was old friends, and it was proof that life survives even the darkest days. At one point during the show—when "Kiss Chase" blasted into full, wall-of-sound *Lush*—I actually had to fight back tears.

I guess I've always been emotional. *Too* emotional, perhaps.

When I got home, I told Tobie and she ribbed me, but she smiled proudly, glad to have pulled off another perfect plan. I wish I was more like her: less selfish, more willing to sacrifice.

"You deserve more," I told her.

"We're fine," she denied. "We've got a nice little house in a good school district, and we've got two happy kids."

"You deserve more than *me*. I wish we didn't have to sweat over every single penny we spend."

314

"I didn't marry you to be rich, Jack. I married you to stay young."

I paused and looked at her. She was being completely sincere.

"I couldn't do this without you, Tobe—you know that, right? And I don't mean 'without help.' I mean, without *you*."

She grinned winsomely and tapped my hand. "I like when you drink your beer too fast and tell me what you're really thinking."

"I felt like crying at the Lush show," I blurted, earning an odd look from her. "I did. It was so *good*, and so good to see Niz and Jolly, and so good to see *Lush* back on stage, like all those years and torments had never happened. It all felt *so good*, and it was all because of *you*. And I realized, you're the only reason I *ever* feel good."

She patted my hand. "I think you're drunk—"

"I'm serious, Tobie."

"I know."

"I guess we're doing okay, aren't we?"

"We are," she agreed, grinning happily.

"We made it, huh?"

"But not without each other."

315

the cracks and light
in the darkness

Summer's end, when you have to drive south from Cleveland to find the heat. That wasn't why I'd headed to Columbus, but that's how it worked out. I'd got four tickets to see Chvrches for twenty bucks total, and I almost talked Tobie into going, but she decided she didn't want to have to drive two hours home after a show. Me? I told you I'm an addict, and I have a rule about bands from other countries: If they drag their asses to within a couple of hours of your house, you should go see them. Chances are, they won't be back.

I talked my brother into driving up from Cincy and meeting me in Columbus to go to the show, and I roped in a guy from work and his wife. Straight up, I invited the guy because I knew he loved to drive, so that I didn't have to deal with driving home after the show either. Also, he loved luxury cars and he liked to drive fast—he lived in a small apartment and drove a Mercedes, so I got to ride in style.

By the time we got to Columbus it had started to drizzle, and the late-summer clouds hung heavy and dark with a storm. As we walked from the parking garage to the restaurant where we were meeting my brother, the lightning splayed across the distant clouds like tree branches. I counted the seconds like I always had as a kid when lightning popped up on the horizon: Each second after the lightning and before the thunder equaled one mile, and that told you how far away the storm was, so you knew if you had to run home. I have no idea if that's true, but we believed it as kids and I still believe it now. As we entered the restaurant, I'd counted forty-five and was pretty sure I wasn't going to hear the thunder.

After dinner it had stopped raining, but the clouds still looked dark and the winds were gusting. I didn't know the weather patterns in Columbus to know how storms traveled across the city, but I was hopeful that it had missed us. My brother didn't agree—he looked at some app or other on his phone and said we'd be slammed in about an hour.

The concert, you see, was outside.

And dammit, he was right on the money. Almost as soon as the opener had exited and Chvrches took the stage, the weather pattern brought the storm right over us, booming thunder toward us from behind the stage and licking the sky with tongues of lightning over our heads.

My friend from work and his wife left before Chvrches played a note, and found a coffeeshop or something to hang out in. My brother headed to some kind of speaker or lighting tower at the back of the venue—a series of grassy plateaus cascading to the stage like green waves—and managed to find some semblance of cover. I stayed put and got soaked, out in the darkness, out in the open, watching the lightning play to the beats and feeling the thunder hold down the low end.

It was one of the best and most memorable shows of my life. Despite the rain, Chvrches played to perfection and the crowd only seemed to love it more, dancing with the raindrops, chanting with the music, and twirling in the puddles.

Standing there in the dark and the rain, alone, with the

music washing over me in undulating waves of bass support-
ing the crystalline vocals of Lauren Mayberry, I felt really
and truly alive in a way I hadn't felt for decades. Catching
cold, getting struck by lightning, dying in a tornado—none
of those things occurred to me. All that mattered was the
lights—purple and green, to match the sky—and that voice
like angelic lightning and the whirling sounds from the boys
in the band and the beats and the fact that I was *there*, experiencing something I'd not experienced before and never
would again. And when Lauren admitted that we were the
band's biggest crowd to date, it made it even more special
that *this* show—the show I was at—would probably always
be special to the band, too.

I felt *alive*. I felt recharged.

And my friends that had driven down with me had
missed it.

Moments like that can never be planned or fabricated,
they simply arrive and you either seize them or you let them
slip away. Don't hold back, don't look for cover, don't say
no—go with it, see where it takes you.

But those moments of whim and inspiration also go both
ways: Living in the moment is as easy as dying in one. Be-
ware of the night and the darkness, because sometimes
whims can cut and moments that could last forever end too
soon.

My mom always said she was going to keep me safe—
maybe not out loud, not in so many words, but that's the
faith all children have. For some reason, I lost that faith, and
by the time I was sixteen, I didn't believe her anymore. And
when it came down to that second of deepest need—that

318

whim; that wrong moment I seized—she wasn't even there. That's what scares me the most about my own kids, because I know damn well the only reason she hadn't been there is because I hadn't asked her to be.

I stared out the back window of the car on the way home, at the press of black outside as we sped down a highway somewhere between Columbus and Cleveland. We were the only car, it seemed—maybe the only life for miles around. No stars, just distant pulses of lightning in the clouds.

Will my own kids refuse my help when they need it? Will they assume, like me, that their parents never lived, never loved, never got hurt, never wanted to die? How can I show them their father can also be a friend, someone who can listen without judgment and without looking for a sermon to dispense? Because I got lucky. I know that as a cold, sobering fact that still haunts me: I knew Tobie Malloy and she probably saved my life that night.

I slumped down in the seat and put my headphones on, my head lolled to the side, my eyes searching that darkness for something bright.

There are those albums I always turn to for solace: for the nostalgia and the melancholy and the deep resonant echoes of a time when they gave me the kind of comfort all insecure teenage boys need. *Led Zeppelin III* is one of them, and the Cure's *Disintegration,* and *Book of Days* by the Psychedelic Furs (the first line of "House" a mantra I always repeat when things look dim)—but I didn't need those albums then. I didn't need anything to give the void substance.

Certain other songs float to the surface as often, for different moods on the other side of the same coin—instead of melancholy, sometimes there is anger. Or at least a healthy dose of American indignation that refuses to believe anything can slow me down; that takes it as a dare that anything thinks it can try.

It's easy to give up, and that's exactly why we choose to fight. I understand now that taking the hand you're dealt and powering through the low points is what *carpe diem* actually means: *seize* the day. *Fight* for the day. For you and for everyone else.

I understand that I really *hadn't* changed, but the thing that had been dogging me had. It wasn't the lingering sting of that knife blade from when I was sixteen anymore. Now it was a fear for everyone else—my wife, my friends, my *kids*. I was afraid that the emptiness would get *them* not me. I knew firsthand how close it was to all of us, all the time. I'd been folded into the woods at night and I was still here.

At that moment, bombing down the dark highway in the back of a Mercedes Benz, driven by a man I barely knew, still wet from the rain and hopped up on the energy of the show, I needed to hear "Escape and Run" by 7Seconds right to my very core. Not one of their typical tracks, but I'd often turned to it, even as far back as when everything was happening for the first time, back when I was sixteen and learning to walk again. Because beneath it all, that became my undying desire whenever the pull seemed too great and my horizon began to turn black: *fuck it*. Get out, get away, dump responsibility, have fun.

Escape… and run.

I listened to it twice, then let the album play through. I

pulled out my phone and I found Penny Harper online and I unfriended her. After all those years and miles and darkness, software designed to mine and sell marketing data had allowed me to find that semblance of closure I'd always needed. It had allowed me to consciously pluck her from my life, however virtual the move was. And I suppose it had given Penny closure, too, for letting her find me again in the first place.

But if Penny Harper symbolized the lingering emptiness that has always followed me, then making the conscious decision to cut her out of my life must have done something to move the void away; to let a little light creep in—a scrim along the borders and boundaries that proved it was a finite construct.

That asshole Perry the Prick had told me to be careful about who I chose as my friends, and I know now that I always have been careful, and that the people I surround myself with are all the cracks and light in the darkness. My children. My wife. My friends. They're there and they're real and they need attention.

In the end, I realized there had only ever been one cut I had to make: And so I cut off the emptiness at the shadows and left it dangling like a dried milkweed husk hanging on the vine past summer.

"Relax, man," the roadie at that Ambrosia show had said. "Enjoy yourself."

All is not darkness.

All is life.

ephemera

Acknowledgements

Thanks again to my proofreaders who happily ensure that my books are worth printing. This time around it was Kristin Benninghoff, Elizabeth Powers, Alex Sberna, and Eric Anderson. If you didn't like this book, it's because I ignored their valuable insight and did it my way instead.

And thanks, of course, to you, the person who bought and read this book—and especially the person who tells their *friends* to buy and read this book. I may never gain wealth and accolades, but knowing that even one person enjoyed it enough to share it is truly reward enough for me.

A Note on Continuity

One of my minor goals with this book was to tour Cleveland's best venues and hype the most memorable shows I've seen at them.

All of the venues named in this book are real, and if you ever find yourself in Cleveland, Ohio, you should head to one or all of them:

> **Beachland Ballroom & Tavern** (Cleveland)
> **The Grog Shop** (Cleveland Heights)
> **Mahall's 20 Lanes** (Lakewood)
> **Now That's Class** (Cleveland)

Mac's Backs, around the corner from the Grog on Coventry, is also a real place. And while you're in Lakewood, stop in at My Mind's Eye Records on Detroit—tell Charles I said "hi."

The concerts themselves were all real shows that I attended, but a careful documentarian will quickly realize I have played extremely fast and loose with the timelines. They did not all happen in a single summer, and in many cases couldn't have happened at all the year Jack turned thirty-six. But that's why it's called fiction—that's my license to bend the truth to fit the narrative.

For you perfectionists, the shows mentioned actually ran like this:

> **Ambrosia** *at a dead club*
> July 13, 2011

Bass Drum of Death *at Mahall's*
January 31, 2014
The Soft Moon *at the Beachland Tavern*
April 15, 2015
SWMRS *at Now That's Class*
March 16, 2016
Bleached / **Beach Slang** *at the Grog Shop*
October 21, 2016
Lush *at Union Transfer in Philadelphia*
September 22, 2016
CHVRCHES *at LC Pavilion in Columbus*
June 10, 2014

Penny Harper Soundtrack

1. Louder Than Hell— Mötley Crüe
2. The Perfect Girl—The Cure
3. Biggest Part of Me—Ambrosia
4. Jungle Boy—John Eddie
5. I Wanna Be Forgotten—Bass Drum of Death
6. Lost Years—The Soft Moon
7. Dreams—Fleetwood Mac
8. Brb—SWMRS
9. Raise Your Hands To Rock—Mötley Crüe
10. Stay Hungry—Twisted Sister
11. Looking for a Fight—Bleached
12. Warpaint—Beach Slang
13. Diary of a Madman—Ozzy Osbourne
14. The Last in Line—Dio
15. Kiss Chase—Lush
16. Make Them Gold—CHVRCHES
17. Last Dance—The Cure
18. Friends—Led Zeppelin
19. House—The Psychedelic Furs
20. Escape and Run—7Seconds

Spotify user: jackofbells
mixcloud.com/jackofbells